Rothya James has written his entire life. He can recall in the third grade the teacher asking the class to write a short story. He remembers what fun he had with thoughts of maybe doing such things as a vocation. But life has a way of pulling you in directions, unpredictable directions. Life also seems to move in cycles: the rotating seasons, the shifting day to night, the ocean tides, bird migrations, and so on. Somehow, Rothya has found his circle in writing and rediscovered the love he always had for it. He hopes you love it too.

**Rothya James**

# Bloodborne

AUSTIN MACAULEY PUBLISHERS™
LONDON * CAMBRIDGE * NEW YORK * SHARJAH

**Ordering Information**
Quantity sales: Special discounts are available on quantity purchases by corporations, associations, and others. For details, contact the publisher at the address below.

**Publisher's Cataloging-in-Publication data**
James, Rothya
Bloodborne

ISBN 9781645758624 (Paperback)
ISBN 9781645758617 (Hardback)
ISBN 9781645758631 (ePub e-book)

Library of Congress Control Number: 2021911831

www.austinmacauley.com/us

First Published (2021)
Austin Macauley Publishers LLC
40 Wall Street, 33rd Floor, Suite 3302
New York, NY 10005
USA

mail-usa@austinmacauley.com
+1 (646) 5125767

I would like to thank my daughter Tricia for the wonderful job she did putting my website together. Thank you, dear. If you go to www.rothyajames.com, you will find the different things I dabble in: songs, short stories, poetry, screenplays, as well as, books.

I would also like to shout out my friends, two brothers from Nepal. Sabin and Saroy of their shop Gadget Repair. They helped me big time with the electronics I used to bring this book to finish. Thanks guys.

And last but certainly not least, a thank you to my cousin LaWayne for her support, which gave me strength and conviction.

# Chapter 1

Another long night was in the forecast. Not that Tilly was complaining, but she knew how weary the nights could sometimes be. There were evenings when the hours seemed to crawl by like dragging bricks. Already signed in for work, she was getting ready to make her rounds; the first of the shift.

Even though the hours could slowly creep by, she was thankful for the job. It matched her real concern, pursuit of an education at the university. She was after a B.F.A. in her sophomore year, but the actual sights were on a master degree in the criminology field. Working as a security guard at the hospital gave a mental prep to her interests. Grateful for the gig, she could go to classes in the day and make a little money at night, acting like a cop. It was not difficult, just time-consuming. But some of that time could be used to study as long as she kept the bases covered. The only regard Tilly really had was finding a moment to sleep. That pleasure would come when she finally had the degree she wanted in hand.

She stood in the staff locker room and observed herself in a full-length mirror. It was part of her ritual to make sure her gear and outfit was properly organized. The heavy leather belt she had on was secure, and the tools of her trade; cuffs, a night stick, and pepper spray was in place. She took a good look at her image, satisfied at what she saw.

Tilly was not a classic beauty, but she never found it hard to gain the notice of boys. Thick auburn hair was balled up under her cap, and the dark-blue uniform she wore set off the dark-brown eyes she sported. Red lipstick on pouty lips accentuated the whole appearance. With her garb on, she looked authoritative and taller than her five-foot, five-inch frame; including beautiful which she liked in a silent pleasure as she scanned herself with a smile.

She made sure her school books were in order and put them away in her locker. Exams were around the corner, and exercised preparation was the purpose of the books. A second glance at the mirror and she was out the door.

* * *

Nurse Bree had started her shift as well, busy checking the logins and floor schedule for the night. Sitting at the front desk, going over responsibilities, her concentration was broken by the sudden arrival of Tilly.

"Hi, Tilly; I see you're wide-eyed and bushy-tailed."

"I'm bushy-tailed anyway."

"You want some coffee?"

Tilly leans over and reads what the nurse is occupied by. "No thanks; might have some later. I'm fixing to make some rounds."

"Do me a favor and take a close look downstairs. The custodian was talking about funny noises down there."

Tilly has a mild reaction. "Funny noises?"

Nurse Bree looks up at her and grins. "Hope it's not a zombie or something."

Tilly turns and saunters off. "You should be a standup comic. It's spooky enough down there without you coming up with goofy stuff."

The nurse grins broader. "Don't worry, you can outrun a zombie."

* * *

Tilly goes down several flights of stairs and walks the length of a dim hallway. She comes to a big metal door and, with some effort, pushes it open to reveal the basement of the hospital.

The industrial lighting is not sufficient for this space. There are bright spots directly under light fixtures set randomly on the concrete floor surrounded by a murky vastness. The skeletal ribcage of the building is located here; pipes of assorted sizes, ranging from two inches to a foot in diameter, zigzag throughout the massive volume. Huge valves with big, iron, steering wheels to open and close the flow of these pipes are mounted everywhere in the network. Air ducts big enough to crawl in run wall to wall above the whole assembly. Among it all are large concrete columns like so many sentries standing silently, supporting the ceiling. The giant chamber is a mishmash of turns, dead ends, and strange passageways coupled with a conglomeration of hidden nooks, shadows, and damp, stale air.

Tilly picks a dark avenue on the perimeter of the metal salad with a cinder block wall at her right shoulder. Pulling the nightstick out, she slaps it in the crook of her hand and searches for anything amiss. The careful footstep she takes resonates in the hallow quiet. The only thing that seems to disturb the stillness is her footsteps and the rhythm of the nightstick softly thumping in her hand. She walks slowly for countless moments until a pathway appears. It leads to the interior of the maze of pipes, and she veers left on it to resume the survey.

The calm is oppressive and eerie. The repose so heavy, it settles in like wet, stodgy moss. It makes the ambience unseemly and uninviting. So still, it is as if there was a purpose to it. She strolls down the wide berth of the footpath and peers on both sides of the trail into the crisscross patterns of the pipes and the shadows beyond.

While she walks deeper into the carnival of shafts and piping, a sinister-looking figure clad in black flutters across the walkway behind her and disappears. Tilly abruptly halts and turns quickly while her intuition ignites like a flare. Perplexed by the strange feeling, she sees nothing in her view and stands motionless, considering the situation, unsure if she sensed or heard anything at all.

"Is someone there?" She waits for an answer. There is none, nothing but a deathly quiet dripping with a burden.

"Hey, really, is someone around here?"

All that responds is that unholy serenity. Shrugging, she starts out again on the rounds. Up ahead on her left is a large concrete column waiting on her approach. When she comes to it, a faint sound, a sound like someone laboring for breath, consumes the quiet. The breathing gets louder and more discernable as she moves closer to the support.

Apprehensive, she calls out, "Who is that dammit?"

Again, she pauses, and nothing but ragged breathing is the answer. It fills the quiet like sour milk pouring into it. She nudges forward, scared and anxious. When she takes a step past the big column, a hand with long, black fingernails strikes out and grabs her left wrist. The reflex is to swing the nightstick immediately, and another black fingernail hand stops it with prompt authority. The hand wrenches the nightstick away and tosses it harmlessly down the path till it clanks to a stop.

Her right hand free, Tilly reaches across her belt and fumbles for the pepper spray. This attempt is thwarted as well, and she lets out a scream of futility. Before the scream subsides, it is followed by a blood-curdling howl that gluts the basement and shocks the strained quiet. It seems to come from a deranged wild animal, and it echoes off the cinder block walls like a waterfall. A dark frame then emerges from behind the concrete column and, with both hands, takes hold of her left wrist.

The imposing figure in black exhibits an uncanny strength and begins to swirl Tilly in circles. So fast, she cannot maintain a balance. She seems to hydroplane from the speed, the toes of her boots gliding along the surface of the concrete floor as if it were ice. The pepper spray in her holster is useless from the momentum.

In a sudden thud, Tilly smacks into the column with a violent impact. She drops to the floor, limp and unconscious from the blow. The ebony thing then pounces and covers her with a black trench coat like an ink spot. Helpless and stunned, Tilly lies at the mercy of the presence. It hovers over her like a black vulture's wing. Her legs flail pathetically under the swathe of black cloth; her arms weakly beating the back of the creature to no avail. A mechanical noise starts up, reminiscent of an old iron lung. A sucking suction sound envelops the quiet and indicates some kind of evil doings is in progress. Her kicking legs and slinging arms slowly become motionless. The machine seems to absorb the essence of Tilly. It is obvious she is losing her life source, ounce by critical ounce, pint by precious pint.

# Chapter 2

The sign read 'Fasten Seat Belts,' and passengers reacted by clicking their belts in place. It sounded like popcorn in a microwave while the airline began its slow decent for landing. Billie Jean took her eyes off the sign and gazed out a tiny window full of daylight next to her left and enjoyed the view of her hometown. It was always a wonderful sight, and it was ages since she had seen it. It seemed like a lifetime, but, in reality, just a few years. She had plans to look up all her old friends, at least the ones who were still here. Her mom and dad would be waiting for her arrival, happy to see their only child back in Dallas. She anticipated grins, waves, and hugs when she walked off the plane.

She gave the fellow sitting to her right a slight poke with her elbow. He slept and snored softly the whole flight, and when he responded to her nudge, she pointed at the sign. The man woke to her intrusion with a yawn and a quick snap of his seatbelt, coupled with a thank you. Billie Jean gave a welcome back, clipping her seatbelt together, and resumed her observation of the city below.

The skyline was still as magnificent as she remembered. One of the loveliest she had ever seen and in the last years she had the opportunity to see many. The trek she was reminiscent over started way back to her high-school days when she graduated. After that, she went to Austin and started her college at the University of Texas, working toward a law degree.

By the time she was a junior, the country was in the middle of a presidential race. She volunteered her services at a local campaign office, thinking it would be a good credit to her fledgling resume. Acting as an intern, she gained the occasion to witness the inner workings of a political campaign. The office loved her dedication and organizing skills, and, over time, she became an important component to the cause. When the election was won, she was surprised at the chance that was given her. The staff asked Billie Jean to join them at the White House. She jumped at the offer, realizing the coup it would give to her background and resume. An easy decision to make, it took no effort to put her education on hold with the opportunity it presented.

It was not long before she found herself with a personal office in the White House. She was put in charge of assigning the seating at the press conference held each day. She took the appointment at hand and mete out the responsibility with relish and efficiency. The personality she expressed and her attention to detail soon made her a favorite among press and staff.

Along with these abilities was the fact she was an attractive girl; a tall, dish-water blonde with catlike-green eyes that were framed by soft feminine features underlined by a strong jaw. Her figure was a perfect fit for a bikini with shapely legs that seemed to never end. Eventually, she noticed a young F.B.I. agent assigned as security haunting the hallway to her office; a good-looking fellow that was a few years older. Dark, tall, and handsome, it did not take long before they were sharing lunch. By degrees, these forays began to be evening dinners and drinks at a bar.

During their dating, the young man put forth the opinion that Billie Jean could become a topnotch F.B.I. agent. After countless conversations with her guy, she began thinking that the notion might be a serious one. She found herself contemplating the idea more and more in the privacy of her home. After a while, the thoughts cultivated to the point that she left the job at the White House and joined the F.B.I. academy.

Billie Jean spent two years with the F.B.I., specializing in profiling killers. She gained an extensive education on the subject before she decided she was not cutout for the rigid discipline and commanding subscription the F.B.I. required. After a personal problem made the whole situation intolerable, she left the academy. For the moment, that brought her to this seat on this airline landing in Dallas, Texas, at D.F.W. airport. She had plans to reacquaint herself with her old stomping grounds, regroup, and see about getting that law degree.

The huge tires of the plane touched the ground, and there was a sudden hiccup in the ride; followed by a distant roar as the large craft slowed down quickly to a manageable speed. While she waited for dock, she thought of the conversation she had with her uncle over the phone. The call held unforeseeable timing and was a big part of her decision to leave the ranks of the F.B.I.

Uncle Max was not her real uncle. He had been like an uncle since her earliest memories. He has always been a part of the family, but he was not really a blood relative. He was actually her father's business partner, a lifelong friend to him, and the enterprise they shared made them both very wealthy. They were always more like brothers and have become regular golf buddies over the years. When they sold their business, Billie Jean's father went to retirement and settled in the Highland Park area of Dallas. Uncle Max ran for mayor of Highland Park and won. Since then, he has gone on to become the mayor of Dallas. The reason he called was for her expertise in profiling. She was in the right frame of mind to accept Uncle Max's offer and seal the deal her doubts about the F.B.I. Now, she was going to get off the plane and see her parents in Dallas. It would be the first time to visit them in Dallas since she left the place. It will be good to see her folks at home for a change, and it will be fun to tangle with the challenge of this new adventure.

# Chapter 3

A throbbing beat pulsates through a bar like a giant's heartbeat. Alcohol-filled glasses sit randomly on numerous tables, jumping to the rock music so loud, it makes the ice cubes dance. Men cheer and chatter in the dark where women scantily dressed walk among them with trays, serving and flirting. It is a typical strip joint with several men stationed around the place, drinking and generally enjoying themselves in a boorish way. Suddenly, the music quits and leaves the ambience in a veil of silence. As if that giant dropped dead from a heart attack and shut the life out of the party.

The main focus of the room lies where the only light is a five-foot high stage. It is big enough for three girls to strut their stuff with a thick brass pole in the center to gyrate on. Mirrors are in the backdrop to multiply and enhance the cheap show till the wee hours of the morning. Little round tables crowd the floor with more seating at the cradle of the stage. These are filled with wide-eyed louts waving dollar bills at the strippers looking to buy some close-up attention.

A fresh song hits the sound system with a new driving beat and the men all roar with delight for the next showcase. An exceptional beauty dashes out on the stage from the side curtains and the audience lets her know the pleasure they all have at her appearance.

She is a tall woman with telephone poles for legs and ample breasts harnessed in a red, satin, halter top. Exaggerating those long legs is a red, satin miniskirt with black fishnet stockings that lead a wandering eye to elevated, black, high heels. The shoes enhance her height to Amazon proportions and match her long, black hair streaming down to her waist. She slings her hair in wide sweeping circles and tantalizes the men with swings on the brass pole that excites them to a small frenzy. The sudden pelt of rock music coupled with the men's uproarious response to the dancing woman makes the bar seem to fill with electricity in a matter of moments.

A pretty waitress sporting short, spiked, blonde hair and bright-red lipstick crosses the floor with a single drink on her tray. Along with the drink is a scrap of paper crumpled slightly next to it. The waitress picks up the paper on her way to a remote table in the corner. She eyes the note, checks the drink, nods to herself, then crunches the paper to a ball and lets it fall to the floor. A strangely dressed man is at the table, watching the stripper dance with fierce attention. The waitress gets to the table, sets the drink in front of him, and waits for her money.

The man is in his late 20s all robed in black. Black hair is slicked back tightly to his scalp showing off a pronounced widow's peak. He wears a large, black, trench coat wrapped around him like a black flag. A snow-white silk shirt with a black string tie gives him a look of a Renaissance man among all the neon and Nike. The waitress stands impatiently above him, waiting on her money. The odd-looking fellow has kept his observation of the stripper intense, seemingly oblivious to her presence. He finally reaches into his black trench coat and procures a ten-dollar bill, ignoring the waitress when he hands it to her with a wave of dismissal. The waitress sees the money before her and snatches the loot from his long, black fingernails. As she walks away, he never glances at her but keeps his eyes locked on the stripper.

He sits very still except for his hand turning the drink on the table. His eyes fixed on the dancer. They are dark orbs, so dark, they seem to be made of nothing but pupils. So dark, they seem to be other worldly; an eerie, supernatural, piercing display. The alarming eyes brim with desire as the stripper he watches finishes her dance. She steps down off the stage with help from many of the patrons and starts talking to three men at a nearby table. She laughs and flirts as the collective life of the establishment does the same around her.

Out of nowhere, the bartender's voice blares out over the intercom, "Last call everybody, last call!"

The man in black responds to the voice quicker than anyone else. He gets up from his untouched drink and gracefully crosses the floor, heading for the front door. His trench coat follows him, streaming in length to his sharp strides, giving a look of someone that seems to be out of context to the times. He gets to the door, abruptly stops, and looks back. The stripper that captured his interest still flirts with the three men. His eyes are glazed and bloodshot, but there is no mistaking the covet in them as he watches the girl in red satin.

He steps through the door onto the sidewalk, turns left, and darts for an alley that borders the outside of the building. Getting to it, he splits quickly into the shadowy lane and tramps his way to the backside of the structure. There, he finds an old dumpster that provides concealment and stands in a darkened spot, his form barely discernible. It is utterly quiet except for a peculiar sound emanating from the obscure hide. A loud, difficult breathing penetrating the shadows like the razor edge of a handsaw cutting wood.

* * *

Discarded garments lie on the furniture, tossed with neglect and uselessness. Down a long wall where a makeup table matches its length and light bulbs circle mirrors, more garments are found. Unused lipstick and assorted colors of makeup pads cover the table top as well. Positioned among the litter is the woman who drew so much attention from the weird fellow in black. Her name is Samantha, but everyone calls her Sam. She took off here red satin outfit and stands naked except for her G-string. Her long, lithe legs glisten with sweat from the night's hard work while she peels down the pair of fishnet stockings. Sam is in a hurry, though she appears to be the last dancer to leave. Spending time on the cellphone, talking to the babysitter was what set her back. Her five-year-old boy was fighting a cold, and when she left the house, he was drowning in sniffles. He was not too sick, but his temperature was worth keeping an eye on. That was the purpose of the call.

She almost did not go to work because of her son. The boy complained all day about the way he felt, and she tugged at the notion to call in sick. But Sam knew the manager would give her a hard time from missing work. He always did. The management acted like the girls who danced there were slaves to whatever whim that tickled their fancy. She also knew they would take it out on her when she came back. Giving it some thought, Sam figured if her son got worse by tomorrow, it would be better to call in sick then. So, she would play the two ends as best she could.

She phoned the babysitter not only about her pride and joy but to see if the boy needed anything before she got home. Packing away her work clothes with the conversation on her mind, a sudden shout from the boss intrudes her musings and startles her.

"Hurry up in there! We're close to locking the door; I want to get out of here!"

Sam climbs into a pair of old blue jeans. "Okay, I'm on it. Be right there!"

Pulling on a tattered T-shirt, she grabs her bag, sticks her cellphone in the hip pocket of her blue jeans, and slings a light jacket over her shoulder. Another shout from the boss thunders out.

"Are we done yet damn it?"

She dashes through the door of the dressing room and ambers down a hallway. "I'm leaving through the backdoor."

The boss yells a retort, "Make sure you shut it good and tight."

She stops at the door and puts her jacket on quickly. "See you tomorrow."

The man calls out, "Yeah, yeah, tomorrow."

* * *

Sam steps out on a concrete porch and slams the backdoor good and tight. She turns to see another pride and joy of hers from the advantage of the perch the back porch produces. A brand-new, shiny, red Ford Mustang. The custom chrome wheels set the car off perfectly and compliments the striking paintjob the automobile possesses.

She goes down the steps of the porch, grinning at her ride. Sam always parked in the back to avoid the inevitable dings that come in a parking lot. She knew the drunken patronage from the bar at the end of the night would not be sympathetic to the car. Pulling out her keys, she evokes the familiar Q-quirk sound an auto security system always makes.

Just as she does, she realizes another sound coming from the direction of the trash dumpster. It seems like someone having difficulty breathing; an agitated and overwrought commotion. She stops her course to the car and stands there, listening to the curious noise. A man wrapped in something heavy and black unexpectedly strolls out in the open from behind the dumpster. By doing so, he becomes an obstacle between her and the car.

"Who the hell are you?"

Both of them stare at each other like gunslingers surveying the predicament. The stripper is in a spill of light from the back porch lighting while the bizarre character in black hangs in the shadow. His ragged breathing fills the silence like the grinding of a hangman's rope.

Sam is tentative, standing very still, trying to figure out the encroachment by the strange, dressed man before her. She decides on a bluff.

"Look, fella, I don't know what this is about or what you're doing, but I've got a gun and I know how to use it."

The only response is that damnable heavy breathing. Moments tick by like lead dominos falling. The dark shadow is motionless, to the point Sam is not sure if she sees him clearly. The image seems to blend in the darkness.

Without warning, the presence takes a menacing step forward and a splash of light reveals his head. She can now see he has part of a trench coat held across the bottom part of his face. All that is disclosed are his penetrating eyes; two black orbs staring fanatically at her. Unyielding, the hollow eyes glare at her with the dead gaze of a shark along with that infernal breathing.

Remembering she has a knife in her purse, she begins to reach for it in a panic.

"Okay, mister, you asked for it."

The man springs at her with astounding speed. In a blink of an eye, he is on her while she fumbles in her purse. Driving into her full front, he does so with such force, the woman flies off her feet and slams to the alley floor with a weighty thud. Sam, on her back, the black fiend on top of her, hammering her into the ground with all his bulk. The radical thrust has smacked the back of her head so hard against the concrete, it leaves her unconscious. What remains is complete and total silence except for a torturous breathing attacking the still quiet.

After some moments, the stirring of cloth shifting around on the woman disturbs the calm while the black intruder adjusts himself to carry out his evil intent. That abominable sound of an iron lung erupts into the stillness and begins the work of a devilish thirst, extracting the stream of life inside her.

# Chapter 4

Across town, on the same hour, two men sat in a midnight-blue Chevrolet Impala. The car is in excellent shape for an older model, and the guy sitting behind the wheel owns it.

Chris Malone is a good-looking dude who likes hot cars. Has so for most of his 27 years of life. A police detective of two years, he made the detective grade as one of the youngest in the department. Chris was a sandy-haired fellow with an athletic build and a good-humored, animated personality. Both men and women liked him. He was a fast-lane, snap-bang, quick-draw character destined for what some in the police force determined as great things to come.

Next to Chris is his partner in crime, Jack Degree. Old enough to almost be a father to Chris, he has been the only partner Chris ever had. Jack can't say that. It would take two hands to count up his partners. Jack is a tough-looking guy with rugged good-looks, dark, short, cropped hair, and a natural build that would rival a weightlifter. His blue eyes project a mischievous glint, conveying his humor.

Jack became a detective by default. Or it should be said by inheritance. His grandfather was a cop; his dad was a cop; his two uncles were cops. The only person he knew growing up that was not a cop was his mother. She was a sweet and nurturing woman, while his dad was a strong and structured father. Jack still went to their gravesites on a regular basis.

Coming from a history of cops Jack was, some would say, born for the job. The only thing that separated him from the rest of the men in his family was the fact he became a detective. All the Degree men walked the beat all their lives. They never hung up the blue suits; they were uniformed cops for the duration of their careers. Jack became the pride of the clan when he attained detective and evolved into a highly decorated policeman many times over.

The two men have been sitting in the Impala for hours, staking out an old, rundown hotel located in a bad part of town just blocks from the strip joint. Night air cools the inside of the car because both men have their windows down, listening to a swarm of crickets sing about the weather. Chris takes a long look at his watch and smirks at the time.

"Man, our boy is way late, and it's still a no show. Are you sure about this?"

Jack keeps his eyes on the hotel. "I have a hunch, besides, my best source put me on it."

The worn-out hotel across the street has alleys on both flanks, with old air-conditioners in each window. It's a dirty, seedy place you can rent by the week; six stories high with several steps leading up to the front door. A big, long, vertical sign hangs above the stairs, expressing the name, Arrow Hotel, with a neon arrow in red pointing at the entrance.

Chris looks at the place. "Your source has been wrong before."

"Hey, my hunches are what, 80 percent? My source I know is 90 percent."

Chris looks at Jack with a grin. "Numbers, you always got numbers; numbers and odds while we sit out here counting crickets."

Just then, a shabbily dressed, lanky man appears from one of the bordering alleys and walks briskly up the stairs for the hotel's front door.

Jack sticks his finger at him. "The odds just showed up."

Chris spins his head toward the stakeout. "I'll call for backup."

"We'll give him a little time to settle in."

Chris picks up the radio and calls dispatch. While he is busy, Jack gets out the car and stands on the sidewalk, hitching his pants. Chris finishes the call and gets out to join him.

They both start across the street. Chris looks up at the building and the big red sign.

"What floor?"

Sam looks up at the sign too. "The fourth."

Chris smiles, "According to your source."

Sam smiles back. "90 percent."

The two men trot up the stairs and enter the lobby. It has a wide berth with wooden benches and chairs lining the walls to the enclosure. Old posters, announcements, and small tables deck the walls as well. Newspapers, cigarette butts, crumpled tin cans, and other assorted trash litter the floor everywhere.

Straight ahead is the check-in counter with a fellow in a grubby shirt, watching a dilapidated television. The T.V. is loud and fills the lobby with nonsense. The detectives ignore the clerk and make a beeline for an old, smudgy, elevator door. Jack pushes the elevator button, the door dings open, and they each step into the chamber.

The elevator rises to the floor they need and opens to the same tacky ambience the lobby offered. Rows of doors occupy the walls proceeding to dead ends in each direction. Chris checks out the sequence of the room numbers.

"Which room?"

"Room four-three-two."

"It's this way."

Jack and Chris walk down the corridor toward the designated door. In short order, they come to it and give each other a nod. Pulling out their weapons, they stand on either side of the door, and Jack gives a soft knock next to the door number.

Nothing happens. They both wait a few moments, staring at each other, and Jack knocks again with more command. Chris follows that with a vocal gesture.

"Police business, open up!"

Several more seconds slip by with Jack and Chris looking at each other, shrugging. All of a sudden, gunshots blast through the door and splinter it. Both the men lean back from the assault, then Jack leaps to the door and kicks it in.

The place is a standard low rent; barren with cheap furniture. The kicked-in door is leaning on one hinge, and Jack drops on one knee in the doorway, pointing his gun. Chris takes a standing position, pointing his gun above him. They both acclimate in an instant, scanning the space for their target and finding it empty.

Jack spots an open window. "The fire escape!"

Chris bolts to the window before Jack can get to his feet. He looks out and starts climbing through it. "He's going down!"

Gunfire thunders, and a bullet strikes near Chris in the window frame.

"I got him here; take the elevator and cut him off!"

Chris returns fire, then disappears while Jack runs to the window.

"Chris! Chris!" He looks down from the window. "Shit!"

Jack turns and tears out the room as gunfire erupts outside. He runs down the hallway to the elevator, but the door is just closing. Getting to it, he frantically pushes the button, but the thing is gone.

"Shit!"

Jack looks about and sees a stairwell door, sprints to it, and takes off.

He runs, skips, flies down the stairs to get to the ground floor. He swirls endlessly around the stairwell stairs for what seems like a lifetime till he gets to the lobby door. Busting through that, he veers for the hotel's front door.

Jack blows down the outside stairs and gets to the sidewalk. Just as he does, gunshots once again ring out in the cool night air.

"Shit!"

He runs around the corner to the alley the gunfire came from and finds Chris and the culprit lying on the ground. Sirens wail in the distance as Jack first walks up to the man being chased. He kicks his gun away and kneels down to feel for a pulse. The man is dead.

He stands and immediately goes to Chris. When he gets to him, Jack puts his gun down and pulls Chris up in a sitting position.

Chris looks up at him with a weak grin. "Did I get him?"

"Yeah, you got him."

"Am I hit bad?"

Jack takes a fast inventory. "Not bad, your odds are good."

Chris coughs thru his grin. "90 percent?"

Jack looks up at screeching police units coming to a stop. "95."

# Chapter 5

The morning traffic was always grueling at rush hour; most of the time, it was exceptionable, considering the size of the city and the score of people on their way to work each day. But, this morning, it was intolerable and on the verge of causing an emotional breakdown.

For the first time in all the rush hour congestions Janet Cross had been in, she was now cursing it. For the first time, she got the phone call this morning she always viewed as dreadful. For the first time since she met Chris Malone, she was now in tears.

She got to know Chris a year-and-a-half ago on a blind date. When she found out he was a cop, it gave her mixed feelings about the news. On one side of the coin, she was proud of him and the risks he took protecting the very people who were now in her way from getting to him. The other side was the fear of what the nightmarish reality would be if she got the phone call she received while having her coffee. When she heard Chris had been shot, her heart simply sank. It fell to the pit of her stomach and left her breathless. It felt like she carried a heavy stone in the very core of her being, and the weight of it kept her from being reasonable, sensible. She was so hysterical, afraid for the guy she loved.

She wiped tears from her eyes and saw an advantage in the traffic jam. Without hesitation, she gunned the car and swerved around the vehicles in front of her to gain some field in the road.

* * *

The hospital waiting room was quiet, except for an occasional intercom announcement. The place was empty but for Jack Degree who sat in the corner next to a plastic plant. He was motionless with his face cupped in his hands, bewildered by the turn of events. He looked weary and beaten; disheveled and in need of a shower. Spending all night in the waiting room left him on pins and needles, wondering how Chris was and if he was going to be okay.

Jack had been here before. Three times to be exact. He was partnered with more than a dozen detectives over the years and never got so much as a scratch. But three of his partners ended up in the hospital. One of them never left it. This would be the fourth, and he hoped the last. No matter what, he was here for the duration of the outcome. He did not think the day would break before he knew how Chris Malone was doing. Yet, here he was, still waiting at dawn. He decided to call Janet Cross when the daylight came and tell her of the situation. She said she was coming right away. He figured to see her any minute.

* * *

Janet made an exit off the freeway and was heading for the hospital Chris was taken to. She could see the tops of the buildings in the distance to the right. Still weeping, the tears did nothing to alter her natural beauty. A tall, lithe woman, she walked with a confidence that only denoted her knowledge of personal success. She made exceptional money as a commercial real-estate agent and had done so without relying on her degree in advertising. A striking feature was her long, straight, blonde hair that reached the lower part of her back and held the look and color of spun gold. Along with her golden hair was a perfect match of dark brown eyes that shone with intelligence.

She turned into the parking lot of the hospital, parked, and jumped out in a hurry. Dabbing at her tears, she scampered toward the front entrance. Janet had never felt about a man the way she felt for Chris. This bridge she was now crossing was all new to her, something that seemed from another world that might be seen on television. Never had she loved so profoundly, coupled with the stunning possibility of losing it in a bat of an eye. It was all she could do to get to where her man was without dissolving into grief. But she had to be strong. Strong in order to answer the circumstance they were in; he stricken on a hospital bed, and she running to his aid for support.

* * *

Jack had gotten up from his seat and was pacing the deserted floor. He was lost in his thoughts, roaming the area, consumed with guilt of getting his partner hurt. At least he felt that way. He was old school, the one to supply the rudder in their skirmishes. It was up to him to be responsible for showing reason out of experience. He should have yanked that kid by the collar and brought him back through the window. To let him go after that guy like he did was foolish. It all happened so fast, but, still, he felt it was on him.

Jack liked Chris. He liked him a lot. In fact, Chris had become one of the best partners he ever had. Just a couple of years produced one of the most reliable colleagues Jack has ever been with. He proved to be a gutsy, resolute, and resourceful detective. All those long, boring hours spent on stakeouts slipped by easier with Chris's sharp observations and sense of humor. And he was the first partner Jack would go through a door with without question and under any situation.

He stopped his pacing and peered out a window, swimming in his thoughts. Worried over the fact that it was well into the morning and he had not heard a word on Chris's condition. What was taking so long in the operating room? Were there complications he was not aware of, and were those complications threatening his life? He should have been informed by now, and as the clock ticked away, Jack could not help thinking it was all a bad omen. In the middle of these thoughts, he heard a voice calling out behind him.

"Jack!"

He turned to see Janet Cross coming toward him.

"How is he? Have you heard anything?"

Jack hugs her. "I don't know yet, but we should be finding out something."

She broke down for another round of tears. "I can't believe this; I'm so afraid."

Jack held her. "Hey, hey; he's going to be okay, I promise. I saw his injuries, and he's strong; he'll be okay."

"How did this happen?"

"You know Chris; we came into a room, and before I could stop him, he was out a window after the perp. By the time I got to him on the street, it was over."

"You saw how bad he was hurt?"

"I've seen a lot of these things; he'll be okay. I know he will."

Jack kept holding Janet, trying to comfort her while wondering if he was correct in his assumptions. Suddenly, a doctor came lumbering their way from a wing of the building, and Jack saw him approaching.

"Doctor, how's he doing?"

"Are you two here for Chris Malone?"

They both blurted out, "Yes!"

"He's going to be all right, but it was touch-and-go at first."

Janet steadied herself. "Thank God, can we see him?"

"He's under sedation right now and being moved to his room. It shouldn't be long before he comes out of it, but he'll be awfully weak and more than likely unable to talk much."

Jack crinkles his brow. "Why was he on your table so long, Doctor?"

"The wound to his arm shattered the bone; we had to reconstruct; the wound to his stomach damaged the diaphragm and ruptured the spleen. There was a lot of internal damage."

Janet was tore up again. "But he'll be okay?"

"Right now, I'd say he's going to be fine. He'll be bedridden for some time, but he should have a complete recovery."

# Chapter 6

The morning was as common as any other in the police department lobby. People were scooting to and fro on self-proclaimed errands and speaking on phones in anxious tones. Aside from the activity, the only thing out of sorts was Jack. He was up all night at the hospital and spent the best part of the morning trying to get to where he was at right now. Without sleep, Jack came into the lobby, looking like he had just been untied and let loose from the whipping post. He walked to a stairway and climbed the rise in heavy, solemn steps, contrasting to the bustle that was playing out all around him.

Jack made it to the second floor and headed for his office. Along the way, fellow detectives inquired about Chris, and Jack was happy to give a thumbs-up. He still felt guilty. Chris was special to him, like a little brother. The loss of his parents left Jack without a family and a deep void that Chris was able to fill. He filled it like the little brother he never had. When the knucklehead got on his feet and back on the job, Jack was determined to change how Chris approached being a cop. No more daredevil acts, jumping through windows under gunfire.

Finally getting to the squad office, Jack made a sharp and sluggish advance for his desk and ploped hard in the chair. A man sporting a bowtie with wavy, snow-white hair sat nearby at one of the many desks that occupy the room. Sam was the old trooper in the office, full of sage remarks and tidbits of wisdom. He watched Jack closely and set a newspaper he was reading down on his desk with a knowing smile.

"I've heard Chris is going to be just fine. If that's true, it's good to hear."

Jack glanced at him. "A lucky boy; he's going to be okay. Tough little nut that kid."

"I figure to go by sometime in the next few days for a visit; he probably needs the rest right now. I have to say, you look a little frazzled, my friend."

Jack threw his arms out for a good stretch. "I've seen better days."

"You don't need to be here; go home. No one will think a thing of it."

"I need to fill out a report. You know, internal affairs, when somebody gets hurt."

Jack started rummaging around his desk for the paperwork when an exceedingly large object filled the doorframe. It seemed to shadow the whole room.

Captain Parks was a huge man, as big as a park; a towering, rotund fellow whose demeanor insisted command and respect from anyone that stood in front of him. He stood quietly in the door, watching the two men at their desk. A fair man that held a tight grip on his crew, he dictated dedication and took no gruff. On the flipside, Captain Parks would not hesitate to place his head on the chopping block for any of his men. He stood in the doorway a long moment with eyes locked on Jack.

"You don't look so good, Jack, are you okay?"

Jack looked up, surprised. "Nothing wrong with me."

"Well, since you're here, I need you in my office."

"Let me finish this report first; I'll be right there."

Captain Parks turned on his heel. "Now, Jack, pronto."

The captain was gone, and Sam picked up the paper again. "No rest for the weary."

Jack stared at the leisure recline Sam is in. "No weary for the rest."

* * *

Captain Parks sat behind a big desk, facing the only door to his office, reviewing a file he had lying on it. All the walls are covered with framed documents, credentials commemorating his personal achievements, and pictures of him shaking hands with city officials. To the rear of the desk is a giant window with an American flag draped on a pole in a corner. Running down the adjoining wall to his right and toward the office door is a brown, leather couch. Tracking the whole length on the left opposite wall is an unusual-looking fountain. Water streams down embedded rocks, cascading into a small pool. It is a large apparatus with a variety of orchids growing randomly in the display. A Garden of Eden; Captain Parks liked to say that he had custom made to ease the tension of his daily work. The gurgling water is the only sound in an otherwise-silent room. In the midst of the tranquility, a soft knock disturbs the door, and the captain turns his attention to it.

"Yes?"

The door opens, and Jack enters the office.

"Come in, Jack, sit down."

Jack takes a chair in front of the desk. The captain drops the file he was looking at, props his elbows on the desk, and interlocks his fingers.

"You look tired."

"I've had a long night."

"I think maybe you're going to have an even longer day. The long night is part of the reason I called you in here."

Jack studies the captain. "What's up?"

"It looks as if Chris will be out of duty for several months."

"That's what the doctors say."

Captain Parks gets up from his seat and goes to his water fountain. He fiddles with the orchids growing in the configuration while discussing the topic.

"I'm going to assign you a new partner till he's able to come back."

"Sure, Sam will do just fine."

"That's not exactly what I had in mind."

"Okay, what then?"

Finished with the orchids, Captain Parks goes back to his desk and stands, looking down at Jack. "I'm putting you on special assignment with someone from City Hall."

Jack flinches. "You're giving me a rookie to work with?"

The captain picks up the file he had. "A rookie in the field but, according to this, tops in the class, no one better qualified, and a genuine City Hall project."

"Great! So I get stuck with babysitting."

"No one's better qualified, not to mention you need a temporary partner for this job."

"What job are we talking about?"

The big man sits down at his desk. "Like I said, it's a special assignment."

"What's so special about it? Come on, Captain, quit dancing around; tell me what's going on?"

"I'm not at liberty to say. You'll have to wait for your new partner to brief you."

Jack grins to himself. "Okay, if that's the way it is. What's the guy's name?"

Captain Parks grins back. "Dobbs, but you've got it all wrong."

"What do you mean?"

Suddenly, a second knock occurs at the door, and the captain stands up.

"Speak of the devil; that must be Dobbs. Come in!"

The door slowly opens to reveal a beautiful woman. It is Billie Jean, and she comes in wearing a light-gray dress suit, carrying a black briefcase. Captain Parks walks around his desk to greet her.

"Detective Dobbs, this is Jack Degree. The man I was telling you about."

# Chapter 7

An immense space lies in the dark and buried in a deep silence. The only window in the expanse are painted black, sitting at the top of a 12-foot cinder-block wall at one end of the chamber. They line the wall in three by one-and-a-half foot rectangles, shaped like vertical dominos, and the black paint defuses any light that might creep in from the outside. The dim atmosphere creates a stale, damp, musky odor that permeates the air like an undisturbed cellar that time forgot. Large, concrete, support beams reach to the high ceiling, and the whole place appears to be a deserted warehouse with a stillness that grabs the conscience.

Odd pieces of furniture adorn the floor, exhibiting a handful of bookshelves set side by side on the concrete. They brim with old books and curious objects that seem to come from secondhand stores. Between these shelves are dust-laden armoires, stacks of worn trunks, and assorted wooden tables and cabinets that compose makeshift dividers. These partitions are set in two columns creating two walls running the extent of the area from the wall where the basement windows are and approaching a solid brick wall on the opposing side. They all stand facing each other some 30 feet apart.

In the heart of this arrangement is what seems to be a made-up living room. An old, tattered refrigerator humming with effort to keep its innards chilled sits facing a shabby, leather easy-chair torn and ripped. Next to the refrigerator is a hat tree bare of coats or clothing, and near the hat tree is a large, full-length mirror standing tall with an elaborate, carved, wooden frame. Behind the chair is a tarnished brass floor lamp with a shoddy lampshade. Beside the chair is a small table with a knife and journal lying on it. To the right flank of all this is a long, old, beat-up oak table that could seat ten without chairs. On one end of the table is an ornate, silver candelabrum dripping with white wax candles that spot the board surface. Along with the candles is an inkwell and quill gathered on the other end of the table.

Heavy breathing forecasts the appearance of an ebony figure approaching the big oak table from out of the gloom. It is the Renaissance man from the strip bar, and when he gets to it, he slouches over the large table and fights for breath with deep heaves. While he toils for breath, he takes off his black trench coat and throws it on the surface. The coat spreads on the tabletop like a big, black, oil slick. He looks around with dark and sunken eyes, red-rimmed and bleak with lifelessness.

Next to the candelabrum, a pair of mirrored sunglasses can be found. He picks up the glasses and trudges toward the wall of painted basement windows. He goes to a six-foot aluminum ladder waiting to be used, the only object leaning on that wall. When he gets to it, he sets it right, then climbs the steps with a slow and methodic motion. At the top of the ladder, he puts the sunglasses over his ghoulish eyes; all the while struggling for breath as if he is reaching for life.

He gingerly places a hand on one of the painted windows and peels a piece of black foam board from a corner spot on the window pane. It reveals a square of clear, bright viewing to the outside. The sidewalk can be seen at eye level, and a splash of light slashes onto his pale face. Mirrored sunglasses give protection from the brightness for his light, sensitive eyes. Slogging for breath, he peers out the glowing hole, mystified by what he sees.

# Chapter 8

Jack and B.J. were tooling down the hallway after leaving Captain Parks's office. Neither of them were speaking, preoccupied in their own thoughts about what unfolded in the captain's quarters and what to expect. Another reason they were not speaking was the simple fact that both of them did not know what to say to each other, what topic to bring up, or how to approach it.

This was completely new to Jack. He never had a woman for a partner; for that matter, it was quite some time he had a woman in his life at all. From out of nowhere, he was suddenly stuck into a situation where he was aligned with this gorgeous woman next to him on a daily basis. It was going to take a different kind of consideration. He could see this whole affair might be a vexing proposition that could lead him to a little uncertainty.

One thing that was crossing his mind was the demeanor he would now be forced to exercise. For example, he would have to watch his language or blunt comments he sometimes made from observations at a crime scene. Something off the cuff that would mean nothing to him but perhaps offensive by her measure of standards. It meant he would have to walk on eggshells till Chris got back on duty. On top of that was this special assignment he unexpectedly found himself on. And just what qualifications did this new partner have that warranted her appointment to the case. In other words, what the hell was going on?

Tinkering in the mind of Billie Jean was a set of values far removed from Jack's concerns. This was not the first time she found herself in the realm of men and their male-dominate domain where she was pressed to elbow a place in it. She would have to prove her capabilities as a detective and the right person for the task. She knew she was more than capable, but the captain or this guy, Jack, did not have a clue. It was just another hill for her to climb, one in which she had climbed many times before. Aside from Jack appearing to be an even keeled individual and a down-the-line professional, Billie Jean could see the possibility of friction in the predicament. She would be happy to show this new partner she was saddled with her own brand of professionalism and knowledge that may bring some revelations to him.

Coming up on the left was the break room in the building, and Jack points a finger at it. "There's coffee in there; you want some?"

She appears detached to the suggestion. "Sounds good."

They both pass through the doorway, and Jack heads for the coffee pot. Styrofoam cups are stacked next to it, along with the customary accessories to compliment the drink.

"You take cream and sugar?"

Billie Jean watches him. "Just cream please, camel colored."

The place is large for a break room. Kitchen cabinets with a sink occupy the back wall where the coffee is. The parallel walls are crowded with a refrigerator, coke, candy, and sandwich machines including a water cooler. A big, round table with six chairs sits in the middle of the room. Jack pours the coffee with a question in mind.

"How long have you been out of the academy?"

Billie Jean looks surprised. "How'd you know about the F.B.I.?"

Jack returns the surprise. "I didn't. I was talking about the police academy."

"I wasn't in the police academy, but I've worked for the F.B.I. I've thought about joining the C.I.A."

Jack hands the woman her coffee. "I'm impressed. Is this recent history?"

Billie Jean takes the cup. "I just left the F.B.I."

"What brings you here to the Dallas Police Department?"

"I was asked by my uncle."

"Your uncle; who might that be?"

Billie Jean shows a knowing smile. "You know him as the mayor."

"Your uncle is the mayor of Dallas?"

"He's not really my uncle, but I've always thought of him as an uncle. He's like a brother to my dad."

Jack peers over his cup. "So, I guess that makes you a special guest on this special assignment."

Billie Jean gets the underlying meaning of the comment. "I guess you could say that."

Jack studies her a moment, then throws down a big gulp of coffee. “Mind if I ask; have you ever been shot at?”

“Nope, can’t say that I have.”

“So all your experience has been under training; I’m wondering if you’ve ever fired a gun at anyone?”

“No, I haven’t.”

“Have you ever shot a gun?”

“What’s with the third degree?”

“Just trying to get a feel for my partner?”

Billie Jean grins. “Trying to get a feel huh?”

Jack shuffles his feet. “Well, yeah.”

“I suppose it has nothing to do with babysitting a rookie.”

It is Jack’s turn to grin. “Someone’s had their ear to the door.”

“I was briefed on what happened to your partner. Maybe I should have some questions for you.”

“I’m an open book.”

Billie Jean starts for the door. “Question is, do I want to read it?”

Jack puts his hand out. “Ah, can I ask you one more thing?”

Billie Jean stops short of the door, somewhat annoyed. “Okay, shoot.”

“You can call me Jack, everybody around here does. Is Billie Jean the handle you use?”

“No, people call me B.J.”

Jack is a little taken back. “B.J., that’s what you go by?”

“Yes, and it’s not what you think.”

“I wasn’t thinking anything.”

“Come on, we’ve got a crime scene to go to.”

B.J. walks through the doorway with a sudden thrust, quickly followed by Jack. They storm down the hall for the front-door entrance, sipping their coffee. Jack isn’t done with his inquisition.

“I don’t want to be a pain in the ass, but I have another question.”

“Look, I don’t know what to tell you, except you won’t have to worry about me on the streets, and I have shot a gun. As a matter of fact, I might be a better shot than you are.”

Jack smiles again. “Yeah, I figure you can handle yourself. No, I’m talking about the case. I haven’t seen any files; Captain told me nothing about it. I’m in the dark.”

“It’s a special assignment, that’s why you have me for a partner.”

“I know that, but what makes it so special?”

The two detectives finally get to the front door, and B.J. pushes it slightly open.

“About three years ago, three murders with an unusual M.O. took place within a span of a few days.”

“Who was the investigating officer?”

“They didn’t take place here in Dallas, it was in Highland Park. My uncle was the mayor of Highland Park at the time. Another murder with the same M.O., actually two murders, have recently occurred.”

Jack is stumped. “In Highland Park?”

“No, in Downtown Dallas, which red flagged my uncle and prompted him to get in touch with me.”

“So how do you fit in?”

“I’ve got psychiatric training as a criminal profiler up to your eyeballs. All these cases have very weird facts about them.”

With that, B.J. goes through the front door, and it closes gently in Jack’s face. He is left there, standing, to ponder more.

# Chapter 9

The lair of the Renaissance man has an ambience to it that cancels thought and chokes the ability of cognition. It has such an overwhelming stillness that it stupors and fogs attention. It ensnares the inhabitant with confusion, leaving a bottomless pit of dark, dank delusion. And the entire perspective soaks into the soul.

From this ominous atmosphere, a solitary frame shuffles to a bookshelf next to the old, rundown refrigerator. In the gloomy paragon, the form defines into the Renaissance man himself. Dressed in a black, silk nightshirt, he fumbles around on the shelves till he discovers what he searches for. After finding the object, he holds it tightly in his hand and makes slow, deliberate steps toward a hanging, black, velvet curtain set in a corner off to the left where the far brick wall is located. It is situated outside the realm of the living refuge the Renaissance man has created with the furniture pieces.

In the defused light, the velvet curtain reflects a deep-purple sheen. Down the middle of the fabric is an opening that the Renaissance man pulls apart to reveal something totally unexpected; a large, black coffin. It sits there as if in some kind of sacrificial state, waiting for an entity to rest in. The confinement inside the curtain is small, and the coffin sits waist high on two slabs of stone, taking most of the floor space. Black enamel gleams like cat's eye on the painted surface with bright silver handles and hinges bolted to the coffin, matching the enamel in shine. The coffin is the only obstacle rooted in the tiny space.

The Renaissance man enters the secluded spot tremulously and walks around the coffin in a sloth-like gate. As he drifts in circles about the box, he reaches out with black fingernails of an outstretched hand and glides them sensuously along the slick, glossy enamel, caressing it amorously while paying close consideration to its texture. As if he is stroking a lover. It is the only true possession that belongs to him and all he really needs in this world of humans. The one place where he can be himself; the one place where he is fully at peace.

He stops abruptly and stares down at the coffin a long moment lovingly. Then, with acute care, he uses what he brought from the shelf, a bottle of lemon polish and a rag. He pours the polish slowly and abundantly on the surface and begins rubbing the oil into the veneer like he is massaging someone he cares about. Meticulous with the undertaking, he painstakingly dissolves into the task. A daily chore he relishes. All the while, he leans over the coffin; the calm of the place is pierced with his difficult, struggling breath. It grates in the quiet like broken glass goring into a surface.

# Chapter 10

Jerome Bickers was a quirky, young man. He was a nice-enough-looking fellow with a pleasant face, a friendly smile, and warm, brown eyes. He spent a lot of money to be well-dressed but wore lifts to be taller in his expensive shoes. Another odd trait was his pension on using Chap Stick. He could not go ten minutes without using the stuff on his lips. People thought he had some kind of hereditary affliction that took the moisture from his tissue. It was very distracting with his multiple use of it. If you had any kind of lengthy conversation with the man, it would only take moments to see his obsession with putting the waxen substance to his mouth.

In truth, the habit was formulated back when he was in junior high school. From the very first girl he ever kissed. It all started at a party when the parents of one of his friends went out of town and presented the perfect chance for a get-together that had no chaperone. Somehow, the old spin-the-bottle game was brought up and everyone decided to play the thing on a lark. When it came time for him to take his turn, the bottle landed on a pretty girl he had a huge crush on. The one and only crush he ever had in his short life. Giggles and guffaws were promptly followed when the two of them were paired; some of the boys knew all about his infatuation and gave him a hard time as the couple got up from the circle.

They both retired to the respective closet, and in the cozy den of the spot, he had his first kiss from a girl he was wildly in love with. In fact, it was so good, he took it upon himself to steal a second. She was willing enough, but she did not seem to match the eagerness he expressed. Afterward, they went back to the group, he with a big smile and the girl with a coy reserve.

On Monday, at school, he was mortified to find out the girl had a complaint from the experience. It seems he was so nervous about the ordeal of the kiss that it caused his mouth to dry up. That, in turn, migrated to his lips which created the texture of cardboard. She told her girlfriends about his dry lips, and it did not take long for the boys in school to learn of the rumor.

His buddies were merciless in their attacks. They started calling him a nickname in the gym shower that stuck till this day. Dry lips Bicks. That afternoon, he went to the corner store and bought some Chap Stick. Needless to say, through the years, the habit became a ruling passion bordering on a phobia. Today, all the different flavors the product comes in makes it an enjoyable dependence. It cured his dry lips, but people still ended up calling him Bicks and, over time, it has evolved into a familiar and likeable name.

Another strange thing about Bicks is his constant use of a pocket tape-recorder; a little silver gadget that uses micro tapes. He refers to it for daily observations or as a reference point when he is on research projects. Not a day goes by without Bicks pulling out the tiny device on several occasions and talking into it like an old friend. It has served as a tool to gather information and keep it logged in a handy order of details.

Bicks went to college from high school and got a journalistic degree at U.C.L.A. After graduating, he applied and landed a job as an investigative reporter at the Picayune newspaper located in New Orleans. He stayed at that paper a few years before he was coaxed by the legendary Miami Herald to join their ranks and work as a crime reporter. The next stop was the Dallas Morning News where he wrote as a columnist and eventually found his true form as a writer.

He was following a case involving a Dallas policeman and his wife. It was a story of murder, scandal, bribery, and drugs. The case so intrigued Bicks, he wrote a book about it that ended up on the bestseller list. Since then, he has completed four other books, all successful, in the true crime genre. At this point in time, he was searching for an episode he could shape into a book. It had been a long spell since he was able to find any material worthy of one.

This is how he came to be walking the hallways of his old stomping grounds in the building of the Dallas Morning News. He was on his way to visit George, an overweight, nondescript fellow who was in charge of a place fondly referred to by the employees as the hotwire office. It was an area where news was accumulated on the local, national, and global scale, then distributed to the appropriate departments. George had been in the office ever since Bicks could remember. He was the perfect man for the job because he never got excited about anything except maybe a shortage of doughnuts.

Trucking down the hallway and greeting friends in the corridor that recognized him, Bicks was finally nearing the door he sought. He sees the door is open and soars through the opening like a flying bird. As soon as he gets past the doorway, he spots his old pal, George, sitting behind a desk, reading type. Bicks walks up to him, jerks the type out of his hands, and starts reading. The incident perturbs George till he looks up and gives the culprit a big grin.

"Well, now, look what the cat dragged in."

"How you doing, George? This stuff is crap."

Bicks gives the type back to his host, then reaches in his pocket for his Chap Stick. He quickly applies it to his lips while George takes the sheet with a snap.

"Haven't seen you around for a while, Bicks. I see you're still using that shit."

"It softens my lips, keeps my puckers ready for a kiss."

"Yeah, well, I'll pass on any offers."

"Don't flatter yourself; you don't have to worry about any offers from me."

George leans back in his chair and folds his arms with a smirk. "Still full of spit and fire I see. Where the hell have you been?"

Bicks puts his Chap Stick away. "Out of town on a witch hunt."

"Find a story?"

"Can't say that I did, which brings me here. What's on the hotwire?"

George gets up from his chair. "Take a look for yourself, it's all yours. I need to take a leak."

"Don't forget to wash your hands."

George strolls out of the office, leaving Bicks to his whims. Walking over to a computer screen, he starts fishing through the information it contains. There does not seem to be anything that sparks an interest as he scrolls through a mountain of news. He spends quite some time alone and undisturbed, scanning the machine till George comes back with a cup of coffee and a cinnamon bear claw. Munching on the doughnut, he titters over to Bicks and plants himself off his shoulder.

"Find anything interesting?"

Bicks glances back at him. "Nope, not much; I have to say, pretty disappointing."

"No lottery ticket for my man, huh."

"So it seems. Whoa, wait a minute. Here's something."

"What is it?"

"Something wicked this way comes."

"Say what?"

Bicks pulls out his Chap Stick and twists off the cap. "I've seen this before; it rings a bell."

George replies sarcastically, "Well, ring the bell, but don't expect a kiss."

# Chapter 11

The big easy chair plants in the middle of the armoires and shelving like an island. The quiet so intense in the amplitude, it seems corrosive and chthonic. Like a tomb without death. The Renaissance man sits pensively in the chair with his street clothes on. The silk nightshirt he wore now hangs with the trench coat on the hat tree next to the refrigerator. He is dressed in black fatigues tucked into black, combat boots. A white, silk shirt with large, blousy sleeves drapes his shoulders. Along with that, a black string tie, like Doc Holliday might wear, polishes the attire off to give him a look from another time but a refined appearance. He sits quietly, contemplating his next venture into the land of humans. He breathes with difficulty, then reaches over to the small table, next to the chair where the journal and knife can be found. Picking the knife up, he rolls the blade in his fingertips with fascination. The blade is six inches long, and it glitters in reflection from the activity. The light source comes from the floor lamp spilling brightness above him from behind the chair. Trying all the while as he sits; the Renaissance man makes an effort to breathe in a regular rhythm.

He cups the blade with his free hand and fastens the steel into the handle of the knife. Then, he releases it and allows the blade to jump out. The switchblade complies at his wish, and he repeats the procedure over and over again. Each time the blade flicks out, it points to the ceiling like a lance and flashes to the light. The Renaissance man is deep in thought while he exercises the action of the blade and scrambles for air. He drowns in the thoughts of his personal mission, a mission to repair himself; to make himself whole and strong again. It is the responsibility he has to his kind; the last remaining individual of his tribe.

He has been relegated to this place he finds himself in; imprisoned by the device of humans and their concepts of boundaries and normality. By their standards of what is human. Shunned when he should be revered, he strives to be recognized as such. He is more than human and feared because of it. So, he is reduced to these dismal confinements and stranded in this ridiculous delimit.

Lost in those musings, he suddenly rises from the chair and walks briskly to the ladder at the foot of the basement windows. Climbing up to the top, he pulls back the black foam board that gives him a view of the outside. The sunshine has turned from bright to a dull glow, and he can see it is beginning to fall into the night. He stands there, gazing in a hypnotic spell, waiting for the dusk; working the switchblade while captivated, he keeps flipping the sharp edge out one swish after another.

Eventually, he sets the foam board on the edge, drops back down the step ladder, and goes directly to the oak table. The candles are lit on the candelabrum, and the wicks flutter to a beat of their own while he takes his knife and flings it hard at the tabletop. It strikes boldly and sticks straight up, deep in the oak. He tugs it loose and slams it in the wood again. The knife does a good job at finding the mark and stands tall like a miniature, armored knight. The only sound in the place is the constant thud of the knife hitting its target again and again and his damnable breathing. It demonstrates the Renaissance man's impatience on waiting for the sunset. The all-important and necessary sunset must be waited on before he can pursue his mission. It will conceal his deeds and protect him from detection and harm. The night was his only friend.

# Chapter 12

Busting through glass doors and entering a bright corridor, Jack and B.J. head into a hospital. Everything is white and clean and smells like it. They make their way toward a counter where the staff can be seen. B.J. brings Jack up to speed on the way.

"The first murder we want to check out took place here. It happened days ago."

Jack looks at her. "There won't be much for a fresh crime scene."

B.J. looks back. "No, but this is the place to start."

"What's the name of the victim?"

B.J. refers to her notes. "A young woman named Tilly Grant."

"Was she a patient?"

"No, she wasn't. This says she was a security guard who worked the night shift."

"So the crime took place at night?"

"Yes, going by this. Is this the same hospital your partner is in?"

"No, he's in the Central Medical Center; otherwise we'd see how he was doing."

By now, the two detectives have walked to the counter and two nurses are watching them approach. Jack immediately flashes his badge to introduce themselves to the nurses.

"Hello, I'm Detective Jack Degree, and this is Detective Dobbs. We're here to ask some questions about the assault that took place the other night. Is there anyone we could talk to who may have firsthand information?"

A young nurse responds, "Are you speaking about the security guard?"

B.J. answers her, "Yes, that's right."

"You should talk to Nurse Bree. She was on duty that night."

Jack puts his badge away. "Might she be around right now?"

"As a matter of fact, she is. She's in the back office, I'll get her."

Jack turns to B.J. "Does that file tell you where the crime scene is?"

B.J. replies without looking at her notes, "Down on the lower level."

Just then, an older nurse walks up to the counter and speaks to them.

"Yes, Detectives, I'm Nurse Bree. I believe you want to talk to me about Tilly and the events from the other night."

B.J. responds, "Yes, that's right."

"I've already told the police everything I know. There isn't really a whole lot for me to tell."

Jack puts his hands on the counter. "We were just assigned this case, and we're starting at square one. The two of us would appreciate your cooperation on anything you remember about the night in question."

Nurse Bree bites her lip. "Well, like I said, there's not much to tell. The shift started that night like any other. I was here, making sure things were in order when Tilly showed up to begin her shift—"

B.J. interrupts, "What time was that?"

"A little after ten in the evening; ten was when Tilly clocked in for her shift. When she showed up, I mentioned to her that maintenance had complained about strange noises in the basement."

Jack explores that comment. "What sort of noises?"

"You'd have to ask maintenance about that, I'm not sure."

Jack responds, "Do you have the name of the maintenance man?"

"His name is Mark. Mark Brown I believe. You could probably find him down there right now."

B.J. has a pencil and jots the name in her notepad. "We'll check that out. Go ahead with your train of thought."

Nurse Bree takes a moment to clarify her recall. "We didn't talk long. Tilly always took her job seriously, and when I mentioned what maintenance said, she took off to see about it."

Jack shoves his hands in his pocket. "You're sure she went straight downstairs?"

"As far as I know, she did."

B.J. makes a pointed question. "That was the last you saw of her that night?"

"Yes, it was; that's not unusual. I have my procedures to look after, and Tilly did the same. Many times, we didn't see each other at all in the evening."

B.J. puts the notepad away. "Who found the body?"

"Maintenance did the next morning. I hope you catch whoever did this. I liked that girl. She was a good kid and didn't deserve what happened to her."

Jack reacts with a sad smile. "Most don't."

* * *

B.J. and Jack were walking down a tunnel-like hallway that gave the feeling it was built underground. Their footsteps echo off the walls, creating the only sound to be heard, enhancing the quality of enclosure. Shut doors line the length of the passage with no window to look out of. All the light was given by electrical fixtures that shone an artificial glare which also caused an aura of a cave-like environment.

Jack suddenly blurts out thoughts stemming from the conversation they just had with Nurse Bree. "You know, I've got something to say."

"What's that?"

"I don't know; this maintenance guy might be someone we should take a close look at. I mean, he's the one that got that girl to come down here, and he's the one who may have found her supposedly the next morning. That's when the body was found anyway, right? There's connections to all that."

"His name is Mark Brown, and he's in his mid-50s. That doesn't exactly fit most profiles. And by the way, how does he connect to the other crime with the same M.O."

Jack shrugs. "You've got a point there. All I'm saying is don't discount this guy, at least from my experience. Not yet anyway."

"We're about to talk to him, that last door on the left is where the crime scene is and where the body was found. It's where he should be as well."

"Just keep an open mind on overlooking this guy."

The two detectives get to a metal door, and with some effort, it squeaks open to a huge space full of pipes and waterlines. A man in a green flannel uniform is not far away, mopping the concrete floor. The detectives can clearly see a tag on his shirt with the name 'Mark' spelling out. They move in his direction while he stops the work he is doing and drops the mop in its bucket. The man is weathered and gray and looks to be 65 instead of 50 something.

"You folks shouldn't be down here. I'll have to ask you to go back upstairs."

This time, it is B.J. who brings out a badge. "We're Detectives Dobbs and Degree. We've come to ask some questions on the murder that took place down here."

Brown fidgets with this revelation. "Yes, of course. I didn't realize you were police. How can I help you?"

Jack scans the area they stand in. "This place is pretty secluded, isn't it?"

B.J. joins his observation. "Yeah, I can see how someone could be attacked down here and no one would know."

Jack looks at Brown. "Can you tell us your version of what happened here, Mr. Brown?"

"I'll do my best to tell you what I know."

B.J. puts her badge away. "Why don't you start with the reason you asked for security to check the place out."

"I heard funny noises."

Jack drills Brown with interest. "What do you mean by that? What kind of noises did you hear?"

"Like someone was messing around in all this pipe and lines. You know, climbing and jumping down off something high; bumping into stuff, noises that didn't seem right. It's always real quiet, never a bunch of odd noises. It sounded like someone was around that didn't belong."

Jack continues the thought. "Did you check out what you heard and look around?"

"Yes, I did. For quite a while, till it was time for me to clock out."

Jack is watching him closely. "You didn't see a thing?"

"No, sir, I didn't. And I got to tell you; when I started looking around, it all of a sudden got real quiet; too quiet. It got so, I felt I was being watched. It was scary, so I left and clocked out. When I got upstairs, I told the nurse about it."

B.J. has been listening intently. "Can you show us where the crime scene is?"

"Yes, I can; it's right this way down one of the inner passageways."

The detectives follow Mr. Brown to a spot with a blood-stained pillar roped off in yellow tape. The blood on the pillar is the only evidence of a crime scene.

Brown points to it. "This is it. This is where I found that girl the next morning when I came to work."

Jack checks it out. "Nothing here but that small amount of blood on that column; you'd think there'd be more on the concrete floor. A lot of it; how was this girl killed anyway?"

B.J. refers to the file. "That's something that hasn't been determined yet. The blood you see belongs to the victim. We'll be making a stop at the morgue a little later and maybe there'll be something more to go on. Forensic believes the blood we see is where the victim was slammed into and caused unconsciousness."

Jack intercedes, "And then what; she was strangled. Is there a door here besides the one we used that leads to the outside?"

Mr. Brown looks startled by the question. "Yes, sir, there is. It's right over here. It goes to the trash dumpsters out back."

Once again, the detectives follow the maintenance man through a network of piping till they come to a big, dark, gray, metal door. Mr. Brown shows the detectives.

"What's strange about this door is that it's always locked. I make sure of it; locked tight. Except for the morning the girl was here. I found it to be open or unlocked later on in the day. It don't make any sense that it would be. I remember checking that door before I left for the night."

B.J. checks the file. "Nothing in here says a thing about that door."

Mr. Brown is eager to help with the mystery. "Everybody was gone by the time I found it to be unlocked. You're the first I mentioned that to."

Jack takes a good look at it. "No signs of forcible entry. Who has the keys to this door?"

"Just me; I got a set, then there's a set up in the main office that's always put away safely."

Jack puts his hands on his hips. "I guess the suspect walked down here like we did; through the whole hospital hallways, unobserved, and left by this door. You're sure this door was locked when you left?"

"Yes, sir, I'm sure. I made a point of checking it because of the noises I was hearing."

Jack rubs the back of his neck. "And you're sure it was unlocked the next morning?"

"You can't open that door on the inside without a key. It only opens by a key. Once you open it, you can close the door, but it will be unlocked. And you need a key to open it from the outside too. I'm sure it was locked that night, and I'm sure it was unlocked the next morning."

B.J. holds the file up to read. "According to this, there was nothing on the surveillance tapes upstairs to indicate anyone in the hallways was walking around that didn't belong there."

Jack checks the door again. "You think the suspect entered through this door?"

B.J. adds to the comment, "Yeah, like a phantom or a ghost."

# Chapter 13

The silence was stupefied; the stillness gripping. Standing some yards from the cinder block wall with window was the Renaissance man. The struggle for his breath has become unnerving. He is motionless except for the performance of the switchblade. Sticking it out alongside his right leg, he collapses the thing back inside the handle by pressing it on his leg. The blade folds into its place, and he releases it once again, over and over; the sharp edge spilling out like a tireless machine.

His black eyes are on the window with the missing foam board. The light outside has dimmed by several measures and is closer to his hunt. The black, empty eyes view the lit spot in the window with intensity. They are full of anticipation, need, and want. The time is near, and he is anxious to start.

He throws the blade out one more time, then folds and drops it in the big leg pocket to his black, fatigue pants. The Renaissance man suddenly turns and walks smartly to a huge shelf full of assorted items. He grabs a beautiful, ornate, wooden box off a middle shelf. It has intricate carvings of a tropical scene with silver inlaid integrated into the carved art. Sparkling in the subdued light are inset-colored, semiprecious jewels. The stones come in red, blue, orange, green, and they all gleam with the silver inlaid. It is a large box that he carries to the oak table with care, handling it as if it were some lost relic.

Opening the lid of the box, he sets it all the way back on the table and begins to pull its contents out. It is a bizarre collection of articles. A leather belt of some kind, with four plastic bottles attached to it in leather pockets and a metal box centered in the middle of them. A black wristband with wires connecting to the metal box is laid out on the table. Separate from the wristband are two, relatively long, plastic tubing running from the metal box, then more going to the plastic bottles in short lengths. A stainless steel object the size of a tennis ball is finally brought out that clunks on the tabletop from the weight.

He goes over the inventory of the items carefully and closes the lid back on the carved wooden box. The Renaissance man then reaches in his pant leg pocket and pulls out the switchblade. As he steps toward the basement wall with the window, he fights for his breath and sends the blade out again and again. He stops in the same place he started from and cast his eyes on the open spot without the foam board. The outside has darkened even more, and as the mechanical sound of the switchblade repeats and repeats, an ugly sneer-of-a-grin crosses his pale, gaunt face. He stands there with the misshapen grimace plastered on his mouth, breathing as if there was a storm in his lungs.

# Chapter 14

Driving in downtown Dallas was no easy feat. No matter what time of day or night, it was a process that called for an operator's full attention. Jack was at the wheel of Chris's midnight-blue Impala while B.J. sat shotgun next to him. He had been shooting around the Dallas streets all day and took extra care with the ride because he knew there would be hell to pay if so much as a scratch was put on it. Jack ended up with the hot rod after Chris landed in the hospital from the gunfight.

He never had the chance to drive the car before. Chris would not let him touch it. But while his buddy was in the hospital, it kept him from knowing about his little prank. Jack now understood why Chris was so protective of the ride after going through the gears and feeling the power of the machine. It put the fun in motoring, and it sure beat that piece of crap his old truck had to offer. In spite of this, Jack still felt a little naughty and would have to come clean with Chris when he would be able to talk to him on the next visit. It was a priority he planned to keep in short order just as long as he was healthy enough to receive such news.

The whole time he and B.J. had been on the ride, not much was said. They hardly spoke on the way to the hospital they went to. This stemmed from the fact they were thrust together as strangers to become partners. They were on the verge of getting to know each other, and a lack of words was a natural course of events for both of them. All their conversing so far had come from the case inside the hospital they just left. The silence in the car was now starting to get uncomfortable. But the shortage of conversation allowed a chance for Jack to check his partner out.

She was beautiful; dishwater-blonde hair cascading over shoulders, with skin that belonged in a fantasy. It has that wonderful tone and texture that seemed to stay in a constant golden tan no matter what the season. Her green eyes were alive with intelligence, and they belonged to a face of a model. Her legs, waist; the contours of her figure was simply divine. Not only was she any man's dream, she was a smart, strong, independent woman, and he was going to be cruising all over town with her in this custom-made automobile. Could it get any better?

On the flipside, B.J. was taking the moments to fill out a list of her own. It had to be ages since she was attached to a man under any circumstance, much less a partner who was a cop and pursuing a murder case to boot. From what Captain Parks told her, Jack was a topnotch detective, one of his best, and a man with outstanding integrity. The captain pointed out Jack was the only cop on the force he would consider putting his own family under his watch. She had to admit the guy next to her seemed to be a standup fellow and a handsome one too. One of the things that made him so attractive was the fact he was not preoccupied or even aware of how handsome he was. She could tell he never thought about it. His masculine, square-jawed face, a straight, well-shaped nose, and those blue eyes of his, coupled with the dark hair; any woman would find nice to look at. His muscles, and the way he moved his well-proportioned body all came natural to him. She suspected he looked even better without a shirt. From what she could gather, he was intelligent and quick-witted which conveyed a sense of humor; the kind of man that could laugh at himself. He did not take himself too serious, and he did not appear to be complicated. To put it bluntly, he was not phony about anything, what you saw was what you got.

Jack promptly downshifts to pass a box truck and goes through the gears, maxing out the R.P.M.s. B.J. grabs the armrest and sat with a stiff stare on the road.

"Are you trying to show me what she's got?"

Jack grins. "What, this? To tell the truth, it's not mine, it belongs to Chris."

"That explains it. How'd you end up with it?"

"He's laid up, remember? He won't mind if I use it. At least, I don't think he will."

B.J. smiles. "Trusting soul or ignorance is bliss."

She opens her briefcase, plucks a slip of paper out, and studies it.

"Take a right up here."

Jack takes the turn and rumbles down the lane. B.J. looks at him a long moment.

"You must be worn out. Are you okay?"

Jack peeps at her. “What do you mean?”

“You’ve had a sleepless night with Chris at the hospital, now you’re here with me into the next day, bordering on the evening. We’re looking at a 48-hour run.”

“I’ve had to make long runs before. Thanks for the concern though. I’m sure I’ll crash and burn when I get home tonight.”

“Your wife’s not worried about you?”

“I guess she would be if I had a wife.”

“Something tells me not to go there. So what did you think of the maintenance man at the hospital?”

“You’re right, he doesn’t fit a profile. I think he’s harmless.”

B.J. refers to the slip of paper. “I agree; he’s not our guy. Take a left into this alley.”

Jack reacts to the request. “Where are we going?”

B.J. waves the slip of paper. “According to this, the last crime scene we’re investigating today. This will be the second of the two recent ones. It took place last night while you were with Chris.”

Jack stokes the car down the alley till they both view the customary, yellow, crime tape roping off an area. A forensic truck is parked not far away and being loaded with the equipment the crew has used on the site. The Impala comes to a stop, and the two detectives get out, shout out to the crew who is about to leave, and watch the truck pull away down the alley. Then, they turn to the crime scene and approach it while their steps click out like a Morse code in the natural canyon of the space; the two of them duck under the tape and walk to little red markers dotted randomly on the concrete. A body chalk is outlined behind a dumpster. It jumps out for attention. B.J. points around on the details.

“A woman left this building through that door to get to her car parked over there. She was attacked here, then dragged behind this dumpster.”

Jack surveys the location. “The car must be at the pound. What time did the crime take place?”

B.J. looks at the file. “Around three in the morning.”

Jack takes notice of the backdoor. “That building’s a strip joint; was the victim a dancer?”

“Yes, she was.”

"The previous crimes you mentioned; the ones that took place in Highland Park; were any of those victims a dancer?"

"No, they were professional women. One victim was a mother and housewife."

Jack ambles over to the chalk outline. "Did this woman usually park her car back here?"

B.J. again refers to her file. "According to this report, all the time."

Jack puts his hands back on his hips. "So it was no secret to anyone she might be back here after work, including the perp."

"It looks that way; the manager of the place says it was common knowledge. No one saw or heard anything."

"There's no cameras back here, no surveillance to look at. We need to go talk to the people that work in there."

"We will, but not now. The place is locked up, and no one's there. I have testimony from the manager and people who work here in my file."

Jack looks at the file. "I need to have a study of that file, pronto."

B.J. smiles. "You can take it with you when you go home tonight."

"How do we know this wasn't a simple robbery, not connected to the investigation at all?"

B.J. is scanning the area for anything that might be in question. "Because of the M.O.; it's all in the file."

Jack sticks his tongue in his cheek. "Because of the M.O.; does that have anything to do with the lack of blood at this scene like the one at the hospital?"

B.J. smirks, then turns back toward the Impala and starts walking for it. "We go to the coroner for that answer. Toss me the keys."

Jack follows her. "I know where the morgue is."

"So do I; take a break and let me drive."

Jack digs around in his pocket for the car keys. "I don't know; Chris wouldn't like it."

"How's he going to find out? I'm not going to tell him."

They both go under the yellow tape while Jack pulls the keys out.

"Do you know how to drive a standard?"

"I learned to drive on a standard."

Jack has qualms tossing the keys. "I don't feel good about this, be careful."

B.J. catches them with ease. “What, are you kidding me? I’ve had a death grip on my seat the whole time you’ve been driving. Like a kid with a new toy.”

“Yeah, but the toy is so cool.”

# Chapter 15

There was always a constant odor in the morgue; the smell of chemical death. The permeated air along with a deathly quiet told one they might be in a place far removed from ordinary. This never seemed to bother Edwin Miller. He was, across the board, a very ordinary man. In his private life, there was nothing that was not normal. He was a balding, 35-year-old fellow who married his sweetheart in high school when he was 18. He and his wife lived in a suburban house with a nice, green lawn, a black Labrador, and a white picket fence. Their two daughters went to college and made good grades. Everything about Edwin was extremely common, except for his job.

He was the county medical examiner and hardly spent a day without cutting someone open to find out what happened to them. He managed away his hours, discovering what killed people. The specimen he was working on at the moment was the most unusual case. The second like this in recent days.

It was a young woman; a very pretty, young woman with long, brunette hair and a more-than-adequate figure. What was so curious about the corpse was the total lack of blood. There was such a loss that the cavity of the body seemed to recede. He had never seen anything like it. This included the body that came in not long ago; a mystery that left him befuddled and a little queasy. Considering the nature of his work, anything that made him feel that way was probably vile and detestable.

This cadaver was back on his slab because of the curiosity it held. That, and a report he received this morning. She was a victim from an unknown assailant and was killed for what seemed to be no apparent reason. At least, not the conventional reasons he usually found his subjects to have. There was no sexual assault, no obvious robbery, or an assault through some kind of rage. Blood seemed to be the primary cause for the attack, at least the wanting of it. And blood was an odd motive for something like a killer to pursue.

On his desk behind him was the file that arrived this morning, which gave the basis to examine the corpse once again. He took the liberty to sift through it before his examination of the body. It detailed a history of related cases from Highland Park. He remembered the examiner there calling him and discussing the peculiar incidents and asking if he had ever seen anything like it. Now, he had examples of the same in his lab.

In the middle of the business, Jack and B.J. slam into the place. Edwin takes notice of their presence immediately.

"Jack Degree, one of my favorite detectives."

He adds with a sardonic smile, "Except for maybe my man, Chris; where is that lad, and who, may I ask, is the lady?"

Jack and B.J. ease up to Edwin with the slab table between them.

"This is B.J. Dobbs; she'll be my partner till Chris gets out of the hospital."

"Hospital; my goodness, what happened?"

"We got in a skirmish with a suspect, and Chris got hurt."

"Is he okay?"

"He's fine; he'll be all right, but he'll be on his back for a while. Detective Dobbs is filling in for him. We're here about a recent murder case."

B.J. jumps in with specifics. "The name is Samantha Pearson."

Edwin picks up the file off his desk. "That would be the lady right here in front of you. And, according to this, she matches with another victim I have in the cooler and another three victims from Highland Park a few years ago."

Jack reaches for the file. "Can I see that?"

"Yes, of course."

While Jack takes the file, B.J. looks down at the body. "Was this woman in the middle of her…?"

Edwin recognizes the question. "You've done your homework, Detective. Yes, she was."

Jack is opening the file while observing the body. "I've never seen a corpse like this. It doesn't look right."

"That's because she was bled to death."

Jack looks incredulous. "Come on, Doc, what are you saying—?"

B.J. interrupts, "The blood was taken from her."

Edwin clarifies the comment, "Drained from her would be more like it."

Jack is dumbfounded. "Someone took all the blood?"

Edwin adjusts a sheet on the corpse. "More than enough to kill."

B.J. checks the corpse. "By the same incision?"

Edwin points it out. "These marks here on the neck."

Jack peers at the wound. "Looks like spider bites or something."

B.J. chips in, "It would take a big spider to suck up ounces of blood."

They all take note of two, small, bruised, and red-swollen marks that look like dots on the jugular vein. They are perfect in symmetry and appear to have been administered at the same time, in unison.

Edwin grins. "Maybe I've seen too many midnight movies, but doesn't this seem like a vampire did this."

Jack looks at him. "Oh, I was thinking it was Frankenstein."

B.J. follows the comment, "Maybe the attacker wants us to think it's a vampire."

Jack reacts, "We're not even sure if this connects to the Highland Park murders. Can we see the other body? She's around here, right?"

Edwin supplies an answer, "They all have the same marks, including the two victims I have here. And they all appeared to have died from a lack of blood."

Jack thumbs through the file. "Granted that's an odd point, but none of the victims have anything in common. We have blondes, brunettes, one African American, one Hispanic, three Caucasians; anything from a housewife to a stripper."

Edwin refers to the file. "Read a little more; you'll find we have no fingerprints, blood samples, or D.N.A. on the suspect. It's as if he appears and vanishes like a fog. Except for a boot imprint found at this lady's crime scene. But we're not sure it belongs to the case."

Jack relinquishes. "Maybe I need to hit the rack and get some sleep. It could be I'm not thinking straight. But it seems we have a situation where standard procedure may not apply."

B.J. stares at the coroner. "There is one particular thing all these women have in common besides these marks on their necks; isn't that right, Doctor?"

He smiles at her. "Yes, they do."

Jack waits for an answer. "What, they all had blood."

Edwin gives Jack a summation, "The victims were all killed during their menstruation."

Jack is taken back. "How the hell would the killer know that?"

B.J. supplies a possibility, "You could say he smelled it."

* * *

Dusk fell on the day's light like murky ink leaving a nebulous source of vision. A white Jaguar drives up and parks in front of a formal-looking building. The white of the car makes a sharp contrast in the fading light of the day.

Bicks is the driver of the Jaguar. He shuts his vehicle down and grabs a fedora nestled in the passenger seat. He almost always wore a hat when in public to accentuate his height. It was an extension of the self-consciousness he possessed since being a kid. He was always depreciative about being short, and it plagued him throughout his life; that, and the imaginary dry lips of his.

Sitting in the car, he stares hopefully at the building while applying Chap Stick. This was not the first time Bicks visited the city morgue at such a late hour. It was a common practice in the newspaper days. He found it much easier to gain access to the building as well as obtaining a wealth of information during this time. He looked on pensively and dwelled on the prospects that could be in store for him. Bicks always relied on his journalistic instincts when it came to digging around for a story. What he discovered on the hotwire at his old newspaper haunt gave him a strong indication at getting a line on a tale that could lead to his next book. The potential had enormous value. He had been researching all day in the archives of the newspaper and came across a fortune in book-worthy material. Bloodless bodies found in Highland Park where some of the richest in the country lived. And the mystery descends into a lull, only to resume years later in downtown Dallas.

A new book was something he needed desperately. It was over a year since his last, and the publisher was adamant for another. The pressure was getting to be unbearable, as the shit rolled downhill through his long-time agent and friend. Plain and simple, he needed something fresh and exciting that would transfer into big bucks, and bloodless bodies seemed to be the ticket. He remembered the curiosity that took place in Highland Park while he was in the middle of his second book. The ordeal was so enticing, he almost dropped the book he was writing to chase it. But the sudden halt of murders and the lack of conclusion left any hope of a story. If these recent murders were related to those, it could transpose into his biggest story yet.

He got out of the car, put on his hat, and started down the walkway leading to the glass front of the building. Halfway there, in the middle of his reflections, he sees Jack Degree and a beautiful woman coming out. Jack's bold voice is the first thing that reaches his ear.

"We got a real twist walking around out here, and from the looks of it, he's been walking around for years."

B.J. extends the conversation, "I'll start working on a profile; see if I can't bring an image to the shadow."

Bicks runs into them, with his words cutting into their discourse.

"Well, if it isn't my old pal, Jack Degree; fancy meeting you here."

"Hey, Bicks, what are you doing here?"

"Working like always. And you?"

"Routine rounds, this is Detective Dobbs. Detective, this is Jerome Bickers, but everybody calls him Bicks."

B.J. sticks a hand out. "Pleased to meet you."

Bicks shakes it. "Likewise; I've got to say, Jack, your company has improved."

"Bicks was a reporter for the Dallas Morning News. One of the best, but you never heard me say that."

"Don't let him fool you; I was the best. And he's a damn good detective but don't let him know it."

B.J. smiles. "I'll do what I can."

Jack muses over Bicks. "Now he's a big-time crime writer. That Jaguar over there tells you that. What the hell are you doing around here this time of night; you working on a book?"

"You know me, following hunches; always following hunches. It was nice to meet you, Detective Dobbs; Jack, good to see you again."

Jack smiles. "Same here."

Bicks starts to walk away. "Maybe I'll put you in my next book, Jack, you and the lady here. Who knows?"

The two detectives stand in silence, watching Bicks enter the building and disappear. Jack finally breaks the pause.

"I wonder what he's up to."

B.J. is wondering about the man herself. "Strange hours for the morgue."

"Yeah, for a civilian anyway; come on, I'll take you to your car. I'm going home and sleep before I crash on this sidewalk."

"You'll be okay driving home?"

"I'll be okay. This isn't the first rodeo I've had. It's been a while since I've made a run like this though. Let me have that file, and I'll brief myself on it." B.J. hands the file to Jack, and he tucks it under his arm. "We'll hook up at the office in the morning and see if we can't get a grip on this case."

# Chapter 16

The money from proceeds of the busy day was finally being counted. The doors were locked, and the empty shop was encased in a welcomed solitude. Kathy Summers was proud of her shop. She was proud of the achievement, the long hours of devotion and good, old-fashioned, roll-up-your-sleeves hard work it took to nudge a nook in the commercial world. She enjoyed the merchandise in the shop and how it reflected her own personal taste. The odds were totally against her when she first pursued the quest. Everyone she knew told her it was impossible. Eventually, she found financing for her gift shop, and it became a realization.

Kathy established the place in the lobby of a popular hotel located in the Dallas downtown area. It was situated with two different entrances. One was directly off the street, opened to the public; the other was off the lobby of the hotel itself. Her shop had flourished for over three years and, during that time, became a fixture to the hotel guests, cliental, and management.

The products that were sold varied from anything that was compulsory such as an array of garments and mesh hats to tourism items like key chains and postcards. She had a couple of shelves that contained things you might find in any drugstore and ledges of glassware and figurines.

Pleased with the daily amount made on sales, Kathy takes the money and stuffs it into a bank-deposit bag. Finished with the chore, she collects her purse, gathers the deposit bag, and goes to a large wall mirror just a few feet away. Checking herself, she fiddles with her hair and takes a close look at her makeup. The reason for pampering was anticipation for a business meeting across the lobby in the hotel lounge. It was an encounter she hoped would induce a second and bigger gift shop she wanted to start.

Reaching over to a light switch next to the mirror, she turns off the main lights. It leaves sparse lighting behind the checkout counter; that done, she makes her way to the door leading to the hotel lobby. The entrance to the outside streets had long been secured, and that door had two, large, display windows on either side of it. They each cast a strange illumination like two silver screens produced by thin window shades and the dominate lights behind it from the downtown streetlamps.

Halfway on her walk to the door, an eerie silhouette steps out in front of the silver-screened windows. The outline of the silhouette can clearly be seen, and it is easy to decipher a man wearing a long coat of black cloth. It stands in a defiant ominous stance, still and rigid, and she stops in midstride, startled by the intrusion. The silence that floats between the two of them has gravity, and the oppressive moments drag down as if they were anchored. From this gripping stillness, Kathy calls out with apprehension, thinking she had not noticed someone still in the store.

"Is someone there?"

The moments continue to tick with agonizing burden.

"Who is that please?"

The silhouette does not respond. It stands in the dark, fixed in its stance like stone. Gradually, the tenacious silence is dispelled. By degrees of volume, a creeping sound climbs in the darkness to a jarring crescendo. The sound is that of heavy, ragged breathing seemingly from a demon's serpentine nostrils.

In a panic, Kathy demands some kind of answer to her inquiry. "Dear God, who is that?"

Unexpectedly, the silhouette moves a couple of steps and strikes a beam of light. Stark-black eyes stare out at her with a hideous, stainless-steel mouthpiece covering most of the lower face. Sharp, glinting fangs are exposed like two twin daggers protruding from the mouthpiece. Plastic tubes run up from the contraption, then down inside the clothes, giving him the appearance of an alien from outer space. The mouthpiece amplifies his laden breathing, causing a megaphone effect that parallels the sight of him and creates an even more grotesque picture. He stands motionless in the slash of light, with the resounding breath heaving through the steel contrivance. Then, he reaches for a wristband on the left arm and pushes a button. The mouthpiece opens to a large gape, causing the fangs to be fully revealed as if ready to devour something.

Kathy backs up a step, disarmed by the ghastly image. "My God, stay away from me!"

Without warning, the dark form bolts toward her in a frightening speed, thrusting forward, equal only to the growling roar he wails. Kathy stands next to a display of sunglasses, paralyzed with fear. She screams like a siren from the oncoming rush the figure has mounted.

Out of her horror, she abruptly grabs the display and pulls it down in front of her. The obstacle does the work she intended and causes the nightmarish presence to crash, stumble, and fall. Sunglasses spill like a broken string of pearls scattering the floor. This presents a window for escape, and she scurries off into the shadows of the shop.

She settles at the end of a shelf full of oddities and glassware. Dropping behind a floor display of candy, she quiets down to hide. A cluttered shelf of glass configurations is to her back as she scans the obscurities of the room, her eyes darting about, full of distress. Kathy's breath has reduced to short, quick gasps, being too scared to inhale deeply. Terrifying seconds tick by with density. There is nothing but ghostly stillness while she searches the gray dim, desperate to find the fiend's location. It is so quiet, the pours of her skin seem to soak up the silence, seeping into her bloodstream and embellishing her frantic state of fear.

Suddenly, hands plunge through the cluster of objects on the shelf behind her and grapples for a hold on her. The tiny glass things spray and tumble in all directions while long, black fingernails reach and scratch for a grip. She screams and rises, backing away down the length of the shelves. As she guides herself along the extent of the shelf, a hand snaps through another part of the shelving, clutching at her shoulder. She screams again, fends the hand off, turns, and begins to run.

Almost getting to the end of the shelf, another hand pitches through the articles once more, catching her lapel. She is terror stricken and screams for release, slapping at the fastened hand. The Renaissance man then swings around the end of the shelf, knocking objects away while appearing with his monstrous mouthpiece. The fangs protracting like an animal's teeth. He holds onto the woman with that one hand as items fly around everywhere, emphasizing the frenzy of the moment.

He still has her by the collar when he reaches below with his free hand for her crouch. She screams bloody murder as he picks her up off the floor as if she were weightless. He lifts her high above his head, straightening his arms, with her dangling at his mercy. Then, with a howling roar, he slams her hard on her backside in one horrific motion.

It is instantly quiet except for a loud, laboring breath resonating from the Renaissance man. Kathy lies stunned and helpless at his feet. He drops to all fours and arranges himself so that he hovers over the woman's throat. Fingering a part of her neck with care, he then sticks out his left wrist; the wristband with electronic switches are ready to be used. He presses a button and the mouthpiece widens even more in a mechanical gesture, expanded at the throat of its prey. The fangs twinkle in the unsteady light. His black eyes peer at the wristband. Placing the fangs on a chosen spot, he pushes another button and the metallic jaws clamp down like a bear trap, locking into her jugular vein.

The dead eyes stare coldly at the wristband while he remains attached to the throat like some kind of unnatural parasite. He presses a third button and a pump under his clothing comes to life with a pulsating action. The pump acts like a heartbeat while the plastic tubing turns red with fresh blood and speeds its way out of sight under his clothes. Churning in an unstoppable knell, it sucks the life out of her. During the process, Kathy proclaims a weak, pathetic moan, then slips into a death sleep.

# Chapter 17

Missy liked her morning coffee. She liked the quiet time, the simplicity of it. She usually took it on the terrace of her expensive, high-rise condo. There, she would enjoy the view and soak in the wonderful moments that came before her day started. Before it would steam like a locomotive derailing out of control; before the phone calls, the conversations, the networking and negotiations; before the compliances and settlements, the idiotic and mundane rhetoric with clients, editors, and, of course, the publishers. It seemed to be the only part of her day that belonged to her and her only; private and intimate. On top of that, she had her coffee just the way she wanted it. She was in control.

Missy Hampton was a literature major in college. Ever since she was old enough to read, she fell in love with the written word. Back in junior high school, she started a book club with the help of her English teacher and she, of course, was the president. There were only five other kids in the club, all girls, and they were not exactly the cheerleader types. In fact, they were not any type at all, except for maybe bookworms. This was when she and her club members were first introduced to such writers as Jane Austen, Edger Allen Poe, and Charles Dickens. It was at this time the love she has today for books blossomed into fertile appreciation. By the time she made it to high school, she already had her sights on the field she would pursue in college. What aspect it would be remained to be seen, but she knew it had to be something to do with literature.

After graduating from high school, Missy enrolled at Stanford where she worked at the campus paper. She was just a freshman, and it did not take long to discover that news reporting really was not what she wanted to do. She knew she was interested in being involved with writing, but what vein, what facet in the business continued to elude her. Set with what her major would be, she was clambering for a way to exercise and express it. By the time Missy was in her second year at college, she was taking creative writing classes. It was here she began to formulate the idea she might want to actually write and tell stories.

Unfortunately, it was in these classrooms she found the truth about herself. Missy had no aptitude for writing, at least she felt that way. Patience and the imagination to flesh out a yarn was not in her inventory, or so it seemed. Through a slow turn of events, she came to know she was no author. In short, she realized that even though her great love of the written word prevailed, it did not translate to that ability.

That self-analysis led her to the direction of work she was now in. Right away, she began channeling her efforts toward the business part of the writing industry. The first thing she did was focus on her quest for a degree. During that process, she used her uncanny capacity to sort out possibilities, and, after graduation, she landed a deluxe job at a publishing house. It came about from her mother's friend. She was able to catch on as an assistant, and once she got her foot in the door, she engulfed the work. Missy spent a year with that job when she managed to grab another at a different publishing house as an editor. She stayed there for three years, then moved on to a major publishing house as a senior editor and worked there for six years.

Eventually, she grew restless and bored. She wanted to do more. Over the years, the lady established excellent connections in the publishing industry and cultivated some great relationships with a handful of well-known authors. In time, Missy started thinking about branching into uncharted waters and strike out in a new proclivity. All her dedication and fortitude had brought her to a decision that would reshape her life and career. She decided to become a literary agent. It was a decision that took over a year before it could be acted on.

Clueless to the fundamentals of beginning an agency, she navigated a course through trial and error. After she installed an office and called the agency in her own name, the next objective was to gather clients; people that would produce not only a body of work but also sell copies and create a devoted fan base. After deciding what the genre she would specialize in, according to the publishing and editor connections, she fostered over the years; she got busy on a client list.

One of the very first writers she signed was a young journalist out of Dallas, Texas. He had a sensational, true, crime story about the local police department that involved all the dirty elements that would sell a book. His name was Jerome Bickers, and she saw the potential the young journalist possessed and quickly put him under a contract. A few short months later, she closed a publishing deal, and several months after that, his book was on the shelves. It was not a surprise to see the book become successful and steadily climb the bestseller list.

All these events endorsed the relationship she now had with Bicks. He called her late last night with news of a story that could prove to be original and very profitable. To say the least, she was delighted. He was finally onto a new story, perhaps the best he ever had the opportunity to write about. It was an account of bizarre episodes and intrigue, a tale that was captivating and yet shockingly morbid. Bicks was elated by the prospect when he talked to her. The man had been in a dry spell for many months. So long, she was beginning to wonder if he would ever have another chance to write again. This story seemed to fall in his lap. Not only was he charged about the promise of the book, but he was overwhelmed by how it came to him. As if it was the power of the gods. A gift sanctioned by them, and no one was better qualified than he to deliver it.

Missy was happy for him, and she too was jazzed that one of her best-known authors was on to something. What was really exceptional to the timing was her schedule to go to Dallas by next month. She would be in the city and get updated info from Bicks while there. Missy was to attend a convention held by one of the largest writing societies in the country. It was an annual affair sponsored by the Writer's League of Texas. She would be a key-note speaker as well as an acting agent for the customary pitch session that was invariably held during the occasion.

Looking forward to it, she now had a second reason to be in Dallas. Visiting with Bicks, having dinner with him, and letting him show her a bit of the city. She was also looking forward to a front row seat of his newest book, how it was going to shake out. There was one more thing she was looking forward to this morning, another cup of coffee just the way she liked it. She would languish in her personal, quiet time, reclining on her favorite lounge chair while admiring the view and contemplating the new adventures that were in store for her. She would be in control.

# Chapter 18

The Renaissance man stands next to the big, oak table, stripping his silk shirt off while grappling for breath. His black trench coat drapes the big easy chair close by. He seems exhausted while he heaves through the stainless-steel mouthpiece; pronounced fangs sparkling in the candlelight.

When the silk shirt is off, it exposes a frail, white torso. Luminous in the defused shadows as if there was a source of light coming from within the core. With the shirt removed, an arrangement of simple yet complex systems of the mechanical apparatus he uses can clearly be seen. It all fits to the mouthpiece like the inner workings of a clock.

A wide, leather, belt-like contraption is leashed around his waist, much like a money belt. In the center of the belt is a small hydraulic pump bookended by battery packs. Four, plastic, quart containers (two on each side) flank the batteries sitting in leather pouches. They shine from bright, red liquid filled with Kathy Summers's blood.

Strapped to his wrist is the wristband with buttons; wires leading down a white, inner, left arm can be observed which travels under the silk-shirt sleeve. They are tied to the arm in two places to produce a secure line to the batteries. One set of wires run from the wristband to the batteries, and another set strings from the batteries to the mouthpiece, administering the electronics of the device. The wires that run to the mouthpiece are attached to plastic tubing that affix to the mouthpiece, and both the wires and tubing stream aside the torso under the garment as well. The plastic tubing appears to be quarter-inch aquarium-tubing. They connect to the hydraulic pump in the general area where the wires connect to the batteries. Tiny lengths of the tubes to each of the four plastic containers mounted on the belt lead from the pump and can easily be detected also. The whole invention is arranged to extract blood from the human body. Long, sharp fangs are the focal point and spearhead of the mechanics. A design that manifests a vampire's will.

The stainless-steel mouthpiece glints like chrome as the Renaissance man attempts to remove it from his jaw with some awkwardness. It fits like the red, waxen lips that can be found during Halloween, displayed in commercial stores. The thing slips into his mouth and covers his lips, then settles by the weight. All his actions are drawn and deliberate while he moves. Energy expelled in the night hours explains the absolute weariness. It had been difficult getting back to his lair, unseen by humans. Holding the mouthpiece in his hand, he detaches the plastic tubes connected to the pump. They release from the hard metal in a loud spew of pressure. He undoes the wires to the mouthpiece and puts the contrivance on the table, and it once again clunks heavily on the wood. Turning from the table, he trudges to the refrigerator with the belt sagging from the volume of the blood. The door is opened, and, inside, five wine canisters sit plainly in sight. One is full to the brim, one is half full, and both contain a dark, red substance; oxidized blood. The other three are empty. He takes the empty canisters out, closes the fridge door, and goes back to the table.

Setting the canisters down in a row, he disconnects one of the plastic containers from the pump, and another steamy spew is heard. He then takes the container from the pouch it sits in. He has a driving thirst coupled with a deep yearning to renew his strength. The delicate energy he expunged on his night prowl exhausted his personal stamina. It is the precious blood that will restore him, make him one with his kind. He pours the blood from the quart container into a canister, then gulps it greedily. A tiny sliver of red runs down his chin, unchecked.

Drinking his fill, he empties the rest of the blood from the plastic container into the wine canister. Detaching a second plastic bottle, he tops the canister off. Then, he goes to the refrigerator, opens it, puts it with the other two already there, and closes the door. His cogency is storming back, reinforcing his fortitude. His breathing is becoming easier to bare. The gate to his movement is stronger; the nourishment he just attained is coursing through the fiber of his being and causing a surge of new life to expand like a balloon being inflated. He walks back to the table and starts the procedure over again with the next container.

After finishing the ceremony of replenishing his blood supply and tucking it away safely in the refrigerator, he puts his equipment back in the wooden, ornate box and sets it on the shelf. He goes slowly to the table and blows the candles out. Passing the refrigerator, he decides on another drink. The door swings open, and he pulls one of the canisters out to take a long swig. It tumbles in his throat like sweet velvet, and the charge it gives him seems electric. His strained breath has subsided to a composed gasp. He softly shuts the fridge door and walks purposely toward the corner, past the refrigerator for the black curtains. Each step he takes is methodical and focused. When he reaches the dark curtains, he grips the cloth with both hands and jerks it apart.

Inside, the ebony sheen of the coffin beams like a lighthouse and waits for his entry. The Renaissance man approaches with an encumbered breath, his body just as depleted with need for rest. He lifts the coffin lid, climbs up, and oozes down into the cavity. A slender hand with those long, black fingernails reaches out and drops the lid closed. From within the oblong box, ragged breathing penetrates the chamber like sandpaper.

# Chapter 19

Chris lay in his hospital bed, watching Janet. He looked like an overused punching bag. Black and blue, bundled in bandages on his torso and arm, he lies, still eyeing his girl with a blissful content. Equipment bleeps efficiently next to his bed, flashing digital information on his vitals. An I.V. stands above everything, hooked to his good arm like a sentry on duty.

Janet is reading gift cards from all the houseplants and bouquets of flowers that splash the drab, peril, gray walls in the room with a parade of colors. They are tokens of thoughts and well wishes sent by relatives, peers, and friends. Chris follows the beautiful woman while she moves from one arrangement to another.

She reads one last card, then looks up at Chris observing her. "People really care about you, Chris. A lot of people really love you."

Chris grins. "There's only one person I want to love me."

Janet sets the card down. "Oh yeah, and who might that be?"

Chris, still grinning, confesses, "The girl that comes to see me."

Janet saunters over to him. "By that, you mean me, I hope. What, you need reassurance she loves you?"

"All the reassurance I can get."

Standing at his bed, she bends down and gives him a lingering kiss, then whispers, "How's that for starters?"

He whispers back, "Best piece of reassurance I've ever had. I'm a lucky boy."

She leans in for another kiss. "Yes, you are."

A knock at the door breaks the intimate moment, and it pops open with Jack yelping.

"Knock, knock."

He sees the two lovebirds are nesting and quips, "Didn't interrupt anything, did we?"

The ‘we’ is a reference to B.J. walking in behind him.

Chris responds, “Hey, Partner. Come on in and pull up a chair. Who’s your escort?”

“This is Detective Dobbs. She’s been assigned to me till you’re ready for duty again.”

“Detective, the name’s Chris. This is my girl, Janet Cross.”

Janet nods to her. “Hello.”

B.J. smiles. “Hello, Janet, nice to meet you. Chris, it’s a pleasure.”

“Jack, you never had it so good; by the way, how’s my car?”

“I’ve got a little confession to make.”

“It didn’t break down, did it?”

“No, no, it’s running like a top. I know because I’m driving it.”

Chris looks concerned. “What, you’re what?”

“Don’t worry; I’m taking good care of it.”

B.J. gives support, “He is; I’ll vouch for that.”

Chris eyes both of them. “The trouble with that is I know this guy too well, and, my apologies, but I don’t know you at all.”

Jack is grinning. “I promise your car’s okay. I’d never do anything to hurt it, you know that. If I just left it in the streets, it might get stolen or it might be in the city pound by now, with dents. Keeping it on the road is good for it; I don’t have to tell you that.”

Chris adjusts his position on the bed. It comes with a grimace. “Yeah, well, keep an eye on the water and oil. And keep an eye on the speed limit.”

Janet has been silent all this time. “As far as I’m concerned, you can have that thing. If some criminal doesn’t take my guy, that car will.”

Everyone chuckles to her comment, then the room grows quiet for a moment. Jack intrudes on the pause.

“How’re you doing, Buddy?”

“I’m okay, only hurts when I laugh.”

Janet looks down at Chris. “I’m watching him like a hawk, making sure he does what the doctors say and eats everything they give him.”

Chris smiles at her. “She’s my personal guardian angel.”

Jack checks the room out. “You couldn’t do better; an angel that loves you. Seems to me you’ve got plenty of angels. This place looks like a greenhouse.”

B.J. makes a comment, "Jack told me how you got hurt. I'm glad to see you're going to be okay. Don't worry about this lug; I'll watch over him till you get back."

Janet is bent over Chris, straightening out his sheets. "Hopefully, that will be awhile. At least I know he's safe in here."

Chris takes her hand. "I hope you can get this guy on the right road at being a legitimate cop. Lord knows I've been trying since I've known him."

B.J. puts her eyes on Jack. "I have my hands full, I know. But I see clay in there that can be shaped into something worthwhile."

Jack sputters, "Hey, I'm standing right here."

They all chuckle again. Jack still has traces of a chuckle on his face.

"What are the doctors telling you?"

Chris scowls. "Doc says I'll be up and around in a month or so. At least I'll be able to get on my feet. It'll be some time before I'll be able to get back on duty."

Janet chimes in on that thought, "And I'll be right here step by step. He'll never know how scared I got when this all happened."

Jack looks at her. "I've got some idea. This girl really loves you, Chris, better hold onto her."

He raises his good arm holding her hand. "Don't worry, I am."

Just then, a phone starts ringing, and B.J. reacts to it.

"Excuse me, I should take this."

She sticks her cellphone to her ear. "Yes… Hello, Captain Parks… Yes… We're on our way… Yes, sir; we'll be right there."

She puts the phone away. "Captain Parks, we've got another crime scene to go to."

Jack is astonished. "When does this guy sleep?"

B.J. puts her phone away. "He seems to have an agenda all right."

Chris has to ask, "What's going on? What are you two working on?"

Jack answers, "We've been dealing with a special case. That's why I'm teamed up with B.J. here. It's a weird one that leaves the victims without blood."

"What do you mean by that?"

"If this call ties to the other two, we've got some dude out there with a yen for blood. It seems to be his motive for the murders. We don't know how he gets the blood or why he does."

Chris adds a keen observation, "How do you know it's a dude?"

"Yeah, you're right. We don't even know that for sure."

Janet offers an opinion, "Sounds like there may be a vampire in town."

B.J. regards her, "If that didn't seem so ridiculous, I'd agree with you; there's no doubt this isn't an ordinary case. And it gets more bizarre as we delve into it."

Jack supplies more, "The crime scenes are mounting so fast, it's hard to keep track of them. I can't tell if it's not getting away from us."

Chris can't help himself. "Sounds like you need the expertise I can bring."

Jack responds, "What we need is a clue. Right now, we're like a ship without a rudder."

B.J. points out the time. "We better get going. Chris, get well, sir, and, Janet, glad to meet you, and take care of this guy."

Janet's eyes sparkle. "I will."

Jack opens the door. "Come on, let's go. We'll be back; see you guys later."

Chris opines, "If you need help, you know where to find me."

Jack zings a reply, "That's the only thing I can say I'm sure of. Get better; we'll be seeing you two."

The door closes softly. Chris and Janet stare after it. It is quiet till Chris rips the silence.

"I need to get back on my feet."

# Chapter 20

A murder investigation invokes challenges. Most of the time, starting at square one, standing in front of a pitch-blank wall. There are always obstacles to overcome, and observations are presented to make sound deductions. One is left with the responsibility to decipher those observations and conclude they are clues. To locate them and even the need to recognize the fact that it may or may not be a clue at all. It is a taxing and, sometimes, vexing situation. The wrong summation can lead to a dead end and wasted time. A suspect could turn out to be not a suspect at all, presenting a false hope of certainty in assumptions. To resolve a murder, you need proof. And the best proof a detective can have should be backed by science, a relatively modern tool in the world of investigation. In a lot of circumstances, more reliable than an eyewitness may provide. But, first, the science must be applied to the right specifics.

The importance of time is in play as well. The clock starts ticking as soon as the crime is exposed. Lost time gives the culprit advantages like establishing a fake alibi or erasing existing clues. Another murder might be on the horizon; the suspect could be mounting an escape. Time is of the essence to prevent such things. Clues can grow old through time and maybe become obsolete. The colder the case gets, the more unfeasible it makes to solve it and have a conviction.

The demands of an investigation and plain, old curiosity are the elements that always attracted Bicks. It was a driving force that propelled his career as a reporter and, now, a true crime writer. He was consistently the guy that wanted to look under the rock, peak behind the door, sneak down an alley. He was worse than a cat when it came to curiosity, and cunning as a fox when it came to garnishing facts.

Right now, he was busy gathering information in the records department at Highland Park. Dressed dapper as usual in a peach-colored suit with a white carnation in the lapel, he looked more like an interior designer than someone who studied gruesome murder scenes. A matching peach fedora was also sitting next to a keyboard of a computer his fingers were actively plugging away on. He had been scrolling for data all morning and was stuck on a screen he found interesting. Bicks confirmed his reading, then slapped the print button, got up from his seat, and went to the printer.

Retrieving the printed sheet, he goes back to his seat and reads the paper carefully. While he does this, Bicks pulls his Chap Stick out and applies the stuff to his lips. Still reading, he puts the Chap Stick away and brings out his little pocket recorder. He presses the record button and speaks into it with his eyes on the print.

"I'm at the Highland Park's records department, and I've printed some material on the murders that took place in this city. I'm convinced these murders are connected to the murders occurring now in the Dallas area. Both sets of murders have the same peculiar particulars; bloodless bodies, identical marks on the necks of the victims, and most of these murders took place in public buildings. All this is confirmed by the interview I had with the staff at the Dallas morgue. One of the murders in Highland Park took place in a doctor's office and the other in a condo. The very first murder was a housewife attacked in her garage, then taken to the side of the house where she was found. The point about this is the murders in public buildings occurred without any signs of a break in; a curious feature to iron out in my inquiry on the matter."

Bicks clicks off the recorder and taps a finger on it. He spends some moments in his thoughts, then scoops up his printed papers while putting the recorder away in his pocket. Getting up from his seat, he grabs his hat and sets it on his head. Then, he turns the computer off and walks for the door, goes through it, and vanishes.

The outside doors suddenly swing open, and Bicks steps out into the fresh air and sunshine. He blinks to the bright sunlight and makes haste for the parking lot where his white Jag stands out among the parked cars. When he gets to it, Bicks unlocks the door and climbs into it.

Sitting in his car, he puts the printed paper away in his briefcase and pulls out some Chap Stick he keeps in the case for another bout of moisture. While he practices his habit, he reaches over and turns on a police scanner he had installed in his Jag. A friend of his in the police force managed to obtain the radio for him, and it has become one of his key tools in the work he does. It keeps him abreast on police affairs and helps him with getting to crime scenes promptly. In other words, it puts his ear to the ground.

Right now, a broadcast informs him of a bloodless body found at a hotel gift shop in downtown Dallas. In moments, he fires the car up and zips out the parking lot.

# Chapter 21

The crime scene appeared to have had a party in it, sponsored by a troop of monkeys. A handful of shelving lines the floor in a parallel pattern, and one shelf in particular has been severely violated. Broken glassware is scattered and ransacked all over the tile floor. Joining the glass shards are small, boxed items and silly tidbits, found in any gift shop, flung about fitfully. Near an entrance, close to the counter where the cash register is, are numerous sunglasses smashed and demolished. As if a typhoon personally tossed the display stand they came from into a storm of frenzy.

The place was soundless except for a constant popping manufactured by several men jumping around, snapping photographs. Some of them are bagging anything that may seem curious or pertinent to the site. In the middle of all the activity is a pale and twisted body lying lifeless on the floor without a bloodstain. Hands are concealed with paper bags to preserve the purity of the evidence that may be there. The coroner, Edwin, is kneeling over it. He is busy examining the woman's neck for those odd marks he found on the other victims. Each of them has one obvious thing in common; a total lack of blood.

Jack and B.J. step into the investigative fray, wide-eyed and apprehensive. Careful not to disturb anything while casting their eyes about, taking in the annihilated store. The old fox, Sam, is at the sales booth, fishing around with surgical gloves on, rifling through the deceased's purse. He gives a nod to the two detectives, then finds a pocket purse and holds it out in plain view.

"Here's the victim's driver's license. Her name is Kathy Summers. 33 years old, Caucasian."

B.J. observes a tagged item on the floor. "I see a bank bag here."

Sam looks at her. "Yeah, full of money from daily sales more than likely."

Jack glances at the bag. "Which rules out robbery; do we know if she's the owner of this place?"

Still searching through the purse, Sam answers the detective, "She does, according to the janitor who found her this morning."

Jack is alerted by the comment. "Janitor, what janitor is that?"

"Right now, he's in the hotel somewhere, working. I talked to him earlier. He said he came in to sweep the place and spotted her the minute he opened the door. As soon as he did, he ran off to notify management. I got his name and number for a follow-up interview."

B.J. is watching Sam. "He said he didn't walk around in here?"

"Nope, he never got past the doorway."

"That keeps the integrity of the crime scene. Nobody else on the staff came in here, did they?"

"I asked; the janitor said no."

Jack chimes in, "He's sure of that?"

"As far as I'm concerned, he is."

Jack surveys the room. "No bloody foot imprints, no fingerprints to lift that can be assigned to the crime; there doesn't seem to be any useable evidence."

Edwin looks up from his inspection of the body. "The wounds aren't big enough for a blood imprint to occur, not to mention the absence of blood to cause a bleed out. There must be hundreds of fingerprints in here; when I get the body to the lab, I can take a closer look for D.N.A. or any fingerprints on the body or somewhere perhaps on the jewelry or maybe the purse, the money bag."

Jack stands with his hands on his hips and takes in the huge mess the floor displays. "From the look of things, she put up a hell of a fight. I can't figure how the perp is able to take blood like he does without leaving blood everywhere."

B.J. moves next to Jack. "What do you mean by that?"

"I don't know, taking blood while fighting the victim, like this place seems to imply, and leaving no blood residue anywhere? How the hell can you do that? What does the perp use to take the blood?"

Sam quips, "Maybe a stun gun was used."

Edwin stands up from the body. "I may have the answer to some of what you speak of."

Jack looks at him. "Yeah, enlighten us, Doc?"

"This woman and the girl from the alley both have the backs of their heads split open. I think maybe they were thrown with such force, it slammed their heads against the ground, knocking them senseless. The girl at the hospital was slammed into a concrete pillar so hard, it did the same. Now, what he used to obtain the blood taken is another matter. I don't have an answer for that."

Jack looks mystified. "It would take muscle to knock people out like that."

Edwin looks down at the body. "Extraordinary strength; there's bruising on this woman's inner thigh, along with bruises on her collarbone the girl in the alley didn't have. She might've been picked up above the head, then thrown down to the floor so hard, it left her unconscious."

Jack is dumfounded. "That sounds like a stretch. What sort of freak are we talking about?"

B.J. answers him, "Someone with abnormal motives could produce abnormal physical qualities. And going by Doc's theory, I'd say our perp is a man."

Sam puts in another quip. "I'd use a stun gun."

B.J. adds, "I don't think he would use a gadget like that to subdue his victims. It's not personal enough."

* * *

Bicks was checking his watch. He was stuck in downtown traffic and was not happy about it. Sitting idle for some time, he reaches in his pocket and puts the Chap Stick to his lips. The road ahead was jammed pack, but he did not have far to go. The hotel he wanted was just a few blocks down the street. He thought about parking the car and walking. But that could turn into a bigger nightmare than what he was already in. Considering it was downtown Dallas anyway. His car was framed in the position he was in, and by the time he got to a parking spot, the traffic could be moving, and it would take time to get back into the flow of it. Putting the Chap Stick away, he decided to wait. He figured it would only be moments before he got free of the glitch and on to the hotel.

The whole time he had been driving, his ear was on the police scanner. Sure of what he heard, he knew this crime scene was one he needed to be at for the book. And from the info the scanner gave, he would probably walk right into the middle of the affair. Bicks checked his watch again and scowled at the losing time. He glared at the traffic in front of him and tapped fingers on the steering wheel impatiently.

* * *

Jack and B.J. are sifting through the bagged inventory of evidence collected by forensic. Some of the stuff warrants a vague interest to the case. There is a matchbook found on the floor near the corpse; a scrap of paper with what appears to have part of a phone number to be scrutinized.

B.J. is handling the bag with the matchbook. "What do you think of this?"

Jack puts his eyes on it. "If it's got a fingerprint on it that leads to our guy, yahoo; otherwise, it's just debris on the floor like a lot of this crap probably is. It may be the janitor not sweeping the floor might hurt our inspection instead of helping it."

The two detectives are standing at the front counter where Sam searched through the victim's purse. Sam is across the way, watching a forensic guy dust the door for prints that opens directly to the outside streets. The two display windows that bookends the door are shinning from the day's light and filtering the gift shop with a bright source. Things are winding down, and the investigation is on the verge of wrapping up. Edwin and most of his crew are outside on the sidewalk for the moment. The pale remains of Kathy Summers laying on the floor still forms the nucleus of the space, lying in a chalk outline, waiting for removal.

Jack quits his study of the bagged items. "I've had enough of this. The pickings are slim."

B.J. watches him leave. "I've got a couple of things here that needs a close look."

"Good luck to that." Jack heads for the door that leads to the lobby of the hotel. He takes a good look at its operation.

"There's no forcible entry on this door. What about that one over there, Sam?"

"Nada, this door was locked, and it hasn't been tampered with. It's got a bunch of smudged prints but nothing solid to use as evidence."

B.J. is finished with her inspection of the bags. "When are these doors normally locked for the day?"

Sam drifts back toward the heart of the shop. "The janitor said they were always locked after hours. A sign out front tells you the place closes at ten."

B.J. puts her eye on the bank bag. It too is also part of the bagged items on the counter. "This money bag tells you it was after hours."

Sam adds to the notion, "The janitor mentioned he used his passkey on that lobby door to get in this morning."

B.J. is at the sales booth where the victim's purse was spilled out. "The store keys are right here."

She picks them up to show the keychain for all to see. It too is in a plastic bag.

Jack looks at the bag of keys. "That doesn't make sense. How could the doors be locked after the killer leaves with the keys in here? For that matter, how can the perp enter if the doors are locked?"

B.J. answers with a question, "Can that door be secured by closing the thing and it shuts locked?"

Jack has surgical gloves on and examines the door. "No, it can't. You need the keys. What about your door, Sam?"

"It operates the same way. It could be the murder took place before the store was locked."

Jack makes an assumption, "Then explain that bank bag full of money. We'll ask Doc for a time of death, but it still doesn't make sense; the doors were locked and the keys are in here."

B.J. makes a point, "Remember the backdoor to the hospital was supposedly left open unexplainably too."

Jack reacts, "Yeah, that's right."

Sam sticks a finger in the air. "Maybe the janitor was wrong. He was pretty scattered when I talked to him. Maybe he got things jumbled around and walked in here this morning without using his keys."

Jack responds to Sam's point, "Double check with him. Don't press; let him think about it but see if he can get a clear picture."

Sam pulls out a pad and pencil and jots a note down. "I'll go talk to him right now."

Jack summarizes the conversation, "So we have some interesting questions. What's the time of death, were the doors locked after hours, and how the blazes did the doors end up locked with the keys lying right there?"

Sam heads for the lobby entrance, going by Jack, when he runs into Edwin entering with a crew and gurney. They get through the doorway and direct themselves to the body.

Sam slides through the doorway after they clear it. "I'll go find the janitor."

Jack walks over to Edwin. "Hey, Doc, you got any idea at the time of death?"

"Preliminary estimate puts it at between 10:30 and a little after 11."

Jack and B.J. eye each other. Jack invokes a result. "That means, in theory, the doors were locked."

B.J. drops the bag of keys back on the counter. "What about a hiding place? He could've been hiding around here somewhere. Like the bathroom or a storage room. Is there a broom closet?"

Jack follows that train of thought. "Good idea, we need to see if there's any place you could hide around here. Any nook and cranny someone could wait till after hours."

The coroner smiles. "We found two places that would fit that bill; the bathroom and a broom closet. The bathroom is small; we dusted it and found nothing. It didn't seem to be disturbed in any way; there was no evidence someone might have stood around in there for any length of time. The broom closet doubled as storage, you can barely get a broom to fit in it."

Jack tugs on his surgical gloves. "We also need those keys dusted for prints."

"They were clean of multiple prints. I suspect the print on them belongs to the deceased. We'll find that out. The wagon's outside, so I'll be taking the body to the lab."

"Okay, Doc, good job. We'll get out of the way."

Jack and B.J. start for the door leading to the hotel lobby. On the way, B.J. has a thought.

"You know, even if a hiding place was established, it still doesn't address the fact the two doors might've been locked with the keys inside."

* * *

Finally, free of the jam he was in, Bicks weaves through the downtown traffic with agile urgency, trying to get to his destination. He shoots the Jag past a beer truck that was blinding his view and discovers a small crowd of pedestrians gathering on the sidewalk halfway down the block. Smiling, Bicks quickly checks the area for a place to park and sees a gaggle of old comrades from the morning news. They are assembled and putting a team with a camera together. A news truck is parked nearby where they are congregated, and, grinning, he finds a niche to leave his car next the truck.

* * *

The detectives are shoving the glass front doors to the hotel open and coming out on the street. A few policemen in blue are keeping the accumulating mass at bay as they make their way to the sidewalk. The day is sunny, and both of them squint to adjust their eyes from the brightness.

With a hand shading his view, Jack looks at the crowd of people. "I see the rubbernecks are here. Listen, as soon as they get the body out, let's go back and check the ceiling for any unknown access."

B.J. follows the suggestion. "We should take a close look at vents and the outside walls too."

Jack announces, "There might be two sets of keys. And the killer took a set with him when he left to lock the door. Assuming the janitor was right in the first place and used his passkey to get in."

B.J.'s eyes light up. "Yeah, a set of keys in the cash register or something; but why would he lock these doors and leave the hospital door unlocked? Assuming the door was left open in the first place."

Jack takes in the throng of people watching things unfold. "It could be because of all the traffic on the streets; as opposed to the seclusion of the basement in the hospital. He figured he didn't need to use any keys to make an easy escape from that site. Not to mention all the people in the lobby of the hotel that might walk in at any time."

Out of nowhere, Bicks walks up on them with a question, "Keys to what?"

Jack turns to see Bicks applying Chap Stick to his lips.

"You're getting to be a familiar face."

"Blood always brings the shark, you know that; keys to what?"

B.J. jumps in with a retort, "The keys to my car."

Bicks sniffs at the answer. "In a cash register?"

Jack quickly intercedes, "It's nothing of interest you need to know."

"Come on, Jack, give me a break. I'm looking for a storyline, and I smell something big in this one."

"Sorry, Buddy, this needs to stay under wraps."

"We've worked together on things before and it was all good; remember? I can help you, you can help me."

B.J.'s eyes dart from one man to the other. "You mean, show me yours and I'll show you mine."

Bicks looks at her with a big grin. "Yeah, something like that."

B.J. grins back. "Something like that huh. Sorry, but it's like my man said, no can do."

# Chapter 22

It was so quiet, you could hear a bug walk. The lid to the ebony casket began to creep open, revealing a rasping sound that conflicted to the quiet. Gradually, the Renaissance man climbed out of his resting place, toiling for breath, and got his feet on the concrete floor. He shuts the casket tight and ambles out of the curtained area into the main living space, still suffering for air.

He goes to the refrigerator immediately and opens the door. Grabbing a canister, he guzzles blood willingly. It is a long drink, and he stops shortly for an accursed choking breath, then resumes his consumption. The canister is emptied and replaced with another. He spends some time on the second, relishing the nourishment. After finishing, he puts the container back in the refrigerator and closes the door.

The Renaissance man then plods to the oak table in his respired state and retrieves the quill and inkwell that is always found there. He collects the instruments after taking the top of the inkwell off and, with care, takes them to the big, leather chair. He sets the objects next to his journal sitting on the small table where he keeps his switchblade. Turning on the floor lamp to full wattage, he eases into the chair and picks up the journal. Taking the quill in his hand, he takes a moment to gather his thoughts, then dips the thing in the inkwell and begins to write. The only sound heard is his laborious breathing and the quill scratching the parchment as he tabulates his resolutions.

* * *

*I am the last of my kind. There is no other individual that can carry my breed to the future. No other that can mount a population and challenge the world with numbers. I have known nothing but struggle, isolation, and sacrifice. The whole of my nation lies totally on my shoulders, but I will prevail.*

*I discovered myself, in terms of time, in a very recent period; a very recent and short period. The discovery was by accident, and as it was revealed to me, it became a measured conception of rebirth. And by this rebirth came the realization that my powers had been taken. Actually stolen, robbed by humans. Through a grinding process of repetition, a repetition of a performance through what humans created, I came to know who and what I was. A walking, vibrant vampire to scour the earth and take what belongs to my clan.*

*The powers that are my birthright will be restored. The loss of their memory came through a procedure that was clouded by an overload of drugs, by confinement and restriction; by psychoanalysis brain draining, by persecution, and last but not least, physical amputation. The humans have systematically changed me or at least have tried to change me. And it was a change to something that is less than my status in life, my stature and position, my creed. They have been trying to make me human. Now, I am alive; alive as a child of the night. And I will only get stronger; stronger and more powerful and invincible. The humans will know my wrath by night and fear my powers by day.*

*Slowly, I'm becoming the prince that I was born to be. The humans managed to take my shape-changing powers, my mystical allure; my enduring and compelling force. But most of all, they have taken my mark of the vampire. The tools used to feed; the holy grail of my identity, my fangs.*

*Blood will bring all these traits back; blood, the eternal stream of life; the essence of life itself. The life-giving source of strength and health that are mine to have, and I will obtain my birth's right. The more I consume blood, the closer I become to the manifestation; the crux of my real worldly being. I will claim my top of the food chain and evolve to the king that I am. And it will all be done through the acculturation of blood. And, with it, my tribe will be restored, and I will be the paramount I was meant to be.*

* * *

The Renaissance man stops writing and reviews his words. Satisfied with what he has done, he sets the quill down and closes the journal. Putting that away on the small table, he grips the switchblade lying there and releases its steel. The blade glows in the light, and he folds and sends it free several times, deep in thought. Each time the blade appears, it shines with authority. And, with each time, his breathing gets louder.

Finally, the Renaissance man puts the knife back in its place and gets up from his seat. He moves to a tattered trunk he noticed and studied while playing with the switchblade. Catching his attention with a curious aspiration, he goes to it on intuition. It is next to where the hat tree stands, and he wonders what it might contain. The trench coat that is used on his night prowls hangs on the hat tree, but he ignores it and opens the trunk. He gets down on his knees and methodically pulls garments from a wardrobe of what looks to be from different periods of time. He suddenly stops his activity and stares down into the cavity of the trunk. With care, he brings out something significant from the containment. It is a large, black cape. Instantly, he realizes this old costume piece has been waiting for him to be discovered and used. He shakes the fabric loose, and it spreads like the wings of a bat.

# Chapter 23

Speechlessness produced a calm in the midnight blue, disturbed only by the stop-and-start motion of the engine. Jack wheels through the downtown traffic while B.J. sits across from him, frowning in thought. They just left the crime scene and found nothing suspicious in the gift shop that would parley to a concealed entrance or exit. This left the standing question of how the shop door was locked and the key to it remained inside. Aside from the theory of a second set of keys, it was very perplexing. Both detectives pondered over what Sam would have to say after talking to the janitor again.

Along with that little quiz was the needling conversation they had with Bicks out in the street. B.J. could not get it off her mind. She kept mulling it over, trying to decipher if it was worth bringing the subject up to the partner next to her. It seems because she was nothing more than audience; she stumbled into something unknown to headquarters or Captain Parks. Jack did not seem to give it a passing thought, but it haunted her like some dark secret had been revealed. She sat there, musing over the occurrence and brooding about it when Jack's voice interrupts the tranquility.

"Why are you so quiet? What are you thinking about?"

B.J. is startled. "Nothing, nothing important anyway."

"Don't give me that. I can tell something's eating at you. The vibes have been pretty evident since we've been in the car."

"I'm not sure if I should even mention it."

"Anything would be better than the silent treatment I'm getting."

B.J. turns to him. "All right, I do have one thing to ask."

"I'm waiting."

"It's got to do with the conversation we had with that Bicks guy."

"I'm still waiting."

"All right, how much information have you managed to leak to him in the past?"

Jack chuckles. "What do you mean?"

"Have you turned over confidential material that may have compromised a case?"

Jack glances at her with a grin. "Are you kidding me?"

"I want to know. I'm wondering if there's been a breach of some kind on standard procedure; if it can potentially happen in this case."

"Well, you know what a stickler I am for standard procedure."

B.J. sits by quietly, waiting for some kind of answer to his cavalier behavior. Her stare imposes on him, and it burns so hot, Jack can feel it. He finally mounts a reply to her inquiry.

"I wouldn't say that I leaked anything."

"What would you say?"

"I'd say it's been more like a cold war. I never told him anything I didn't want him to know, and I'll lay a bet he's done the same."

"How can you be so sure?"

"You can't be sure of anything. But I do know there's never been a breach on anything to do with a case. I played him; he never played me."

B.J. turns back to the traffic. "Oh, what are you, a bullshit pimp?" In a mock voice, she quips, "I played him; he never played me."

She projects her focus on the traffic and cars. In a slip of time, a slight smile unfolds on her face.

"Cold war." She looks at Jack. "Mr. Diplomat."

The both chuckle a bit, then fall into a silence with a comical smirk. Several moments tick along while they take in more of the heavy traffic. All of a sudden, B.J. happens to view a strange disruption on her side of the street. Her forehead crinkles from the sight.

"Do you see that? What is that? What's going on?"

* * *

Three young men wearing ski masks were leaving a convenient store, waving guns. One of them had a large bag dangling in one hand. An old Asian woman was hanging onto it, screaming words in her language while the man drags her by the knees through the door.

The old woman shrieks like a parrot as fearful onlookers scatter like geese, getting clear of the ruckus. The other two robbers run for a Ford double-cab truck parked nearby. The man struggling with the woman is not keeping pace with his pals, slowed down by the old lady clinging to the bag. He starts to pistol whip the woman when Jack and B.J. pull to a screeching halt and jump out with their revolvers. Both of them hunker behind the opened car doors.

Jack roars out an order, "Freeze, police!"

The two men are behind the truck on the driver's side and immediately start firing their weapons. Absolute chaos follows, and everyone with a gun starts shooting. During the fierce battle, the man with the bag jerks free of the old woman and escapes for his buddies. Blasting away while running for the truck, Jack takes a quick aim and hits him in the upper thigh. He tumbles and sprawls on the sidewalk, losing his weapon. It skitters off on the concrete, several feet away. The bag flies up in midair and lands in the center of all the bedlam. The new situation does not deter the men at the truck as the gunfight thunders on like the old west in the streets of Dodge City.

The old woman, still on all fours, scrambles to the bag like a crab and grabs it. The gunfire spits bullets all around her; they wiz everywhere, smacking brick walls, breaking glass window, and drilling car metal. The woman retrieves the bag in the middle of the raging gunfight and crawls back into the store, untouched.

The two guys at the truck have been banging rounds off furiously. When they see the loot is lost and their partner who is shot has the truck keys, it leaves them with little to do but abandon their cover and run down an alley next to the store. Firing over their shoulders, Jack and B.J. walk steadily after them, returning fire just as intensely while they disappear around a corner. B.J. kicks the gun further away from the man that is down and kneels to cuff him.

Jack yells at her, "Call for backup!"

Then, he tears out after the two men. He dashes into the alley, expecting to be shot at. He looks about hastily and spots a door swinging loose. It is halfway down the alley, leading to a neighboring building. Jack cautiously heads for it.

* * *

The open door felt like a trap. Jack pulls himself through it and is confronted with a host of wooden crates. Mountains of stacked crates fill the floor like a vast sea. Too numerous to count, they leave an ominous maze to walk in. Jack moves into the warehouse among all the boxes timidly, taking heed from exposure and alert for any sight of his quarry. He nuzzles up to a chest-high cover when gunshots explode and peppers his location with missiles.

Jack drops behind the wooden barrier and returns a blind volley. Tucked down in his nook, beads of sweat form on his forehead; his breath shortens, and his heartbeat pounds like a drum in his ear. The excruciating silence that follows acts as a villain in the hothouse of the building, and he wonders where the culprits might be. It is oppressive and burdensome with the unknowing consequence of what his opponents are up to.

Peering through the obstacles of his protection, Jack spots one of the men through an open gap and sees him pointing a direction for his comrade. The man unwittingly gives him a clear target. Jack nestles his gun into his empty hand and takes a careful aim. The gunshot rings out, and the young man is hit. Jack hears him yelp and watches the man lope away, holding his arm. The other man retaliates, clipping several rounds off and sending a hoard of metal in Jack's direction. Then, the shooter moves hurriedly on an opposite course his buddy took.

Jack starts tracking the man who is not hurt, thinking he is the dangerous of the two for the moment. He goes down a line of crates stacked so high, it is a virtual wall. Moving with stealth, Jack crosses a lane and runs down the length of another huge stack. Peeling around a corner, the silence stifles every decision made. It becomes despotic and heavy like a lead cloak.

The man he is looking for is darting through a clutch of boxes, out of breath. Sweating profusely from the tension of the predicament his shirt is soaked from it. Pointing his gun at anything he hears or anything he thinks he hears, the man works himself into a small clearing on the floor; unsure of which way to go, he stands rigidly in place, trying to figure out his dilemma. The unsettling silence blankets everything, and his loud breathing penetrates the stillness. Jack's voice suddenly erupts, disturbing the eerie equipoise.

"Don't move, don't think about it. Now, real slow, lay that gun on the floor and kick it away."

Jack has placed himself directly to the man's rear, and the young man hesitates to the command.

"You can't win, Son. Don't do something stupid; give it up."

He still does not comply. A moment lags by like a creeping predator. Anticipating the actions of the individual, Jack sends his right leg kicking while the man turns with his gun. Just as the turn is finished, Jack's kick and the gun meet. The pistol fires off harmlessly and sails some distance away. In a flash, Jack matches the kick with a left hook and slugs the fellow senseless.

Looking down at the guy, Jack shakes his hand to pacify the pain, then sucks on the knuckle for relief. Without warning, a voice staggers the quiet.

"I got you now, Cop, drop your gun."

Jack contemplates the alternative, then decides against it and lets the revolver plop to the concrete. He turns toward the voice. The young man shot in the arm stands there, bleeding.

"Look what you did to me, Asshole. You fucking shot me, and it fucking hurts. You, son of a bitch, you're a dead man. But, first, I'm going to make you pay, and you ain't going to like it."

He sets his pistol on a straight aim at Jack's crotch.

Out of nowhere, B.J. pops into the scene from behind a bunch of crates with a big, red, fire extinguisher. Quick as a cat, she blows white fog in the boy's face. He flings his arms around in the cloud of mist, confused and disorientated.

B.J. then slams the extinguisher into his gun hand, and he yowls with pain. The weapon clanks to the floor, and B.J. couples the assault with a bash to the head. It puts the guy out, and he drops to the concrete.

Jack stands a few feet away, watching the chain of events. They stare at each other for a few seconds, then Jack grins big.

"What took you so long?"

B.J. sets the fire extinguisher on the floor and inspects a finger.

"I think I broke a fingernail."

# Chapter 24

The squad office was as solemn as a classroom in the middle of an exam. Captain Parks was used to his men filling the air with noise and nonsense when he came into this room. His huge bulk roamed around the desks like a buffalo in a suit; scoping out things lying on the desktops and generally surveying the area without the bustle of detectives grabbing his attention. He checked the walls in the place for what seemed like the first time. They were cluttered with memos, wanted posters, alert notices, and personal reminders. File cabinets and framed documents occupied the spots where no paper hung. In a small breeze, the papers would flap and rattle from lack of being completely tacked. It gave the room a shoddy appearance that produced the feel that nothing could bloom here when it came to results. But, in reality, this office had one of the best arrest and conviction records in the state.

Captain Parks found himself standing in the middle of the space like a big tree, all alone, with a gallon of idle time. His hands stuffed deep in his pant pockets. He still felt a little at odds with the empty room. The captain's right hand jiggled loose change, causing his right pant leg to jump up and down. It gave the impression a pet mouse was bouncing around in all that cloth. Almost at the end of his wait, because time was short, he was about to walk out when voices started floating into the office. The voices get louder, and it tells him that someone is on their way to join his solitude from the hallway.

They belonged to B.J. and Jack, and as the two of them scamper into the office, they see Captain Parks immediately. Both are jazzed from the gunfight they just had and chattering about it. Jack throws a comment at the captain on his way through the door.

"Hi, Captain, we just had a hell of a shootout. B.J. and I rode up in the middle of an armed robbery."

The captain still jiggles his change. "Yeah, I heard about it on dispatch, one of the reasons I walked in here. Everyone's okay?"

"Yeah, we're okay. My partner did a great job. Thanks to her, I'm still here."

B.J. looks to the captain. "It all came down pretty quick. Neither one of us got hurt, the only ones that did are two of the perps. There were three all together, and they're being booked right now."

Captain Parks takes his hands out of his pockets and folds his arms. "That's all good news, but I have another reason to be here."

Jack realizes what the captain wants. "Let me guess, a bloodless body at the Crown Fountain Hotel."

The captain puts his attention on Jack. "Give the man there a teddy bear for a prize. These cases are getting more press as they grow in numbers, and this one took place in the heart of downtown; in one of our most prestigious hotels no less."

The detectives go deeper into the office to find a seat. The captain remains in his spot like a boulder. Jack goes to his desk. He falls into the chair, opens a drawer to get a pencil, and pulls a sheet of paper out as well. B.J. has no desk to sit at, so she perches herself on one near the door. Crossing her long, lovely legs and allowing the hem of her skirt to ride high above her knees, it gives the two men something to look at besides old furniture.

Jack starts his report to the captain, "The case at the hotel connects to the other two. Forensic has dusted the shop, but it's unlikely anything will come of it, since it happened in such a public place. This scene is like the others; no physical evidence was found. The corpse will be checked at the lab along with bagged items. What the findings will be remains to be seen. The only thing we do have right now are what we already had, a bloodless body without a customary motive."

Captain Parks shuffles his feet. "Any idea how the blood is taken?"

"Nope, no idea; we think maybe the women are unconscious while it's done; how or why, we don't know."

B.J. speaks out, "One thing that sticks out is the matter of keys."

Captain Parks turns to her. "How do you mean?"

"The deceased, Kathy Summers, owned a gift shop off the lobby of the hotel. She was found inside the shop along with her keys. What doesn't fit, though, is the doors were locked and her keys were inside the gift shop with her. Those doors can't be opened or locked without the keys; you simply can't leave them locked without the keys to do it."

Jack chimes in, "A backdoor at the basement of the hospital was found open where the victim was, and no one knows how it was open. The custodian at the hospital didn't know why it was unlocked; he made sure it was when he wasn't using it. And you can't open it without a key, inside or outside; and you can't leave it locked without a key. Besides the lady in the alley, we keep finding doors without any keys to explain their function."

The captain ponders the dilemma, "Who found the body at the hotel?"

B.J. answers, "The janitor when he unlocked the door to clean the place."

Jack adds to B.J.'s reply, "There are two doors; one goes to the lobby of the hotel, and the other opens to the street. We checked them both; there was no forcible entry. No evidence of any kind they were tinkered with. For that matter, there was no forcible entry on the door at the hospital."

The captain circles his steps. "The janitor is sure they were locked, both of them?"

"Sam is double checking that testimony right now. Forensic established the victim was attacked after she closed the store. It stands to reason the doors were locked while she counted money.

"There's no evidence he waited for the store to close. So, the question is, how did he gain entry, and how were the doors locked after he left?"

B.J. puts fuel on the fire, "We had the super show us blueprints of the building. To see if there was a way in or out without the use of a key. Nothing came of that. There is a possibility that another set of keys exists, and he took them with him after the crime, but that doesn't answer how he got in there in the first place."

Jack throws more gasoline on the fire, "It's a big, red flag that needs explaining. If all this lines up, that means the suspect had his own set of keys not only for the hotel but for the hospital as well. If that's true, where and how did he get those keys?"

B.J. jumps off the desk and walks to the men. "We're waiting on Sam to see what he found out from the janitor about another set of keys we don't know about and if the doors were locked for sure when he came in."

Captain Parks steadies a gaze on both of them. "Very well, keep working the case. Let me know what Sam digs up."

He starts walking for the door. "I'd like what we've been talking about on paper please."

Jack looks at his back. "I'm doing that right now, Captain."

The captain gets to the door, stops, and turns to B.J. "I'd like to see a profile on the suspect as soon as possible."

"I'll have one, Captain, like Jack said, I'm doing that now."

The captain walks away and leaves B.J. and Jack to stare at each other. Jack smiles with knowing eyes.

"Paperwork; the drudge of police work; wish I could wave a magic wand and it's done."

"Speaking of magic, you sure are lucky all that shooting didn't hit Chris's car. Not one bullet."

"Yeah, that was magic, wasn't it? And it will stay magic if no one tells Chris it was in a gunfight."

"I won't tell if you don't tell."

"Good. I'm hungry, how about you?"

"I'm starved."

Jack puts the paper and pencil back in his desk. "I'll do this later at the house. I know a great place we can get something to eat; it's called The Blue Note."

"Can you get a drink there?"

"That goes without saying."

"Great, I could use one."

Just then, Sam strolls into the office. "Hope I'm not intruding."

Jack lights up when he sees him. "You're always intruding. So, what did you find out, did you talk to the janitor?"

Sam walks to his desk and sits. "I did. He's sure the door was locked. He's sure he used his passkey."

B.J. asks a question, "I assume you got our message on your cellphone about an extra set of keys. Did he mention if there was another set somewhere aside from what the deceased had?"

"Yes. Ms. Summers had an assistant, a manager if you will. Her name is Beverly Peters. I talked to her, and she has her own set of keys which she has possession of. There's no other set she knows of."

Jack surveys the information in his mind. "So, I guess you could say, if we find that third set of keys, we find the killer."

Sam smiles to the deduction. "A sage remark, Detective, a very sage remark."

"Did you hear about our little excursion on the way back to headquarters?"

Sam nods to what Jack said. "I heard some scuttlebutt on the subject. You two walked into a big skirmish I believe. I see you're both okay though."

Jack points a finger at B.J. "She saved my ass, literally. If it wasn't for her, I wouldn't be talking to you."

"And this is a good thing."

Jack gets up from his seat and heads for the door. "I'm serious. I owe this gal my life. Come on, B.J., we're going to the Blue Note. The food there is excellent. I'm buying."

Jack goes through the door and is gone. B.J. looks at Sam. "Does this mean he likes me?"

"He's never bought a meal there for Chris, or me, for that matter."

# Chapter 25

It was a beautiful loft. Ultra-modern with a spacious, hardwood floor dotted by big, round, support beams in white. Large palms in huge planters also adorned the floor. In the dining area, next to the all-white kitchen with stainless-steel appliances, was an immense, black, metal, dining table with a glass tabletop. It seated eight, and it had a giant, glass vase with assorted colored flowers centered on it. The walls there were painted a dark winter-green, creating a serene ambience. In the living space, there were enormous pieces of black, leather furniture with glass tabletops on black metal for the end and coffee tables. The walls were painted butterscotch, with an assortment of original paintings on them in bright colors leaping out and begging to be noticed. The contrast of the black furniture to the butterscotch walls gave the room a feel of sophistication and money. Glass brick surrounded a spot where Bicks used as his office. He was sitting in a black, leather, swivel chair at a glass-and-black metal desk, busy scrolling a website on his computer, garnishing information he thought could be used for his book.

Enthralled by what he was reading, he pulled Chap Stick out of his shirt pocket and smeared his lips. When he finished with the Chap Stick, he dropped it back in his shirt and grabbed his little recorder. Turning it on, he had his eyes on the computer screen while he spoke into it.

"I've found some pertinent material I think could be used for the book. A paragraph or maybe even a short chapter; at any rate, it's stuff that will bring some history to the story I'm working on.

"Over the recent past, there has been several murders called vampire murders. Dubbed, I'm sure, from the infatuation in modern times of the vampire myth. I believe the crimes I'm interested in for a book may be a part of this phenomenon. If so, this website I'm reading supplies a bevy of vampire myth and legend that might end up being good fodder for the book.

"The vampire myth goes back centuries. One of the earliest comes from the Far East in China. Supposedly, there was a man named Che who killed his victims by touch, then drained their blood. This sounds familiar, doesn't it? In 1632, Scotland, a man named James Spalding was hung for his crimes. The legend says he rose from the dead. It's believed he wasn't actually dead when he was buried, just simply unconscious. He rose and walked among the living.

"Early Christians were accused of vampirism because of their reference to drinking from the body of Christ. Jesus himself rose from the dead which perpetuated the myth. In the early 1700s, a European fear of vampires ran rampant because of the Black Plague epidemic and other unexplained deaths. In 1715, a strange incident took place in a Hungarian village. An old farmer and his family invited a soldier to stay the night. When they sat down to the evening meal, an uninvited guest knocked at the door. Without saying a word, the individual came in and sat down at the table. Needless to say, this put a damper on the festivities of the evening. The uninvited guest was said to be dead for ten years. When the meal was finished, the soldier and the rest of the family retired to rest. The odd guest and old farmer remained at the dinner table. The next morning, the family found the farmer dead with no blood.

"In retaliation, the villagers went to the gravesite where they believed the strange guest was laid to rest all those many years ago. They dug his grave up and found fresh blood around the mouth of the still-intact corpse. To make sure he would not walk among them again, the villagers drove a stake into his heart. Not to kill him, but to pin the creature to the ground. As an addition to break the curse, they also decapitated the intruder, then reburied the corpse."

* * *

Bicks turned off the recorder and set it down. He sat a moment, contemplating what he had found and the curious content of it. He then got up from his seat and walked to the kitchen. Obtaining a glass of chilled wine, he took some sips, thinking about his research. Pleased with what he had so far, he goes back to his office and looked at the computer screen. Smiling from results of his effort, he puts the glass of wine down, then retrieves the Chap Stick from his pocket. Applying the stuff once again, he sets it on the desk next to the wine and takes the glass. He sits down, drinking the wine, and views the computer screen. Bicks reaches over and picks up his recorder again, turns it on, and goes back to work.

* * *

"Perhaps one of the weirdest incidents happened in 1613, Paris, France. A young man took heed to a woman on the streets of the city. It was rainy, and the woman didn't seem to have a place to go. He invites her to his room to get out of the bad weather. She willingly accepts the invitation, and they share a meal and wine. The two end up in bed together that night. The young man rises the next morning and finds the woman dead in the bed. He calls a doctor who informs him that the woman was hanged and had been dead for several weeks. The young man was astonished to realize he had made love with a woman who supposedly came from the dead.

"But the most bizarre occurrence was committed by a royalty woman named Countess Bathory. She married a favored nobleman to the king. Their castle was located in the Carpathian Mountains. The rule was held in the late 1500s where she outlived her husband and took over the kingdom. A lesbian by nature, after her husband died, she surrounded herself with beautiful girls. What started her blood lust was by accident. It ignited by slapping a chamber maid and cutting her cheek. The cut came from a large ring she was wearing, and it left blood on the back of her hand. When she rubbed the blood into her hand, she thought it revitalized her skin.

"For the next 20 years, she practiced her sadism with a variety of tortures and different methods of killing her victims. Aided by her man servant and three of her maids, she tricked young virgins to her castle, under the pretense of a job. She would bathe in their blood, believing it kept her young-looking and beautiful. She murdered over 600 virgins, making her one of the earliest and most prolific of serial killers. Her demonic behavior was exposed after she had just about expelled all the village girls and started in on fellow noblemen's daughters. She ended up incarcerated in a room to her castle for the rest of her life. She died in 1614.

"The interest and belief in vampires has been passed on from generation to generation, immortalized by myth and legend but also in the modern era of Hollywood and bestselling novels. Vampires have been romanticized by these current ploys and have become a big, sexy business.

"In 1996, a reporter named Susan Walsh started haunting the dark corners of New York City by going underground. She visited the popular vampire clubs and lifestyles that prevailed in them. On one of her excursions, she met a mysterious man that called himself Christian. Through him and because of him, she was seduced into the lifestyle of the Goth movement. Eventually, she claimed she was being stalked. The woman vanished on July 16, 1996, and was never heard of again. The subculture of vampire is very real, and some individuals can be dangerous. Vampire has become more than a myth; it's become a lifestyle.

"Today, I am investigating what could very well be a person caught up in this vampire lifestyle. He leaves bloodless bodies with strange marks on their necks. This isn't in the mainstream news; I know this from my own personal connections. And it's knowledge that will stay with me till I reveal it in my book; where this investigation will lead, only time will tell."

* * *

Once again, Bicks turns off the recorder. Tired from the concentration expelled on the task, he applies more Chap Stick and takes a big drink of the wine. Happy and pleased with the research discovered and deductions made, he removes the tape from the recorder and puts it away in a nook on his desk.

Then, he rises from his seat and saunters to a wall near the living-room furniture. It is about ten feet in length, with a black shelf covering the total of the wall, maybe six-feet high. A custom-made shelf he had made, there are many different sorts of shapes in the shelving, which makes it unusual in looks, and used for placing decorations. There are squares, elongated shelves, vertical-sized shelving; all kinds of geometrical shapes make up the shelf for his prized pets. All living in their own miniature glass containers of different sizes and shapes with an assortment of color schemes for their environments. They appear to be snow globes, perhaps from trips taken, but something inside the glass moves. They are Siamese fighting fish more commonly known as Betta fish. The little creatures are living jewels in their myriad of colors, swimming happily in their individual glass homes. They are stunning in brilliance and calming in temperament. When he gets to them, he reaches for a vile of fish food to feed his small friends. He talks to the fish and himself while he sprinkles the food in each tiny glass world.

“You guys hungry? I know you must be. You’ve been very patient, and I’m going to reward each and every one of you with a special treat; brine shrimp for my babies tonight.”

# Chapter 26

It was deathly still in the chamber; complete silence except for the din of a metallic whisk; a sharp, slinking noise that duplicated itself over and over again. The cadence of it seemed the projection of a machine. No break in tempo, no fluctuation in the rhythm. It just kept a recurrence with the same beat. Like the blip of a heartbeat; perfect pitch, perfect time. It was also married to a harsh breathing knell that struggled for any kind of air it could muster; the persistence of it almost to the point of violence and certainly disturbing to anyone who heard it while it penetrated throughout the quiet.

The Renaissance man stood like a statue. Stiff and erect, focused only on one thing. That spot of light from the high window. The single pane was exposed, and it showed a fading day outside. He stood there with his chin raised as if he were watching a live performance. Holding the switchblade in his hand, it attacked with precision each time he released the blade. It was all done without thought. Like driving a car while one's attention was elsewhere. Just coasting in the action, and in the stillness, the sound echoed on top of the sound; repeating, repeating, and, once more, repeating; drowning the atmosphere with a repetitious drone.

Then, suddenly, the Renaissance man spun around and walked smartly to the refrigerator. As he approached the object, his toiling breath disrupted the feel of the mood; the charm of the repose broken and depleted. He gets to the icebox and throws the door open. Reaching into it, he desperately pulls a half-empty canister of blood out and slams it down his throat. Putting it back, he takes the switchblade, goes to the big oak table, and slings the knife into the wood. It stands straight like a chess piece, and the Renaissance man leaves it there.

He begins to pace; slowly at first, but with every step, more forceful and more frightful than the one before. The pacing runs parallel to his breathing, each step coincides to the deep draw he makes in his lungs. And the pulse of the movement swings to a frenzy. His fists ball up, and in harmony to his step and sucking breath, they begin to pummel his upper thigh. Each moment of this behavior escalates and transcends into a fury. Fighting for the breath he desperately needs.

Out of nowhere, he almost leaps to the table where he left the switchblade. He raises his fists high above his head and drives them into the table with such force, it shudders from the blow. He stands with his fists in the wood, heaving for breath. A long moment goes by with him slugging for air. Then, he spins from the table and almost runs to bookshelves across the way. He comes to a shelf where the top half is closed off with cabinet doors. He flings the doors open, and inside the cabinet are tiny brass hooks imbedded into the doors and back panel of the little closet. Hanging on the hooks are keys glittering to the light; nothing but keys of all sorts. Hundreds and hundreds of keys; all of them pointing as if little fingers to a direction. They glisten to the shallow light like dew drops in early morning sunshine.

He stands there, gazing whimsically at them. Pondering on the choice he has to make and where that choice might lead him on the next hunt.

# Chapter 27

"This is a district in Dallas people call Deep Elm." Jack flies through the gears of Chris's hot rod on the downtown streets, giving B.J. a little tour. "It's the answer to the Sixth Street party Austin has every night."

B.J. takes in the proceedings. "Yeah, I know this place. I use to party here back in the day. The Blue Note is around here?"

"Yep, right up the street."

"Isn't that strip joint somewhere close by?"

"It is. As a matter of fact, it's right there."

B.J. looks to where Jack points. "I didn't recognize it from the front."

"I'm going to park across the street over here. The Blue Note is just up the block."

B.J. is dubious. "What do you have in mind?"

Jack is turning the steering wheel. "We haven't talked to anyone about the murder in the alley yet; thought we'd kill two birds with one stone."

B.J. eyes the strip bar. "Can't eat a stone; but I've wanted to do that."

Jack sees a spot to put the car. "With all the crimes on top of each other, we haven't had the time."

"Now, we do."

The midnight-blue pulls into a parking lot, and Jack sticks out some bills through the car window to an attendant. They get the car parked, climb out, and head for the strip bar. Dashing across the busy street, Jack opens a door to the joint, and B.J. takes the invitation to walk in.

The place has the same overpowering beat of music pulsating heavily into eardrums. B.J. and Jack take a moment to orientate, then they weave their way through the crowd to get to the bar. A girl is on the stage, moving to the manic sound, with plenty of eyes checking her out. The two detectives ease up to the bar, and the bartender approaches them.

"What can I get you?"

Jack flashes his badge. “We’re here about the incident in the alley the other night.”

The bartender scopes out the badge, then looks the two over. “Yeah, okay.”

At the same time, the waitress who served the Renaissance man comes to the bar to get some drinks. She watches Jack show his badge.

B.J. shoots a question to the bartender, “Did you notice anything unusual that night?”

The bartender gathers empty beer bottles on the bar. “I’ve already told the police. There wasn’t anything out of the ordinary that I saw. It was your typical bullshit night.”

Standing nearby, the waitress examines the detectives. “You two cops?”

B.J. responds, “Yes.”

“I noticed something weird.”

Jack enters the conversation, “What was that?”

“This guy I served a drink to. He was at a table on the back wall over there. He had trouble breathing.”

B.J. is curious by that observation. “He had trouble breathing, what do you mean by that?”

“He just had a real hard time drawing a breath. So much so, the first thing I thought was this guy needs a doctor. But the really weird thing was how he watched her.”

Jack intervenes, “The girl that was killed?”

The waitress looks at Jack. “He never took his eyes off her; just kept staring at her; never even looked at me, just her. Another weird thing was the way he was dressed.”

B.J. leans on the bar and places an elbow on it. “How do you mean, how so?”

“I don’t know; like he was in one of those swordfight movies. He was wearing a white, silk shirt and the sleeves to the shirt was big and puffy like a swordfighter. He also had on a black string tie; I can’t remember a time I saw something like that in here. He also kept this big, black, trench coat over his shoulders like he was some movie director, like it was a cape. His hair was slicked back tight to the scalp.”

Jack jumps in. “What color was his hair?”

“It looked black in this light.”

B.J. makes a comment, "Sounds like he came from the Renaissance period or something."

The waitress' eyes light up. "Yeah, it was like that."

Jack steps closer to the woman. "Did you get a good look at his face? Could you give a description to one of our sketch artists?"

"I never saw his face, at least not clearly. It was dark. And another weird thing was he never talked to me. Never looked me square in the eye, just kept watching the girl; and something else. When he ordered his drink, he did it by passing a note to me."

Jack is curious. "He never said a word?"

"Nope, only ordered that one drink by using a note; and I don't think he touched it the whole night."

B.J.'s attention has been steady on the woman. "Do you have that note?"

"Oh no, I threw it away that night."

Jack regards the back wall where she serviced the individual. "You remember what he ordered?"

The waitress thinks a moment. "A Bloody Mary."

By that statement, Jack and B.J. look at each other, the answer strikes a chord, coupled with a knowing response.

* * *

On the same night, amid the same streets, at the very same time, the Renaissance man is marching among the people there in Deep Elm for the night's revelry. He walks briskly along, set on a destination, moving forward like a ship at sea. He has on his white, silk shirt with the black string tie, but draped on his shoulders is the black cape he found. The puffy sleeves are exposed from under the cape as it flows freely to his stride. In the crowd, he seems to be someone from another period, another era.

He veers through the folks on the sidewalk like a man walking through a gaggle of sheep. Bumping and shoving his way, ignoring the patrons that share the street with him. People turn as he goes by, wondering about his clothes and rudeness. But those who take the moment to look into his eyes are stunned by what they see.

* * *

Jack and B.J. are strolling down the street, blocks from where the Renaissance man is. They are on their way to the Blue Note for dinner. B.J. has been pondering the conversation with the waitress at the strip bar.

"What do you think about that guy the waitress was talking about?"

Jack glances at her. "The Renaissance man?"

"Yes, what do you think?"

"I think he's the only reasonable suspect we have at this point in the investigation. His acute interest in the girl that was killed, his odd way of dress, and ordering a drink by a note; I wouldn't call all that normal behavior. Not to mention it was a Bloody Mary he had for the drink."

"Nor would I; that stuff about his breathing is also something that might be important."

"Yeah, we should mention that to Edwin, see what he has to say about it."

"I agree; he might have something of a slant on the subject. So, where's the Blue Note, I need to eat."

Jack points in a direction. "It's right up there."

"The food's good?"

"Got the best pot roast in town; all the guys come here after hours. Have for years."

B.J. sees a blue neon sign in the window of a bar and grill, exclaiming the Blue Note. "Will I fit in?"

Jack grins at her. "You're a cop, aren't you? Come on, you'll like the place."

Once again, Jack opens the door, and B.J. enters the establishment, followed closely by Jack.

The joint is teeming with cops. Hard to see at first, the detectives let their eyes adjust to the dim. An abundance of neon beer signs on the wall helps with the process. A big screen television is above all the liquor bottles, facing the bar. There are some fellows sitting at it, watching a ballgame when they turn heads and yell greetings. Jack introduces B.J. to them, and they all share a gleeful intercourse. Then, Jack and B.J. search for an empty booth to settle into, turning an about face and heading away from the crowd.

A pretty waitress arrives, handing menus out. She's got short, spiked, black hair with red lipstick on full lips and nice curves to match. "Hi, Jack, haven't seen you for a while. Would you and your friend like something to drink?"

"How are you, Nancy? This is my new partner in crime, B.J. Dobbs."

“Glad to meet you.”

B.J. looks up from the menu. “Glad to meet you.”

“So, where have you been, Stranger, and where is Chris?”

“He’s in the hospital, but he’s okay.”

“Sorry to hear that; I like that kid; almost as much as I like you.”

Jack appears uncomfortable. “I’ve been on a big case. That’s why you haven’t seen me lately.”

“Well, don’t make yourself so hard to find. I don’t get my Jack fix; I don’t sleep so good.”

She follows that declaration with a wink.

Jack responds with a sheepish grin and looks at B.J., “Two beers for starters?”

B.J. nods. “Two beers.”

“Two beers coming up.” Nancy takes out a bar rag and wipes the tabletop, “You know I aim to please,” then winks at Jack again and leaves.

B.J. takes her eyes off the menu with a slight pang of jealousy. “What’s that about, Detective?”

Jack looks sheepish again. “She’s been after me to take her out. I guess seeing you with me got a rise in her.”

B.J. is surprised by the feelings she suddenly has. “There’s nothing going on huh?”

“No, not really; I don’t like mixing pleasure with business, and when I come in here, I’m still on business.”

B.J. grins big. “I’d say she wants to make you her business.”

Just then, Sam saunters to the booth with a beer in his hand. “It took you guys long enough to get here, mind if I join you?”

Jack is relieved. “Yeah, Sam, sit down.”

Sam sits next to B.J. “I’d rather sit with you.”

B.J., still grinning, looks at Jack. “I’ll bet Nancy would like that too.”

“You’ve met Nancy; it’s common knowledge she’s got a crush on Jack.”

B.J. drills Jack while she makes a remark, “Knowledge that can’t be ignored.”

Sam has a sip of beer. “How do you like the place?”

“It’s okay; haven’t eaten yet.”

“The food’s great, try the pot roast.”

“So I’ve heard.”

Nancy shows up with two beers. "Hi, Sam, here are the beers, are you ready to order?"

B.J. hands her menu to Nancy. "Let me have the pot roast."

"And you, Jack, what do you want?" Her eyes sparkle with invitation.

Jack gives his menu to her. "I'll have the same."

"You got it, Amigo. Be back in a jiffy." She walks away with the menus and swaying hips.

Sam noticed the flirt. "Dodging bullets again, Jack?"

Jack, embarrassed, addresses B.J., "So, tell me, have you formulated any kind of profile on the guy we want?"

Sam answers the question, "Simple, we got a serial killer."

B.J. picks up her beer. "I don't think so. Not in the textbook sense."

Jack gets his beer. "Explain."

"Most serials kill out of some kind of sexual frustration or blood lust. I'd say this guy is on a personal crusade."

Sam chips in, "It seems to me the dude has got a big taste for blood lust."

B.J. takes a sip of beer. "On the surface, it appears that way, but I'd say his real motive goes far beyond his need and want for the spill of blood."

* * *

There is an opaque stillness behind a large building while the Renaissance man dashes in and out of the shadows with stealth. He moves behind trash dumpsters and along walls, staying relatively out of sight and in the dark while he nears a backdoor to the building. His cape flies when he runs rapidly from one spot to another, trying to keep his behavior unnoticed, and it flutters like a flag when he does.

He finally gets to the door located up a few concrete steps. It is a service door for the building staff to use. His head darts from one direction to the next, making sure of his secrecy. Digging in a pocket, he pulls out a set of keys. He first applies a key on what appears to be the security system found in a little gray box next to the door. Slipping the key in its home, he nullifies the system from any detection of violating the building. Then, he puts a different key in the door and enters through the opening.

* * *

Nancy is just setting down two plates of pot roast in front of B.J. and Jack. "Do we need anything else?"

Jack picks up a fork. "I think we're good for now."

Nancy has a glint to her eye, then walks away with that same sway. "I'll bet you're better than good."

B.J. smiles secretly, thinking the same thing. She picks up her fork and has a bite of pot roast. "Not bad."

Sam looks over his shoulder. "I need another beer; how about you two?"

B.J. is eating hearty. "Please, I could use another."

Jack joins in, "I'll take one. What would be the crusade our guy might be on?"

B.J. realizes the question is hers. "Are we back to our suspect?"

"Yeah, what would be this crusade he has that results in motive?"

"Who knows? I don't know if you would call it a crusade; it's got something to do with taking blood though, and the use he has for it."

Sam is climbing out of the booth. "Like I've said, maybe he's a vampire."

B.J. has a mouthful of pot roast. "Maybe he thinks he is."

Sam leaves to get more beers. The detectives sit quietly for a moment, devouring their meals. Jack is in the middle of a bite when he blurts out an enquiry.

"Why the hell would he want blood? What purpose would it be for?"

B.J. shrugs. "In his mind, for strength of some kind maybe, or some kind of religious-rite."

"You mean, he might belong to some cult?"

"It's possible. But I don't think this guy's mixed up with a bunch of people.

"There's no evidence indicating he is. So what's your profile on the guy?"

B.J. hovers over her plate. "Keep in mind, this is all preliminary for the time being."

Jack holds a fork in the air above his food. "I'll keep it in mind."

B.J. takes a moment to gather her thoughts. "I figure this individual may have a lopsided view of demanding parents. He's always been a loner, an outsider. I think he wants blood for some kind of fulfillment. Negating any and all responsibility he would have to his parents. He's probably a Caucasian somewhere in his 30s or late 20s. I don't think he's ever had a career of any sort. He's just been drifting in life; to the dismay of his parents. I would say he could very well be delusionary which would lead to manifesting a grandiose self-image of who he is. And that, in my opinion, is a reflection of his parents."

Sam suddenly shows with their beers. He sets them down on the booth tabletop and takes a sip of his. "Here are your beers, my friends."

He sits back next to B.J. and takes another sip of his beer. B.J. is occupied at eating her pot roast. Jack is fiddling with his food, ingesting what he just heard from his partner.

Sam notices they are both quiet. "Did I miss something?"

# Chapter 28

Tomorrow was going to be a big day. And, of course, Amy was excited. So amped, she had a large cup of tea laced with a heavy dose of valerian to help her calm down and sleep. She knew she would need the aid to get a good night's rest. Otherwise, it would be tossing and turning, thinking about the events that were going to take place the next day. Mixed feelings swam inside her over those events. On one hand, she could not wait to show her stuff and expose the potential talent her office mates suspected she had, and on the other, there was a dread of things not going well. But she was prepared and confident it would all turn out on the upside instead of the down. It was a kismet she worked hard for all her adult life.

Amy Sanders had not been out of college more than a few months before she landed a career-oriented job. It was a job she had dreamed for, and tomorrow was going to be her first big test; her very first presentation for a client. Needless to say, she was anxious but overjoyed at the prospect and opportunity. Everything so far had turned out as she planned. She got her education by working long hours and sacrificing; she got the job she went after on an important P.R. firm right out of the gate, and, now, she was on the verge of illustrating her talent with the presentation in the morning. She could not help but grin at herself in the mirror while she brushed her teeth. Amy had a lot to grin over and beautiful teeth to use for that grin.

* * *

The Renaissance man was standing in the shadows, hugging a wall behind some large metal shelving, still as a statue and barely drawing breath. He was watching a maintenance man rummage around, straightening and organizing the basement to the building that he entered. He had stationed himself for some time, leaning into the wall, waiting on the janitor to find something to do somewhere else. Finally, the man disappeared around some large cardboard boxes and stacks of five-gallon paint supplies. It was the chance he was waiting for, and the Renaissance man zipped to a staircase, skipped up them, and went through a door at the top of the stairs quietly as a spider. It took no longer than a heartbeat.

* * *

Finished with her hygiene, Amy puts her toothbrush away, rinses her mouth, and leaves the bathroom, turning out the light. She already has on her favorite silk nightgown, which she has kept under wraps in celebration of this night, and walks to the bed. She turns the bed down, then makes one more tour of the apartment, making sure the lights are out and the door and windows are locked. Amy comes back to the bed, climbs into it, and grins to herself once again at a big mirror she has on the wall next to the bed. The mirror is so low, she can lay her head on the pillow and still see those beautiful teeth grinning at her. Then, she reaches over and turns the night light to dim.

* * *

Bolting unseen down the hallway of the first floor, the Renaissance man ignores elevators; his cape whipping the air behind him. Running to the door of the stairwell, he hastily goes through it. Satisfied with the seclusion the stairs offer, he begins a climb to his personal destination. Chugging up each flight while his cape flaps to his motion; every step he takes is noiseless and painful for breath in the narrow passageway. He silently attains the floor he wants, undetected by anyone in the building. When he gets to the door of the fifth floor, he stops and suffers through rasping breath.

Reaching into the deep pockets of his black fatigues, he pulls out the tool of his trade. The mouthpiece flashes in the obscure light of the stairwell. With care, he fits the bit into his mouth and begins attaching the piece to the mechanics of his machine which are already in place. Now, the silence of his presence is broken. Mechanical sounds invade the stairwell serenity while he goes through the procedure of connecting all the instrument details. Clamping noises and the din of valves releasing pressure punctuate the silence. When he has the mouthpiece in place and ready for use, he peeks out the door and sees the hallway is empty.

The Renaissance man then takes off for a certain door down the line of doors he passes. As he makes his way for the objective target, he digs in his right pocket for a key. He gets to the door he wants and his cape falls from the flight and hangs to the sudden stop. Finding the key in his pocket, he puts it in the door and turns the lock with ease.

Inside the apartment, the door cracks open, and a hand with black fingernails grips the edge and widens the opening. The black image of a death stalker slinks into the room, sniffing the air for detection.

* * *

Airless, tireless; drop to a rise. Float below. Stop the motion; wiz through the flow. Where am I? Nowhere that is lasting. Buzz colors. Buzz colors exploding. My eyes; I need to see. I need to; what is that? I'm walking inside an impressionist painter's dream. The colors are brilliant, but the objects are blurred. The picture is clean.

Hi, Amy! Hi yourself, walking down a neighborhood sidewalk on a bright sunny day. It is a calm and pleasant stroll. Flowers are blooming, unfurling with all colors imaginable, the lawns are jaunty green and alive. Up ahead, a beautiful baby boy is watching me come to him. He is around four, wearing a lavender shirt in matching shorts, standing under a cherry tree; his pale-white skin glowing flawless under the sunlight. I walk by him and look down at his face. The boy has shocking blonde hair, platinum-blonde, with piercing, ice-blue eyes. The color of them appears to have been stolen from the sky. Cherry blossoms blanket the green lawn where he stands, and the contrast as he peers up at me with those wonderful blue eyes are electrifying. A bee suddenly flies between us, and I call for the boy to be careful. The bee weaves around us in circles, then lands and stings. I can feel it on my neck. But the sting comes from under my skin. The pain seems to spread from the point of contact throughout my whole body like ripples on a pond. And it spins me into the realm of reality.

* * *

Amy's eyes pop open to see herself in the mirror along the side of her bed. She also discovers something unholy latched to her neck. Some kind of thing locked onto her like a black leach. Staring at her in the mirror with these black shark-like eyes. His left hand, with those long, black fingernails, is covering her mouth, and his body pins her body down under his weight. He reaches over with his right arm and pushes a button on a wristband to the hand covering her face. The sound of an iron lung drums to a start, and it begins to extract blood. It seems to be drinking her blood stream. Her eyes are wide open, witnessing the atrocity. She is helpless, and the helplessness gets weaker every creeping moment. A struggle is futile because of the heavy bulk on her and her expelling energy slothfully slipping away. Her eyes slowly begin to droop. They get heavier and heavier while she watches the black, shark-like eyes watch her. They close, then open, close, then open in a drowsy proceeding. They close, then it takes longer to open and see those black, dead eyes staring intensely at her. Finally, they close for long seconds, then they open once more, and, slowly, ever so slowly, they close forever.

# Chapter 29

Missy was packing. She had a routine in her packing that took years to develop. To begin with, she would start the process days before her schedule to depart. On top of that, she always used her spare bedroom to pack in. Putting her luggage on the bed in that room, she would spend endless hours going to and fro from her bedroom to the other, laying garments out in the suitcases. Being a clothes horse is a big responsibility, and she took care in what she packed because of it, and she always packed three or more cases to insure that reputation. Sometimes, she would change her mind on an article and bring it back to her bedroom, only to change it again and take it back for the trip. It was total repetition and a meticulous procedure that she had perfected to a science; a science that was all her own.

Missy was always somewhat of an eccentric. Her packing habits reflected that. She was getting ready for her flight to Dallas and had started the process the day before. She had it in mind to really get serious about it today, but first, before she got lost in the activity, she was going to check her computer. One never knows what might be in the email, waiting for a discovery. Missy trots off to her office to do just that.

She gets to the office and turns on the computer. Missy could not find much on the email but located a ton of literature to download about today's publishing world, and she garnished material that would put a stamp on her speech at the seminar. She turns the printer on and starts collecting the information. She would stand behind a podium on the middle day of the three-day affair and deliver the facts to a waiting audience. Her plan was to spend a large portion on what she obtained from the internet, then pitch her agency and speak of its history. You never know what you might uncover at a convention. There could be an unknown bestselling author out there, and she should be the one to foster that writer to fruition. This particular convention usually took place in Austin, but, this year, it was being held in Dallas. Because of this, she had a personal forecast of a much larger gathering than she had seen before at this thing. Being how much bigger the city of Dallas was and the prestige such a city held in the eyes of the public.

Satisfied with the research she found, Missy walked into the spare bedroom and put the printed papers next to a suitcase. She would get familiar with the stuff and highlight or jot down interesting points she could use on the flight to Dallas. As for the knowledge on her agency, she could wing that easy enough.

Making an about face, she steps off for her bedroom to do some packing. She comes to her room and heads straight for the closet. The double doors are open, and she pulls out a black, elegant, sheer, and revealing dress she bought on a lark some time ago. It is the sort of dress that screams for attention. She holds it out and thinks of a tall, breezy blonde wearing it. Then, she swings to the left closet door where a full-length mirror is mounted. She tucks the dress under her chin and decides a tall blonde she is not; short and frumpy is more like it.

Missy was almost right. Even though she developed a style of her own, a mixture of intelligence and coquette, when she tucked this dress under her chin, she ended up frumpy in her eyes. But, in truth, she was lovely.

Her hair was a deep silky red, cut short and tossed to fit her round face. Makeup was always clear and immaculate without overdoing it. She liked to keep her lips in an auburn shade, and matched with those big, shiny, dark-brown eyes, it made her look very much the smart and modern woman she was. But, in her view, she would be eternally frumpy with somewhat of a flare.

Swimming in her little disappointments, she reaches to hang the dress back up when she stops dead in her tracks. A thought trips her fancy, followed by a naughty smile. You never know what folly might occur at that convention, especially since it takes place in Dallas. After a moment, she darts off for her packing station, holding the dress.

* * *

Bicks could not stop grinning. Things were rolling along splendidly. Last night, Missy called, and he was going to pick her up in the next few days at D.F.W. His groundwork on the book was pulling together, and he had plenty of detail to show Missy when she got to Dallas. Also, a thought jumped into his mind when that girl, Amy Sanders, was found in her apartment. That same source he had at the police department told him she was another victim with the same M.O. that connected to his investigation for the book. He was also told of how the girl was assaulted without any forcible entry into her place.

He reached over to a catchall he had in his Jaguar car door and drew out a tube of Chap Stick. While dabbing the soothing goo on his lips, he mulled over the thought that struck him like a thunderbolt. If this string of murders started years ago in Highland Park, could the culprit be a resident from Highland Park? He was on his way back to the Highland Park records department to delve into that very subject. And this was the main purpose he was grinning so big.

Bicks enjoyed playing the proverbial fly in the cream, buzzing around murder scenes, bothering the detectives. He liked discovering the things that did not occur to them or what they may have overlooked. One of the reasons he became a crime reporter was for that very aspiration. It gave him a charge to be steps ahead of cops; digging for the truth and coming to a resolution before anyone else. Now that he wrote novels on the subject, it gave him that much more satisfaction to solve cases before the police. It justified his position in the case, and, besides, it paid well; the P.R. that could be gained from it, including boosting sales for his books. But the bottom line to it all, he just got a kick out of being the pain in the neck, the burr under the saddle, the paper cut that annoyed the departments of protection.

Something evil and secret had surfaced in this city. Something malevolent and pernicious, and he was going to open it up like the can of worms it was. The cops were obviously intent on keeping the case wrapped under their thumb. He already had what he felt was a hot item when he overheard Detectives Jack Degree and Dobbs talk of keys. He could only surmise they were speaking about the keys to that gift shop. What else could it be, and if they were talking about keys, did it have something to do with entering or leaving the scene of the crime? That assumption seemed to fit along with the new case Amy Sanders presented. All this intrigue was certainly material for a writer. And it made him grin all the way from downtown Dallas to the outskirts of Highland Park he was now driving into.

It was funny his destination would be Highland Park. The bizarre connection of bloodless bodies is what made this seem out of place and weird silly. You would think such baroque killings would have started in the seedy downtown streets of Dallas or the free-wheeling area of Oak Cliff. Not the illustrious place called Highland Park. Which brought him to the conclusion, did the miscreant come from there? That, and how did a set of keys figure in all this?

Highland Park had features uncommon to any other community. While Bicks drove deeper into the residential canvas, he was a witness to it; house after huge house slides by his car window as he admires their divine expense and caretaker grounds. A home to his right is like a great southern plantation dressed with a row of six, giant, white columns and a driveway bordered by behemoth oak trees. Across the street, a long, winding drive leads to a peach-shade Mediterranean-style home complete with an Olympic swimming pool and tennis courts. Bicks has never forgotten the first time he saw a place that was fashioned after a fairytale with loud primary colors on the outside walls and a roof covered in thatched straw like the three little pigs might have. It looked like an abode from Disneyland. Located somewhere on a corner around here, the unusual imported trees coupled with the outlandish and whimsical architecture surely cost a fortune just to maintain.

What made Highland Park so unique was the small-town city stuck in the heart of the Dallas expanse and one of the wealthiest little townships anywhere in the country. It was a nest for millionaires and billionaires to dwell in, where they could set their own elite standards; with their own utilities, fire department, and police force. Some of the richest families in the United States lived in this oasis. And here was Bicks, driving the charming little streets, looking for a blood-thirsty killer. Could the absurdity get any better for a writer and his book to maintain?

# Chapter 30

Jack and B.J. were sitting in the squad office. Jack is busy on some paperwork while B.J. sits at a desk nearby, scrolling through her cellphone. A couple of detectives are at their desks in the back, speaking on phones. It is quiet except for the gentle rumblings of talk from the detectives in the rear.

Jack suddenly throws his pencil down in frustration and it tinkles on the desktop. He props his elbows on the desk and covers his face with both hands and rubs it hard, trying to dispel the hard-luck feeling he was wrestling with. He hated paperwork. Looking over at B.J. on her cell, he wondered why he was the only one that felt so cornered.

"Don't you have some reports to fill out?"

B.J. answers without looking at him; she keeps her eyes on the business her cellphone has.

"I did it last night at my apartment."

Jack enjoys her beauty just sitting there. "You want to do mine? I'll give you ten bucks."

"I could find a way to get ten bucks from you without doing your work for it."

Jack tries another avenue. "Have you finished writing out your profile?"

"Finished." She looks at him. "So what's on the agenda today?"

He smirks. "First, we need to go to the lab and see what Doc has on the Sanders's case."

In that moment, Sam busts through the office door with an expression of glee on his face. He spots his two buddies and barks out a command.

"You two, follow me."

Jack takes in his appearance. "What's up with you?"

"I've got something to show you." He triggers his forefinger. "Follow me."

Sam spins around and walks out the office seemingly in a hurry. The two detectives jump to their feet and walk out the room in Sam's wake.

As the three of them ramble down the hallway in a flurry, Jack inquires about where Sam is taking them. "Why are we following you?"

"The viewing room; I've been scanning the surveillance tapes from the Sanders's building and came across something you should see."

B.J. blurts out a question, "What was that?"

"I'll let the tapes show you."

They get to a door and go through it. There is a fair-sized room with three flat screens on a wall and taping-and-looping equipment set everywhere on tables. Everything is lit and waiting to be used. Sam immediately goes to a tape player he has keyed up and pushes a button. The middle screen comes alive to the order.

"Check this out. I've been searching these tapes for some time, and I found two frames I think you guys will find very interesting."

As the three detectives stand together, watching the screen, an image begins to appear. The picture shows seconds of what seems to be a man dashing down a hall and slinking through a stairwell door. His hair is slicked back, tight to the scalp, and he wears a white shirt with puffy sleeves along with a string tie. But the signature comes from a cape that flies around to his movement. The body of the culprit is all that can be seen for good viewing. His face remains obscure in the shot.

Jack is not satisfied. "Can you back that up? I want to see it again."

Sam reaches over to one of the machines and recovers the picture for another look-see.

"All I got on this is what you see here and another piece of tape from the floor where the girl was found. What's intriguing is this stuff is recorded at around the same time the murder took place.

"There's not much, it's like he knew where the blind spots were on the surveillance cameras."

B.J. is curious on what she is watching. "Have you got the other piece of tape keyed for review?"

Sam throws a smile out. "Sure do."

He turns the same film they have seen before on, and it comes in crystal clear.

Jack turns to B.J. "What do you think?"

"It looks like our Renaissance man; I don't know what else it could be."

"Yeah, and, now, we know he's got black hair; he looks to be of average size and height too."

B.J. points out, "Can't see much of anything else though, except for his cape."

Jack makes an observation, "I guess he quit his trench coat and got a cape to run around in."

B.J. adds to the observation, "It shouldn't be too hard to spot someone dressed like that on the streets."

Jack follows the train of thought. "That would be my guess. We'll have to put out an A.P.B. with that description."

Sam shuts the tape off and pushes a button on another tape recorder; the screen on the left bleeps on. "This is the second strip of tape I found. I searched diligently for more, but these two are the only ones I could find that may have anything to do with the Sanders's case."

They view the same dark image run to the door of the deceased, and, after a moment, the door swings open. All they can see is his back, with the cape hanging loosely and the door opening. He grips the edge of the door silently, then slips inside, and they watch the door close quietly behind him.

Sam freezes the frame. "That's it. But it's enough to give us a visual on a suspect."

B.J. has her eyes on the T.V. screen. "Good work, Sam."

She looks at Jack. "I believe the waitress at the strip joint really did see the guy we're looking for, the Renaissance man."

Jack replies, "Yeah, and it looks like he opened that door by using keys."

Sam is perplexed. "You two keep talking about a Renaissance man. Who might that be?"

B.J. answers, "That's the tag we've given our suspect until we find out his real name. And it looks like we're one step closer in finding that out. At least we know he's a real, alive, human being."

Sam blinks a retort. "I don't know; he looks like a vampire to me. I mean, he moves around undetected and, like magic, opens doors through his will. That cape is a sure fire-wardrobe of a vampire. I'd tag him as a walking dead."

Jack looks at both of them. "He's the Renaissance man, and, somehow, he has keys to open those doors. And that, ladies and gents, is our key."

* * *

Bicks could see the Highland Park records building loom ahead. He quickly pulls his Jag to a park and gets out. Dressed in a gray suit with a red carnation in the lapel, a red silk tie, and a gray straw-fedora with a red hatband, he jauntily walks up to the front entrance.

Behind a desk, with his feet propped up, sits a lanky fellow with a scraggily beard and long hair. He has on a green T-shirt and blue jeans, wearing beat-up sneakers. Busy reading a comic book, he is halfway through the story. The job he held there was just the sort a guy like him would cherish; where little effort was required except spending idle time on pop culture like comic books. It was a job he held for quite some time, and he intended to keep it for as long as he could.

The entrance door opens, and Bicks storms in with the air; he came to buy a new suit. The clerk looks up from his reading and shows a bland response.

"Back again huh. Can't get enough of this place?"

Bicks grins. "What are you reading?"

"Batman, what else; what do want this time?"

"Oh, you know; the life of investigative writing; I go where the story leads me."

"Yeah, well, the story had you here just the other day."

Bicks saunters to the desk. "I'd like to take another look at your files."

The clerk folds his comic book. "You were just here, damn it, and I let you do that already. I could get in some shit over letting anybody in the back who wants to. This place is for Highland Parkers and city officials. Not jokers with a pencil in his pocket. What the hell are you looking for anyway?"

Bicks pulls out his Chap Stick. "That's confidential, a need-to-know kind of thing."

"Yeah? What a surprise."

"What's the harm? I won't be long."

The clerk drops his feet off the desk. "If I let you go back there, what's in it for me?"

Bicks puts the used Chap Stick in his shirt pocket and brings out some money. "A C-note; you can buy a lot of comic books with that."

* * *

Jack and B.J. were in the lab, standing around, observing Edwin. He was at file cabinets, fishing through one of the drawers. Edwin finds what he looks for, pulls out a file, and walks to his desk. He opens the file and lays it down on the desktop. Then, he smiles at the two detectives with an inquisitive look.

"Would you two like some coffee?"

The two of them glance at each other and decline the offer. Edwin goes to a small table where a coffee pot can be found and pours a cup. Finished with the chore, he takes a drink and peers at the detectives with the coffee cup close to his mouth.

"I've been expecting you two. I have a bevy of information to report."

Jack makes a suggestion, "Start at square one."

"Well, I'll start with those punctures on the throat. The more I look at them, the more I'm inclined to think they're not made by teeth; animal or human."

B.J. is watching him. "Made by what then?"

"Machine would be my guess; mainly because of the lack of tear in the tissue when you study it under a microscope; and the precision of the entry to the jugular vein."

Jack steps over to the desk and picks up the file. "What kind of machine?"

Edwin sips his coffee. "I'm unaware of anything that does that sort of work."

B.J. leans against a countertop. "He probably made it himself."

Jack thumbs through the file. "Custom fit, I'll wager. What else do you have, Doc?"

"You can see, by the file, Amy Sanders is verified as the latest victim. But there is one thing."

Jack looks up from the file. "What's that?"

Edwin pours more coffee. "We found residue of saliva on the victim's throat. We were also able to get a good thumbprint from the apartment door. We think that print could belong to the suspect. It's right there in the file."

B.J. shifts her weight. "All of a sudden, the suspect leaves saliva and a print for us to find. We just saw a piece of surveillance film Sam found with the suspect gripping the front door."

Edwin turns back to them. "It could be he's getting careless, getting overconfident, and he took so long in this particular procedure. He just about extracted every drop of her blood. She was literally dry of plasma."

Jack lies the file down. "He took all the time he wanted. Being no one was in the apartment but the two of them, and it was such a private place."

B.J. adds to the thought, "Let's not forget, there was no forced entry which brings up the question of keys again."

Jack makes a point, "She could have left the door unlocked, but I doubt it."

B.J. bounces back a point, "So do I; she was found on her bed in her nightgown, and I'll bet forensic implies she was attacked in her sleep."

Edwin swallows more coffee. "She didn't have any head wounds like the others. It's in the file."

B.J. sparks to a thought. "You know what? Let's do this. Let's set up a radius around the murder sites. They're all pretty much bunched together in city blocks; let's canvas that area of all the locksmiths and key makers within that perimeter and see if we can find a source to those keys."

Jack nods. "Good idea. It'll take some footwork and manpower, but we can do that."

Edwin walks to his desk, sipping his coffee. "Let's not lose sight on the fact that residue of saliva will give us a D.N.A. result. I've sent the thumbprint to the F.B.I.'s file record. There hasn't been a hit though."

Jack sits on the desk. "That's good news about the D.N.A., Doc. And you never know if that thumbprint makes a hit. I assume you already checked the print in our department records. B.J. and I came across something the other night."

"When I get the D.N.A. results, I'll send that along to F.B.I.'s CODIS too. What did you come across?"

"We went to the strip bar where the dancer was found in the alley. A waitress told us about someone she noticed she thought acted odd. She said he watched that woman all night long the night of the murder. Never took his eyes off her, and he never said a word; even ordered his drink by a note. She also talked about how he had trouble breathing. So much so, she thought he needed a doctor."

Edwin sits at his desk, pondering. "That might be a case of asthma. Sounds like it anyway. Anytime someone has trouble breathing, that's usually the cause. And it's nothing to fool around with; the guy probably needs a doctor to look at it if that girl noticed it enough to mention the problem."

B.J. walks away from the counter and picks up the file on the desk. "She also harped about the way he dressed. Jack and I call him the Renaissance man."

Edwin shifts in his seat. "The Renaissance man; why use that term?"

"By her description, he wasn't dressed in contemporary clothes. In her words, more like a swordfighter from another century. That surveillance tape Sam found came from the building Sanders lived in, and, there, the guy was entering the building with a cape on. That thumbprint you have probably belongs to our suspect closing the apartment door."

Edwin lights up to that news. "You didn't see his face, did you?"

Jack chimes in, "No, we never got much of a look at it. Mainly, we just saw his body and how he was dressed. It followed the description of the waitress."

"Sounds to me like someone with delusional fantasies."

B.J. reacts to that comment, "Funny you should say that. Part of my profile on the suspect points out that he may be delusionary."

Edwin folds his arms. "You know; there have been hundreds of murders referred to as vampire murders. One that comes to mind is a teenager who killed an elderly woman just down the street from his house. He watched her and schemed about his crime for a long time. He waited for his parents to go on a weekend trip, then snuck over to the old lady's house at night, killed her, and collected her blood in a cooking pan. He drank it and expected to wake up the next morning with mystical powers like a vampire. It didn't work out like he planned when the police arrested him. Another case I can recall took place in Houston for Christ's sake. Four young women were enthralled by the vampire myth. The leader got them to pick up this middle-aged guy they found staggering drunk on a road. They took him to a pier out by a lake, and the leader slashed his throat so she could drink his blood. The old guy had somehow got ahold of her credit card and stuck it in his sock. When the police found the body, it didn't take long for them to trace it to the leader and the rest of the girls. Needless to say, that ended badly for those girls; would-be vampire wishers and their strange motives to become just that. It brings a whole new meaning to the phrase, vampire myth."

B.J. puts the file down. "For a while now, it's been rolling around in my head this guy might think he's a vampire."

Edwin looks at her. “People don’t realize drinking blood to excess can cause an iron overload in your system, not to mention gastric problems. There can also be a sexual response to the taste of blood. The term used for it is called clinical vampirism.”

Jack stands up from the desk. “Maybe he’s drinking blood, thinking it will bring some kind of power. Not to mention a relief to his breathing difficulties or any other weakness he may have.”

B.J. displays a slight secret smile. “Maybe it turns him on.”

# Chapter 31

There is an old, tarnished, work sink at a corner several yards from the black curtains that concealed the Renaissance man's coffin. It is located down the brick wall, and it has been leaking for hours, the drops pounding into the sedate ambience like a base drum. The drops were steady. It had a cadence to it like the tick of a clock. The droplets kept intruding on the quiet like it was supposed to. Like it had a job to disturb the stillness and bring some kind of life to the dead atmosphere. On and on, the bits of water descend in a perfect beat. Plunk; then the end of the faucet would ball with moisture again to produce another drip, and it would fall to a plunk. As if it was the heartbeat of the massive space.

Suddenly, almost undiscerning, the sound of a strident breath invades the smacking rhythm the dripping makes. It overpowers the ear throb with the ugly struggle for breath. The combat makes it seem something is dying; fighting a lost cause against the inevitable grip of death. Then, without warning, a placid calm cloak the asylum of noise and leaves a tempo of peace. The only thing that can be heard is the persistence of the faucet and the intrusion it makes to the tranquility.

The Renaissance man is standing by the opened refrigerator with a canister to his lips, gulping the blood down with a fury of lust. He drinks it like a thirsty fountain till the glass container is bone dry. Finished with the replenishment, he puts the empty bottle back in the refrigerator and closes the door. He stands rigidly there with a perplexed expression on his pale face; his agonizing breath subsided to a small scale and his eyes tripping from one piece of furniture to the next. The Renaissance man studies the parallel rows of shelving, armoires, trunks, and small tables, trying to decide the best place to start a search. He is attempting to decipher where a perceived treasure might be found.

He sprints for an old trunk of suspect on the other end of the chamber, wedged between two shelves. It is located below the window not far from the step ladder. The Renaissance man gets to his destination and throws the tattered trunk open. Then, he begins to fling the contents out like he is looking for a remedy to a snake bite. Casting garments and forgotten bits of objects all around like a buzz saw. The items fly up and out, some drop quickly from weight, other things such as scarves flutter and float to the concrete floor. Finally, the trunk is emptied, and he gets to his feet, staring down at its uselessness.

He scans his domain and spots another trunk across the way. The Renaissance man heads for it, determined to accomplish his quest. Getting to the trunk, he jerks it open and begins the same process. Hurling stuff everywhere to the point the concrete floor fills with discards and unimportant articles. It appears the place has gone through a criminal ransack, gleaned of any value. Once again, he stands with a disenchantment that makes his shoulders droop. Turning from that disappointment, he resumes his hunt and settles on a shelf with cabinet doors. Situated down the line of furniture where the cabinet of keys is placed.

The Renaissance man darts to the shelf and slings the doors open. Inside are assorted objects, obsolete and expired from use. On the bottom shelf, the paragon he has been looking for comes to view; a small, black, leather bag. The little bag is like the kind a country doctor would use. A small, black, leather handle is at the top where the bag opens, no bigger than a handbag. It is old, covered with mold and dust. He grabs it in a frenzy of recovery and embarks for the sink and dripping faucet.

On the way across the concrete, he scoops up a piece of cloth that was thrown from the trunks. He carries both the bag and the rag to the sink and turns the faucet on. It explodes with a torrent of rusty water, and he uses it to clean the leather surface. The Renaissance man dampens the rag and starts to wipe the old doctor bag with care. By degrees, the leather transforms from the mold and dust to a healthy, black shine under the layer of muck.

# Chapter 32

Janet was hovering over Chris while he was lying in bed, eating. She was making sure he had no trouble with his bum arm. His other arm was still hooked to an I.V. and machines for vital readings. Janet was feeding him bites of food, something she liked doing, mothering him. Chris was enjoying the attention, getting fed by his gal, but then he liked any attention he might get from her.

Chris was chewing a mouthful. “I’m really getting tired of this hospital food. It’s all starting to taste the same.”

“I sympathize with you. It won’t be long before you’ll be able to walk out of here and have whatever you want to eat.”

Another bite appears in front of Chris. “Not soon enough.”

Janet pours some juice. “Tell you what; when you’re able to leave, first thing, we’ll do is go to your favorite restaurant. I’ll buy, it’ll be on me.”

“I’ll take you up on that, can’t wait for the day. You know what? Instead of my favorite place, I’d like to go to the Blue Note. I’m beginning to really miss that joint.”

“Blue Note, I’ve never heard of it. What kind of food does it have?”

Chris takes a drink of juice. “I’ve never taken you there, and it’s due time I did. It’s a hangout where all the guys go from the department after hours. Jack and I have been there so many times, I can’t count. The food’s great; steak, pot roast, and I’d get a chance to see all my buddies I haven’t seen for a long time, catch up with the police shenanigans. Not to mention I’ll be able to show off my beautiful girlfriend.”

She winks at him with another bite of food. “We’ll make it a celebration all through the night.”

A knock at the open door interrupts the conversation while B.J. and Jack walk in; both of them with big, toothy grins and eager to grant salutations.

Chris is the first to speak while chewing his food, "Well, well, my partner came to visit."

"Yes, I did. B.J. and I have been busy but not too busy to see how you're doing."

Jack looks at Janet. "Has this guy been giving you any trouble?"

"No, he's been the perfect patient."

Chris drills Jack between bites. "You haven't wrecked my car, have you?"

"What, you think that's why I'm here?"

"It's a possibility. I heard about the gunfight you got my car into."

Jack looks surprised. "Where did you get that info?"

"Sam came by and told me about it. He also told me how your partner saved your ass."

"She did save my ass; I wouldn't be talking to you if it weren't for her. What did he do; come in and couldn't wait to tell you?"

Chris takes another small bite from Janet. "No. But he got around to it. He didn't make it sound so bad. But I've had time to think on it."

B.J. has been mute during the conversation. "You might as well clean the slate, Jack, and tell him the truth."

Chris widens his eyes. "Oh no, don't tell me. How bad is it?"

Jack looks at B.J. and sees the mischievous glint in her eye. Then, he looks down at his feet. "I didn't mean to do it, didn't see the tree."

Chris is beside himself. "Damn, Jack, how bad is it?"

"You'll still be able to drive it, but the frame might be bent. It goes down the street like its sideways. I've got my insurance taking care of it. It'll be out of the shop before you get out of the hospital."

B.J. gives him a report, "We drove up on that robbery, and it ended in hot pursuit."

Chris puts his hands over his ears. "I knew something was going to happen; I knew it."

Jack decides to come clean. "Quit your fretting, my man. We're joking; the car's fine."

Chris stops his self-torture and stares wide-eyed at both of them. A trace of a smile unfolds on his face, and it evolves to a chuckle out of relief. Then, it migrates to laughter, and the rest of them tumble behind his laughter with their own. The laughter brings an ease to the tension that was beginning to boil over into a stew of accusations and regrets.

Janet eases the tension even more. “You two had me going as well; I know what that car means to him.”

Jack reassures her, “So do I; didn’t mean to rile you, Partner, it wasn’t planned. It just played out that way. Your car is being well taken care of, trust me.”

“I know. No harm done. Actually, the jolt is almost a welcome. My days here are as uneventful and bland as this food I’m eating.”

Janet picks up the food tray and puts it on a nearby table along the wall. “And now that I know you’re in good hands, I’m going to go.”

Chris takes her wrist. “You okay?”

“Of course, I need to get back to work. I’ve been spending so much time with you; I’m really behind on things at the office. I’ll see you in the morning; I’ll be working late.”

“You’re sure you’re okay?”

“I’m sure, Silly. I love you.” She bends over and gives him a sweet kiss. Then, she looks at B.J. and Jack. “Make sure he does what he’s told; I have to watch him like a hawk.”

B.J. ensures the request, “Don’t worry, we will.”

Janet scurries out the room and leaves it quiet for a moment. Chris breaks the silence.

“There goes my girl.”

Jack follows the comment, “That woman loves you, Chris; the morning you came here, she was a mess. I wouldn’t want to see her like that again.”

Chris smiles. “I know; I’m a lucky man.”

“You are, Buddy, in more ways than you deserve. So, how are you doing?”

Chris perks up. “The doctors say I’m a miracle case.”

Jack folds his arms. “Why, am I not surprised?”

B.J. walks to the foot of the bed. “When are you going home?”

Chris is relaxed with the company. “Next week sometime, barring no complications; how’s this guy treating you?”

“He can be a jerk ever once in a while. But in the long run, I have no complaints.”

“When I’m back on duty, you can ditch him and team up with me.”

“I’ll think about it.”

Jack seems perturbed, panged by a dose of jealousy. “Hey, you two, you don’t see me standing here? I like to think I’ve got some say in that.”

Chris glances at him. "Why, Jack, I've never seen you in such a twist over a partner. Could there be more to it than just a partnership?"

B.J. peers at Jack, curious about the truth of that. "Jack, I didn't know you cared."

Jack blushes. "I care; you're my partner, so I have to care."

"That's not much of an endorsement."

Jack looks at B.J. with a deep stare. "I care, in more ways than one."

Chris is observing them. "Even if you are a jerk sometimes?"

Jack smirks. "You know what? I've never seen a good man without a little jerk in him. I've never seen a good woman without a little bitch for that matter."

Chris checks out B.J. "I think he's calling you something."

B.J. keeps her eyes on Jack with a twinge of longing in her heart. "Sounds like it."

Jack matches her with his own brand of bullshit. "Is that what the B in your handle stands for?"

B.J. replies lasciviously, "You'll have to be a lot nicer than that to find out what my initials really mean."

Jack reacts with a tint of bad behavior, "Do tell."

Chris has been watching the two of them play with words and adds to the jackass atmosphere everyone has formulated, "Who are we kidding, this guy only knows one thing, and it starts with an insult. Now, me, on the other hand, you couldn't find a nicer guy. One of the best partners a partner could ever have."

Jack rolls his eyes with a retort. "You know; it's getting knee deep in here."

* * *

Shafts of sunlight streams through the room from high windows on the west wall; tiny dust particles, in what seems to be a constant affliction, float through the light source like little soldiers on a march to battle. A loud click fills the place with sound as if some machine was at work. Bicks is at a long, wooden table that nudges a windowless wall. In front of him is a pile of files spread out on the tabletop. He is reading, intensely tapping the forefinger of his right hand on the table and supports his chin with the left. Behind him is a large space where the sunlight blares in, full of filing cabinets and a score of floor-to-ceiling shelving. The shelves are stacked to the brink and covered with dust, disturbed by Bicks rooting around and causing that march of little soldiers.

Crooked from the scrunch his left hand makes supporting his face, he pulls it away and rubs the soreness in his wrist with his right hand. Then, he reaches in a pocket and gets some Chap Stick. Smearing the Chap Stick on his lips, he thumbs through the file he is looking at and stops abruptly with a curious eye. Finished with the application, he puts the Chap Stick away and replaces it with his recorder. The important instrument was like having an assistant at easy access 24/7; a secretary within the simple reach of his pocket.

He pushes a small button, and a red bead of light shines brightly, indicating the recorder is playing. He puts it close to his mouth while he studies the file before him.

"Note: I've been unable to find any connection to someone that lives or might have lived in Highland Park to the murders that took place here. Nothing in the Highland Park records department indicates anything or anyone. But I did find some information that may be pertinent. I've run across an article on the Becker Building's tenth anniversary. It's the building where the doctor was found in Highland Park. According to the article, it was once Crown real estate. The Crown outfit is well-known for its property in Dallas. Now, on the surface, that doesn't mean much except for one thing, the woman that was killed in the gift shop. That gift shop was in the Crown Fountain Hotel. It's the only connection I've been able to come across so far. I'll be going to the tombs and see if I can dig up more information on the subject."

Bicks grins to himself, turns off the recorder, and slips the gadget in his pocket. He starts to gather all the files he has laid out on the table and begins to organize them in the order he found them in.

* * *

Missy was standing in her spare bedroom with hands on her hips. Suitcases were on the bed, filled to the brim and locked in preparation for her flight. Her tickets for the plane were sitting on top of one of the suitcases. She was making sure everything was in order, going through a mental checklist for a final tally on the trip to Dallas. In a couple of days, she would call Bicks to let him know the details of her flight and verify he would be able to pick her up and take her to the hotel she was staying at.

Everything seemed in good arrangement when a glitch suddenly entered her mind. Did she pack those shoes she wanted that matched the black dress she had second thoughts about; the one that made her feel mousy when she stuck it under her chin for a look to surmise the garment on her? She took off for her bedroom in a flurry. When she got to the big closet, she looked for the shoes. They were not to be found, but to make sure the assumption was correct and she did pack the lovelies, off she flew back to the spare bedroom.

Getting to one of the bags, she unclasped the latches, opened it, and rummaged around the articles packed. Discovering the shoes, she gave a sigh of relief, reclosed the suitcase, and latched it tight once again. Then, she looked down at the suitcases, put her hands back on her hips with a pensive expression, and spoke to herself, “Okay, now I believe I’m ready.”

* * *

A nurse is just leaving the hospital room after checking in on Chris. Satisfied with her assessment, she goes through the door while B.J. and Jack surround the bed. After she leaves, Jack steps over to the window to take in the view. It is several stories high in the building they are in. He looks down on tiny people from all walks of life like little miniatures going to and fro along the sidewalks of the hospital that lace the green lawns. Some are coming into the hospital; some are departing, maybe visiting loved ones for the last time. Jack ponders to himself how life goes on like a river. The ebbs and flows of it seemed impossible to stop even when life is stifled and shut down in a sudden act of violence. And a hospital was a leeway station for that river to flow through with all of life’s frailty and drama, heartaches, and joy; the inevitable deluge of life with a one and only purpose, to live. He is also wondering over the conversation they just had and the feelings he has come to know and somewhat revealed about B.J. Sentiments that brings the worth and marvel to living life. And he speculates whether or not he has disclosed stuff to his friends that he would rather keep to himself. Chris is observing Jack’s back while he muses on the thoughts.

“How’s the case going?”

Jack jolts out of his introspection and turns from the window. "It's going. We still don't have much to go on. Edwin came up with a D.N.A. sample and a thumbprint though. Sam found an image on surveillance tape, but it doesn't show much."

"Well, damn, Jack, that's something, isn't it?"

"We don't have a suspect to match it with."

"Catch 22 huh."

"Yeah, that's the way it stands right now."

B.J. has been listening to the two of them. "What's that; catch 22?"

Jack goes to the bed. "It's a term Chris and I use. Sometimes, you may have a case that leads to nowhere but dead ends. So you wait for the next crime to happen with hopes of finding something more."

B.J. stares at nothing. "Catch 22."

Jack sticks his hands in his pockets. "Except, in this case, it may mean someone loses their life. We need to get going."

Chris responds, "Yeah, get out there and find the bad guys."

B.J. walks over to Jack. "Its great news you're going home soon."

"Thanks, looking forward to it."

Jack starts for the door. "You'll see us soon enough."

Chris is sarcastic, "Thanks, looking forward to it."

B.J. follows Jack. "Take care, Chris, and watch out for those catch 22s."

# Chapter 33

Dim light made the vision veiled, and the stillness was so heavy, it felt like a damp membrane. The solitude the place invoked was purposeful. It stayed that way hour after hour, day to day. The resident wanted it to be just like that. It was customary for the atmosphere to be dark, quiet, and cemetery calm. That was the way of the undead.

Over by the old, ornate, wood-framed, full-length mirror on casters was the Renaissance man. He recovered and rolled the piece from an obscure corner and set it in the place it now stood among his living quarters some time ago close to the refrigerator. He was preparing for a night hunt. Straightening the string tie on his white, silk shirt, the sleeves danced in the shallow light from the lavishness of cloth. Dressed with the black fatigue trousers tucked into his black combat boots, the Renaissance man was near the ready. He threw the cape over his shoulders and swirled it out in a furl while the cloth unfolded to its length. Then, he attached the cape around his neck and let that settle. The Renaissance man studied his image in the mirror for several moments, trying to decipher whether it was fading or not. This was a ritual he exercised mostly every day since he found the mirror. It marked the value of his labor and any progress he was making in transforming into the entity he wanted to be. He was supposed to be. The image looked back at him with definition to his dismay. The struggle to right the animus the humans had bestowed on him was still evident. It will take time.

Turning from the mirror, he walked to the big, oak table, gasping for breath. There, his tools were waiting to be used on the hunt. The leather belt with the small pump, plastic containers, and strands of tubing were next to the wristband with its wiring and switches. Above all was the mouthpiece and fangs sitting idle and flashing in what light there was. Placed in the center of the table was the old doctor's bag. Black and cleaned, it was ready to receive the tools used on his escapades. The doctor bag was wide open at the top, resembling a baby bird wanting to be fed. Sidled up to the table, the Renaissance man begins to load the bag with his goods, and, when finished, he closes the little black bag and clasped it nice and tight. Then, he hovers over the business with his hands spread and resting on the tabletop, eternally fighting for breath.

The chore of the evening had been depleted. He looks at the square of light where the windows were and sees the time is near to depart. Trudging back to the mirror, laboring for air, he sweeps the cape out in one majestic motion and it complies to gravity and falls behind him. He is ready and only waits for the dusk to turn darker. He runs his hands over his slick black hair and takes into account the pronounced widow peak. The Renaissance man stands motionless, observing his own double in the mirror once again and toils for his breath. He wishes he could not see any of this. Looking at his image in the mirror is a measuring stick. Until he sees himself fading to nothing, his rebirth is not complete. Each day, since the mirror was discovered, the Renaissance man had checked his reflection, searching for any signs in his recovery. Blood was still the element of need. Blood was the answer to it all.

Done with the time taken, he turns from the mirror and goes back to the big, oak table. The black stalker grabs the doctor bag with one hand and, with the other, the switchblade as he passes the small table next to the easy chair. He steps toward the windows and watches the one window pane exposing the outside. Standing at a spot, he sets the doctor bag down on the concrete and gazes at the square of light, breathing heavily, drawing hard for a breath to bring relief. With deft precision, he flicks the blade of the switchblade out while waiting for the dark to show itself through the tiny pane. The dark was his only friend, his ally in his bloody pursuits, and he always embraced it like a lover. This was the fate of his kind, the counterpart of his deeds, and he too embraced it with impunity.

# Chapter 34

Jack was going through the gears of the midnight blue without thinking. He hit them forcefully, then maxed out the R.P.M.s whenever he could to the fluid adjustments of the traffic. He was preoccupied in his thoughts while he jostled for position on the busy street. Downshifting to a clog of cars that appeared at an intersection, his mind was really on that bit of conversation that took place while visiting Chris. He kept tripping on the fact he may have shown too much of his feelings about B.J. It was a small revelation, in fact so minute, it might have gone unnoticed, but, then again, professionalism was important to him, and he prided himself in maintaining it. Always had in the past, and, so far, he had managed to keep the attraction that had blossomed for B.J. hidden from observation. At least, until the conversation in the hospital room, it was embarrassing; he had never been so uncontrolled about anything in his life. But in this case, he just could not help himself. And it was getting harder to hide it. In plain, simple terms, Jack had become crazy over the heels for this woman.

When he first met B.J., it was on obvious terms. She was his partner, that was all there was to it. But as the days went by, in her company on the job, he came to appreciate qualities in her that were enchanting. He loved her sense of humor and the intellect that shined through that wit. She was tough and more than capable when things got in a squeeze. It was easy to recognize the strong character she possessed, and he found himself relying on her as much or more than any partner he ever had. When he was off duty, alone in his room, thoughts of her filled his mind. He could not stop thinking about her. It had not interfered with his performance as a detective so far, but it was getting more difficult to keep it under wraps when it came to their partnership. She was just so familiar and easy to be around.

On top of that was the way this woman looked. It was impossible to ignore. You might as well try not to notice a bright blue sky on a sunny day. She had the kind of beauty that slapped you in the face. The kind even a blind man would see because of that indomitable spirit that radiated from inside. Her skin, her eyes, and hair, that killer figure; it was all he could do to keep his hands off her. Yet, she was his partner. The dilemma was crushing, and it kept him standing on an island.

While all this was swimming through Jack's thoughts, B.J. was dealing with her own turmoil. She was thinking of Jack. Dwelling on him while pretending to watch the city blocks dash by in the car window. B.J. took note of the slip Jack made that suddenly erupted in the conversation while they were talking to Chris. He said he cared. But the way he phrased it, the emotions in his eyes that seemed behind the words was what struck her. From what she felt after he uttered the words, it seemed he meant more than what the topic encased. It seemed he really did care for her. This was news she had no idea existed. To say the least; it was titillating.

She had found herself thinking of Jack a lot since she met the man. Crowding into her thoughts, even to the point of obstructing her attention on the investigation they shared at times. She would lie in bed at night, imagining what it would be like to be in his arms, to feel his warmth and strength. She tried not to; she knew how Jack felt when it came to a partner and the internal structure of it. But all of a sudden, it seemed he was on the same track as she was on.

What she loved about Jack was his simplicity. He was an intelligent man, observant, with a keen, deductive mind, but he was easy to read. He had no faces; he was not manipulative or devious in any way. Jack was real, no games and no bullshit. She also loved the way he moved, the smooth way in which he worked his large frame, not to mention he was drop-dead gorgeous. The beauty of that was he did not seem to be preoccupied with his looks, did not even seem aware of it. But she was, and the whole package of the man was what any girl would want. At least this girl would.

The bonus of all this and even more was the fact he said he cared. What else could a girl ask for except maybe backing it up with those strong arms around her; speaking of ask, she wanted to explore the subject of caring with this guy. Delve deeper and dig up any nugget that might still be buried. And now was as good a time as any to do that.

"I've got a question."

Jack was jerked out of his thoughts from the sudden probe. "What's that?"

"You said you cared back there at the hospital. I'm wondering what you mean by that."

"The statement explains itself."

"How much do you care?"

"I'd rather keep that to myself."

B.J. is persistent, "Even if I may have a right to know?"

Jack makes a turn on the street. "Even though you may have a right to know."

"Maybe I care too. Have you thought of that?"

There is a pause. "No, I haven't."

B.J. turns and looks at him. "So what do you think about that?"

"I could easily say it makes my day. But I'm not sure if we should be talking about this."

"Come on, Jack, we need to take the fuzz off the picture so we can see it clearly."

Jack looks back at her. "What's that supposed to mean?"

"It means we're both adults. How many times do you meet someone that you share feelings for, something hard to find, I might add, and you don't want to talk about it?"

"Okay, you're right." There is another long pause in the midnight blue that hangs in the air like soft rocks.

Finally, Jack comes clean, "I care about you, B.J. It's gotten so, it's the only thing I do care about except for getting the guy we've been looking for."

B.J. grins. "You know what, Big Boy, I care too. More than I have for any man for a long time. So what are we going to do about it?"

"I think it's definitely something we should check out. But not while we're partners."

"How are we going to do that?"

Jack pulls the car over to the curb and stops. He turns to her and looks into her eyes. "I want to get to know you, B.J. I want to get to know you well. And I'd like for you to get to know me, everything about me. It's all I can do right now to reach over and kiss you. To hold you and kiss you many times."

"So why don't you?"

"We're partners, B.J., and we're trying to find a guy that's going around taking people's lives, and that's really more important than what we've discovered for each other. It's something that needs to be taken care of first;

the city is waiting on it; something that needs to be solved and tucked away before we should go on with a relationship or follow out the impulses we may have for each other. Otherwise we'll start this whole thing in the wrong way. It doesn't fit with me. I believe you probably feel the same way if you think about it."

B.J. stares at him a moment. "Part of the reason I feel like I do about you are your values, who you are. Yes, I think maybe we should do that. Even though expressing our feelings for each other; that it would interfere with our duties might be questionable, I respect your stance on that. I understand how you feel, and I have to say I see what you mean."

Jack continues after a moment, "The only thing that concerns me is you getting cold on all this before it's the right time to act on it."

B.J. smiles. "I think maybe that's the least of your problems."

# Chapter 35

The hour was getting late; the day starting to fade. Striving for breath and standing in the same place for some time, the Renaissance man was recognizing what he had been waiting on. That lone window pane had darkened, giving him the cue to haunt the streets. His switchblade was still performing its purpose, slinging the blade out on command into the diffused light. He stops the function, and the silence coats the area like paint. The only thing penetrating the quiet is his taxing breath sawing into it mercilessly. At his feet, the doctor bag sits, poised, to be swept away on an excursion. He drops the switchblade in the leg pocket of his fatigues and keeps the window pane in his eyesight. The outside has become more intangible in the last moments. It was a gateway to his own personal hell; his own personal yearnings.

A sudden turn, and the Renaissance man briskly moves to the cabinet that contains the keys. With both hands, he jerks the small doors open, and the keys wiggle and tinkle to the disturbance. Still fighting for his breath, he puzzles over the selection of keys he wants in the massive display. Deciding on a set hanging at the back panel, he plucks them from their location. Inspecting them carefully, he puts the keys in his front pocket and closes the cabinet doors.

He abruptly turns again and resumes the spot where the doctor bag is; picking it up, he regards the window pane while dragging on his breath. By degrees, it has gotten darker. The Renaissance man snaps a turn and strides out of the limited spirit of light deep into the shadows. The only evidence of him being there is that tugging breath.

* * *

A young woman is working late at an office building. The office she is busy in belongs to her. It is positioned in a building situated at the outer skirts of downtown near the Deep Elm area. The entrance to the office is all glass, providing a clear view to the inside from the hallway. Etched in the glass door is the name of her company, City Sight Real Estate. It has the customary trimmings any business might have. A reception setting is the first thing to encounter while entering, with a small desk and seating facilities to the right. In the corner where the glass front joins the inside wall, a large fig tree flourishes with its giant leaves.

Through the doorway of the inner office that is just ahead of the entrance door is a woman's backside that can be seen with long, straight, blonde hair cascading to the small of her back. Standing at some black, filing cabinets facing the inner office door, she is engaged, searching for something in need. Down the length of the cabinets where that wall adjoins a corner to a wall leading to the inner office door is a big, leather, beige couch that fronts her desk, and by the door view, the left end of the seating is easily seen. Above the couch is a painting of a beach and tide. At the end of the couch, near the door, is a small table with some green ivy in a pot, a tall cast-iron outline of an owl about ten inches high and a good-sized, black, metal lamp. The lamp is the only source of light found in the space.

The woman shuffles through the files and determines what she wants might be in the drawer below. She closes the top drawer and opens the next one down, intent on finding the file she needs to complete her chore.

* * *

Treading the city streets with his cape flowing in the wind, the Renaissance man is on a mission. Stopped at a city intersection, he waits for the pedestrian light to allow him to cross the road. While quietly waiting, holding onto his doctor bag and the action of his flapping cape blowing around him; fellow bystanders who are on the same corner gawk at him. He seems oblivious to their attention. A handful of people are checking out the strange individual with curious wonder without any concern of being noticed by the odd apparition. They all stand behind and to his flank, and most try hard not to be obvious in their speculation. But those who do stare do not seem to care if they are perceived while he labors for breath loudly, committing the only sound in the crowd; complicating the whole scene with an alarm of catching something contagious, they awkwardly stand nearby with small fears.

The pedestrian light blinks on walk, and the Renaissance man darts out, the first to cross the street. His fellow patrons are steps behind, with the gap between them and the bizarre fellow ahead widening by the second. All they have to look at is a flying cape, the peculiar doctor bag in his hand, and the noise of his breathing.

* * *

Long, blonde hair falls like a golden fleece down the back of a swivel chair at the inner office desk. The young woman has obtained the file she searched for and has it all laid out for deciphering. She is transposing information the file contains into her computer. The office is quiet but for numerous clicks, as her fingers sprinkle the keyboard of the computer while she reads the screen.

Working on a commercial real estate contract, the bread-and-butter of her company, she is calculating the particulars of the transaction for her client. Reading what she has on the screen carefully, she slaps the print button. The electronics start executing their purpose, and she rises from her chair to retrieve what she has at the printer to her rear.

* * *

The Renaissance man has found his way to a more remote street. Standing in front of a four-story building at the base of a stairway, he looks up at its height, breathing profusely. He turns a 360 and checks the streets to see if he is being detected by anyone; satisfied that he is not, he scuttles down an alley on the side of the building.

Getting to the back of his destination, the Renaissance man quickly makes his way to a metal industrial door. Again, he scans the area for secrecy, then takes the keys he brought with him out of his pocket and uses them. The door pops open, undisturbed, and he slides through the opening.

Once inside, he makes his way to another door, opens it, and dashes down a dark hallway until he comes upon the lobby of the building and hugs the wall. A security guard is sitting at a chair, overlooking the front, reading a magazine. He has his back to the spot where the intruder stands. The Renaissance man searches for the surveillance cameras and determines a route he can use to disguise his presence. He watches the guard for some moments, trying desperately to control the sound he makes while breathing. Content the guard is unaware he is being observed, the black frame sneaks quietly behind the man to a door. He pulls it open quietly and a stairwell is revealed. He silently slinks through the doorway, and it slowly comes to a close.

With the doctor bag in hand, he mounts the stairs of the building in complete privacy. Fighting for breath every step of the way, he finally gets to a door that leads to the third floor. Knowing he is far away from the security guard and feeling safe from interference, the Renaissance man decides on the third floor for his hunt. He sets the doctor bag down and slithers through the door to the third-floor hallway.

Sniffing the air, his nose pointing to the ceiling, he strides sharply along, going from one door to the next, determined to find prey. As he goes by a glass front office, his eye catches a glimpse of a blonde woman as she passes across the inner office doorway. He stops abruptly and places the edge of his hands on the glass to gain a vision without any reflection. The Renaissance man watches the woman walk to the file cabinets, open the second drawer, and thumb through the files to find the correct place for the file she carries. While he drags on his breath, his dead-like eyes spark in recognition of opportunity. Then, he sniffs the air around the glass door-entrance and seems pleased with his find.

Deciding on the blonde-headed woman, the Renaissance man rushes back to the stairwell door; he goes through it and gathers the doctor bag. Unlatching it, he begins to fit his tools on; opening his shirt, he starts with the leather belt, pump, and plastic containers. He pulls the belt around his torso and fastens it tight while the plastic tubing wiggles to the motions that will append to the mouthpiece. Then, he gets busy with the rest of the procedure, fitting on the wristband and running the wires down the loose sleeve. The mouthpiece is the last to fix and the easiest to attach for his purpose.

* * *

An open briefcase was sitting on the desk. The young woman puts things away, including the contract she was working on, printed out and ready to show her client. Finished with the task, she closes the case and grabs her purse. She takes the office keys out of her handbag and picks up the briefcase. Leaving the lamp on, she walks to the glass front door and stops. The woman looks around the office to make sure things are in order, and happy that it is, she opens and goes through the office glass-door.

* * *

Out in the hallway, the young woman sets the briefcase on the carpet floor to lock her office. Down the corridor, where the stairwell door is located, there is a crack in the opening. There, in the crack, is a lone eye showing a black, blank, bloodshot orb regarding her, coupled with a heavy breathing disturbing the quiet. The craving in the eye is chilling as it views the woman with a need and want of a demon. What the eye sees becomes even more alarming. It is Janet, the woman who loves Chris so much. She has been working late, trying to catch up on work after falling behind from spending all her waking hours at the hospital taking care of her guy.

She fumbles with the keys in the door, distracted in thought about Chris. Wondering how he was, did he have an afternoon that was good, and nurturing for his health, did he have a proper dinner and did he eat well. As she finds difficulty with locking the office door, detached from her mental wanderings, the stairwell door suddenly flies open, and a black creature appears from out of nowhere into the veiled and still hallway, running full blast at her, screaming like a banshee.

Janet hears a loud thumping sound coming from his tromping feet on the carpet, married to a horrifying scream. She turns to see the Renaissance man, with his hands reaching out like claws, a pair of black, dead-like eyes glaring at her over a hideous piece of metal gleaming in his mouth. He tears out after her like a rabid, black panther, a cape flying behind him like it is on fire, and the sight is terrifying.

Frantic from the appearance, Janet lets out a scream of her own and drops the intention of locking the door. Instead, she opens it with the plan to lock herself inside for safety. She almost achieves the notion when this black bat-of-a-man gets to the glass door before she can lock it tight and starts pushing hard on the obstruction with both hands.

Screaming like a wailing cat, Janet pushes back, trying to keep the door closed. The struggle between them results in a stalemate while they stare at each other through the glass. His eyes burning with determination, the glass in front of his face fogging from his hot breath effort. Janet's eyes are wide-eyed and tearing from the panic-stricken, desperate situation. What she gapes at is some kind of an intense mad entity; crazed black eyes on a gaunt face with a grotesque set of what looks like fangs imbedded in a stainless-steel mouthpiece.

Both of them grapple at the door for several moments. One trying to open it and the other trying to keep it closed. Without warning, the fiend puts his shoulder into the door and applies his weight to it. This gives him an advantage in leverage to impel the door to an opening for his head. He seems to be winning the tug of war as Janet screams from sheer fright. With free hands, the black thing reaches over to the wristband and pushes buttons. The mouthpiece and fangs react to the programming and begin to snap at her like a deranged beast. It chomps at her relentlessly, the fangs like tiny, sharp, devilish knives and the effect mixes with the horrific screams of Janet. She now sees the situation as even more ghastly.

Terrified by the threat, Janet releases her force on the door and backs away from the attack. The door flings open, and the Renaissance man fills the doorway like a black marauder. Scared to her core, Janet retreats to the inner office and picks up the cast-iron owl on the end table to use as a weapon. With all her strength, she pitches it at the black invader. He easily steps aside and dodges the attempt.

Speed and agility carries the Renaissance man at her unexpectedly. She retaliates by grabbing the black, metal lamp and swings it. Janet connects with the blow, and it stuns and stops the advance for a beat of a second. Janet still has her purse in hand. She reaches in it and comes out with a can of mace. Firing the substance directly in his eyes, he howls with pain like a wolf and leans on the wall. She stands motionless, figuring what to do next while he thrashes in torture and scraps for breath.

All of a sudden, he spins out of the misery and propels himself at her. He body slams Janet, and she falls badly, banging her head on the filing cabinets. Left semi-unconscious and vulnerable, he drops upon her like a black vulture. The sight of her white arms trying vainly to push the black hoard away is distressful. The fangs find their mark on her neck, and Janet yelps to the shock and pain of it. A pulsating, sucking sound fills the silence, and the workings of his machine takes control. Janet attempts to push the black invasion from her but fails at length. The blood she is losing weakens to the point that nothing is left but listless gurgles and final gasping sighs.

There, in the gloom, she lies with a blackness blanketing her like a bad thunder storm. A series of death pants can be heard, filling the inner office while she ultimately drifts away from life and from Chris.

# Chapter 36

The midnight blue drives onto the police-department parking lot in the settled night. It is empty of movement but for the motion of Chris's car stopping at B.J.'s rental. The two detectives had spent the good part of the afternoon checking out locksmiths and key makers in a selected perimeter of where the murders had taken place. They had hopes of finding an origin of where keys to the string of murders might be connected. The day had produced no real leads on the case; nothing to show but a big, fat zero for their efforts. Conversation had been sparse since their talk on how they felt for each other except for the questions in all the shops they visited. That was the only time they seemed to be on the same page with a willing discourse. They both had been musing over their little chat ever since it took place and trying to figure out what was going to come of it. It left an uneasy feel between them that collected thick as icy slush. Jack brings the midnight blue to a full stop, and both he and B.J. sit in the cab, wondering what to say to each other before they depart for the evening. It is like they were frozen in a block of ice, sitting stiff and blank. B.J. decides to break the ice.

"We've still got more shops to check out, quite a few more."

Jack is clumsy. "Yeah, when we meet up in the morning, we'll hit the road and finish the ones left."

B.J. muses over her next statement. "I guess we'll have to see how all this goes between us day by day through the investigation."

Jack fingers the gearshift. "Yeah, I guess that's what we'll do. It seems the only thing we can do. I'd like to keep our arrangement under wraps though. No one needs to know about our private business."

B.J. stares out the windshield. "I see the sense in that. Sam would probably have fun with it."

"He would be relentless. Trust me, I know how Sam is; a good guy, but there are times he doesn't know how to quit."

B.J. opens the car door. "I thought so. Not to mention anyone else who works around here."

Jack turns to her. "Yeah, it would get weird. I'll see you tomorrow."

B.J. hesitates. "Before I go, you think we could at least have a kiss just to seal the deal."

A moment passes like a bouncing ball going down a long staircase. Then, Jack responds with a grin.

"I was hoping you'd say that."

They both eagerly lean into each other and touch with a soft, lingering kiss. In a heartbeat, the kiss migrates to a hungry one, and it carries on for seconds. They finally release with a knowing urgency. Both of them want more but keep their distance and agreement unwillingly. Jack looks deep into B.J.'s eyes.

"Goodnight, B.J. Can't wait till the morning when I see you again."

B.J. climbs out the car. "Imagine waking to see each other in bed first thing in the morning."

"I'll make a small confession. I've already imagined that."

B.J. reveals a smile. "So have I. Goodnight, Jack."

"Goodnight."

They each express a delightful but nervous chuckle, then B.J. shuts the car door.

Jack quietly watches her get in the rental and does not pull away till he sees the car lights blink on. Then, he begins his long and lonely drive home.

He wheels the midnight blue out the parking lot and joins the city traffic. His mind tripping on the events that just took place and amazed that such a beautiful woman would want him. That kiss was still swimming in his blood, and he knew tonight would be a rough one when it came to sleep. Intuition told him that a lack of it was at his doorstep again. There would be long hours of staring at the ceiling, thinking of this woman that had suddenly become the most important object in his life. But he also knew he was going to have sweet dreams of this lovely woman tumbling in his arms. He tries to put his thoughts on something else and realizes his stomach aches for food.

Deciding on a burger, he knows of a burger joint he stops at on occasion that is on his way to the house. He'll get one to go along with fries; a double meat with mustard and no pickles. He knew there was beer in the refrigerator. Everything seemed to be determined and sorted out for the evening except for one thing. How the hell was he going to sleep with the taste of that kiss remaining on his lips like a soft wish?

* * *

B.J. came into her loft apartment, holding a small bag. She had been floating on air since she left Jack. Her loft was located near the police department downtown. She was lucky to find such a vicinage when she first got into Dallas, and it did not take long for her to get home once she left the parking lot. She took the liberty of stopping at an all-night grocery for a fresh salad, knowing she needed something to eat. Otherwise, it would just add to the longing she already ached for in the form of Jack.

She locks the door and heads for the kitchen, humming a merry tune. It was like she could not get off the cloud Jack left her on. Along the way, she passes unpacked boxes and wall hangings leaning against the wall. A few of her paintings were already hung in strategic places in the loft, all originals, and full of abstract images with bright colors.

B.J. gets to the kitchen and sets the bag she came in with on the kitchen counter. Opening the fridge, she takes out a bottle of white wine nearly empty from use over the past few nights alone. She pulls the cork out, gets a wine glass, and pours the remainder of the wine into it. Then, she reaches in the bag and comes out with the salad. B.J. finds a fork in a drawer and spills a packet of dressing the salad came with on the meal. She then sits down on a bar stool at the kitchen bar and starts eating.

While she digs into the salad, she scans the loft and takes into account what she has left to finish her move in. There was still a lot. Several boxes full of sculptures and oddities she had picked up on her ventures were packed neatly in newspaper. Along with that were all her framed pictures of friends, family, and memories. These would be used to make the place more intimate and feel like home. Not to mention her collection of paintings she had acquired that always made the abode familiar and cozy.

Munching on her salad, she contemplates one nice truth. Her loft was wonderful, and it was going to be a really cool place, someday. It was roomy with plenty of window to bring in the daylight. The front room she was looking at was long, and at the end of it was a huge bay window. There was a large Ponytail plant sitting on a wooden, hand-carved plant stand inside of the indented space the big bay window produced. Situated on both sides of the plant were two, glass, brick windows bordering the bay where Birds of Paradise plants with their big, leafy stalks bowing in directions enhanced the whole area with a lush, tropical ambience. To the right of the room was the entrance door, and along that wall were the cardboard boxes waiting to be unpacked. Across the floor on the opposite wall was a large, light-brown, swede couch with dark-red, ruby throw pillows. Next to the couch was an easy chair with its back to the kitchen and a companion ottoman in brown swede as well. Above the couch was one of her favorite paintings from a popular artist, that cost her a bundle, hanging and centered. She loved that painting, and it was situated to be a focal point in the room with its vivid colors and interesting depiction. To top off the little warm cove of relaxation was a dark-brown end table between the chair and couch with a stained glass lamp and a matching coffee table with magazines scattered around on it.

She was close to the end of her salad and wine. Tired of not only admiring her new home but from the endless day spent on police affairs, she cleans up the kitchen and moves for the bedroom. It was going to be difficult to sleep after her revelations with Jack. But there was one good thing out of all of it. She was going to see him in the morning, bright and early, with complete honesty between them. That is, not before dreams of the man she suddenly found herself involved in would dance and play like sugar plums in her head and heart. Soothing the wild spirit of wanting she possessed for the man.

# Chapter 37

The day was brilliant. It was the kind of day where everyone and everything might look like it was captured in a treated photograph. The colors were striking, the clarity crystal clear. All that you saw would leap out in your eyes with profound substance; as if the day itself were alive. And the joy of it made a person feel happy and well. Despite the obvious beauty this day created, the one element that made it appear to be peculiar was what was composed in the form of a ceremony; a total opposition to the celebration of life in the mold of a funeral. And the solemn state of such an event seemed to dampen the vividness.

White tombstones rose from the ground like giant mushrooms. The lawns were a healthy green, the trees tall and bountiful. Among all the glorious features was a black cloud of humanity. Standing and grouped around a casket about to be lowered to a final resting place. All the people were sedate and reserved while a preacher spoke of the last rites. Some of them were seated, placed in a special way to accommodate the relation to the deceased. Chris was in that circle to show a sad appreciation of Janet's life.

He was devastated. His arm still in a sling, and a lone crutch leaning on his chair, Chris was in a deep sense of mourning. The last thing he thought that should occur in his life would be attending Janet's burial. And, yet, here he was, sitting with mostly strangers who had no idea of the love he held for her. The isolation of those emotions made him feel that much more alone and dismal. For Chris, this day would never be forgotten. And it would be a very long time before he could come to reasonable terms about it.

As he sat in his chair, listening to the closing remarks of the preacher, Chris pondered if he would ever love again. He was so happy with Janet. He always felt she was a perfect fit, and he liked to think the same went for her. That wonderful design he had with her will never be matched, at least it seemed that way. And as he sat in his grief, he considered if the void that dwelled inside him could ever be filled again. Would there be light at the end of this dark tunnel he now found himself in? He deemed it was an empty, lonely course he saw ahead before any light would appear. And he was left to wait for any remnants of that light to shine a path for him once more.

He thought about love. What was it really? It was such a rare thing to find and that made it so much more of a cherished… what was love? He could not answer that for himself; could anyone? All the poems written and all the songs sung on the subject did not give a definition of what love was or what it was like. What you might find in a dictionary did not convey the truth of it. Maybe the meaning was different for each individual. Love was something you could not hold in your hand or mind, only in your heart. And in Chris's case, only in the soul. It was like the wind. You could not see it or grasp it; you could only feel it. Whatever it was, Chris knew one thing. The love he had was now gone; at least the manifestation of it which was in the body of Janet.

Across the way, on the other side where the casket sat, Chris could easily see Jack and B.J. They were standing with several other people he did not know. Most of the folks there, Chris had never met; they were friends and family of Janet's. It made him feel better to see his partner there along with his new friend, B.J. Frankly, they were the only familiar faces in the crowd except for Janet's parents; whom he had dinner with on more than one occasion. It made a difference to have buddies from the force attend. He had a pair of sunglasses on, so the two of them were unaware they were being watched. When this whole affair was over, he intended to talk with those two and thank them for being here.

* * *

Bicks was anxious. It was no easy feat finding someone at D.F.W. Airport. He was at the right gate, at the correct terminal, but a hair early. He came in on another flight from visiting his mother. She was ill, and, besides, it had been some time since he went to see her. Bicks was always closer to his mother than his dad. To the point of being tagged a mama's boy, though he hated being called anything like that and would always get riled whenever the term came up. His dad had passed away years ago, and the relationship between him and his mother had grown even stronger, and, needless to say, she was very proud of her bestselling-author son. She clucked around him like a mother hen and she loved to.

He flew in a couple of hours ago and decided to wait for Missy who was scheduled to come in on her flight that very day. It was necessary to go see his mother, and he had no regrets about that, but it did take him away from his work on the book. One of the things that made him anxious was the fact Missy would be curious to know about his progress on it. He did have some leads to follow, and they were enticing leads to say the least, but Missy was not always patient when it came to work.

It had been awhile since he saw Missy in the flesh, and she was due to walk off board any minute. Her flight had docked, and he was beginning to see some of the passengers from the plane enter the terminal. It took no time at all for him to spot her in the cluster of people, and he gave a little wave with a big grin to gain her attention.

She saw him immediately and veered for his direction. In a handful of moments, they were close enough for a hug. Bicks followed with a question.

"How was the flight?"

"Okay, but I'm glad to be on the ground."

"Well, I've got plans tonight for dinner; reservations at one of my favorite restaurants. I think you'll love it."

Missy is acclimating to the bustle in the airport. "Is it a good place to talk business?"

"Of course." Bicks takes her arm. "Come on, I know where to go for your luggage. It's down below on the next floor. It's good to see you, Missy."

"It's good to see you. I've been looking forward to it. But it's always a pleasure to see my favorite author. Needless to say, I'm interested to see what you have on your current project."

Bicks looks at her while they scurry along. "You won't be disappointed. It's going to be a great book."

Missy keeps her eyes on the crowd ahead of her. "I have all the confidence in the world it will be. I'm booked at the Crown Fountain downtown; I'd like to get there and get some rest before we eat if that's all right."

Bicks is leading the way. "That'll be easy enough. The restaurant is just blocks from the hotel, and we've got plenty of time before we eat. I need to get home and unpack myself, feed my fish, and stuff like that anyway. I just flew in from seeing my mother; she was ill."

Missy looks at him. "I'm sorry to hear that. Is she okay?"

"She's fine. Visiting her set me back a little in the research on my book, but I've got plenty to tell you about."

Missy is tramping along, trying to keep up with the flow of the multitudes. "I can't wait to hear about it. I know it's a conversation I've been itching to delve into."

* * *

People were beginning to drift back to their automobiles. Janet was laid to rest, and the group of folks there to mourn her passing was breaking apart to their separate lives.

Chris was still seated, unable to leave the sight. He knew he eventually had to, but leaving brought something final he was not prepared to face. It meant walking away from Janet and starting a life without her; a thought that seemed unbearable at the moment.

Jack and B.J. tentatively walked to Chris and helped him rise from his chair. Jack hands the crutch to him. "You okay, Buddy?"

"I don't know. Yeah, I think so."

B.J. helps him tuck the thing under his arm. "You will be, Chris. It doesn't seem like it right now, but you will be."

Chris takes his sunglasses off. "I want to thank you two for being here. It means a lot to me, seeing familiar faces at this thing. I mean it, thanks for the thought and support."

Jack observes him closely. "We'll always be there for you, man. You're my partner and my best friend. You need a ride, Chris? I'm still driving your car; you need it back?"

"No thanks, Jack. Janet's parents are doing that. I appreciate the offer though. How's my car anyway?"

B.J. sparks to the inquiry. "The car's fine, we're taking good care of it."

Jack adds to the comment, "You can get it back anytime you want, good Buddy."

"I know. I can't drive yet, so keep it for now. I do have one request though."

Jack waits for the request. "What's that?"

"Use the car to catch that son of a bitch."

B.J. reacts to what he just said, "We will. You can count on it."

Chris looks at both of them. “Keep in touch; I want to know what’s going on in the case. I won’t rest till I know the bastard is behind bars. I wish I could be out there to do it myself.”

Jack puts a hand on his shoulder. “That goes without saying; I promise it’ll get done.”

“Get him, Jack, catch him.” Misty-eyed Chris turns; he puts his sunglasses back on and eases toward a handsome couple that was waiting for him.

Jack and B.J. watch Chris go to Janet’s parents, then start heading toward a parking lot where the midnight blue is sitting. The two of them steam along at a good clip; both swimming in their respective thoughts. B.J. suddenly blurts out something.

“Catch 22.”

Jack is surprised of the intrusion on his thoughts. “Huh, what was that?”

B.J. responds, “Catch 22.”

Jack nods. “Catch 22. A number I’m beginning to dislike.”

B.J. contemplates the subject. “What sticks out in the case is the ability to enter places without disturbing anything.”

Jack digs out the keys to the midnight blue. “It hasn’t been established how he got in the building where Janet was found.”

B.J. goes to the passenger side. “Exactly my point; it goes back to what you said, maybe he has his own keys. At least it looks that way, since we can’t find anyone making them for him.”

Jack unlocks the doors. “If he does, he’s got an inventory of the damn things.”

# Chapter 38

A gaggle of detectives was walking out the squad office on their way to lunch; spirited with laughter and comradely. Sam was at his desk and paying no attention to the exodus. He was grateful for the seclusion that came with their departure. It leaves the office empty, and with it comes the unusual quiet. Because no one was now around, Sam relaxed and kicked up his feet on the desk. He was reading the newspaper by the abundant light flooding the room from the wall of window. His sleeves were rolled to his elbow, his tie loosened, with the top button of his shirt undone, and his coat was hanging on the back of his chair. It was a perfect moment and a rare one at that; all because his fellow detectives were hungry.

The article he was reading was on the string of recent bodies found in the metropolis. It was an impressive list with pictures of each victim along with their names. There were no particulars about the case, like bloodless corpses or how they were killed and what the circumstances of their death might be, but their identification and what the police was doing to confront the situation was on the front page for all to see. As he ran through the article, making sure there was nothing that might hurt or hinder the investigation, the phone suddenly rang. The ring cut into the library, quiet like a knife and blared like a fog horn, forcing Sam to drop his feet on the floor and reach for the phone on his desk to stop the damnable ringing.

"Homicide… Yeah, Doc, how are you…? He's not here… He'll be coming in soon; I'll tell him you want to talk… I will."

Sam hangs the phone up while B.J. and Jack stroll into the office.

"I was just talking to the coroner, he just called. He wants to talk to you two."

Jack responds, "Oh yeah, what about?"

Sam puts his feet back on the desk. "Didn't say, just that he wanted to talk."

B.J. looks at Jack. "I wonder what he wants?"

Jack picks up the phone. "Let's find out."

He dials a number and waits for the connection. "Hey, Doc, it's Jack Degree… Yeah, I just missed you. What's going on…? I'll be right there."

He hangs the phone up and starts for the office door. B.J. follows close in his wake. Captain Parks appears at the door while the detectives go through the doorway. He steps aside to let them hurriedly pass.

B.J. ignores the captain. "What did he say?"

Jack does the same. "I'll brief you on the way."

In seconds, they are through the door and gone. Sam sits with his feet on the desk, picking the paper back up. The captain stands in the doorway, a little perturbed from the snub by the two detectives on his presence. He stares back at Sam who is getting comfortable.

"I'm here to get an update on the case after reading that article you're looking at. Since those two are busy, why don't you brief me on the subject?"

Sam appears surprised by the attention. "Ah, well, ah."

He seems confused while a long, awkward pause evolves and hangs in the room like a sharp object. Suddenly, he throws his hands out in exasperation, leaving the paper in his lap, with a big, perplexed expression and eyes the size of saucers as an answer to the captain's inquiry.

* * *

Edwin was at his desk, sipping coffee and reading the newspaper. The sound the rustling of the paper made seemed to exaggerate in the quiet of the empty lab. Just as he sets the cup of coffee on his desk, Jack and B.J. storm in. Edwin looks over his newspaper, reacting to the bustle.

"That was quick."

Jack barks out his haste, "Hey, when the Doc calls, the soldiers come running."

Edwin rattles the paper. "Have you seen this?"

Jack and B.J. look at it, and B.J. asks, "What is it?"

"It's an article on the case you two are investigating."

Jack advances with a purpose. "Let me see that."

Edwin hands the paper to him. "There's nothing in it that the public shouldn't know."

Jack surveys the article, then passes it to B.J. "No harm, no foul."

B.J. adds to the comment, "To look at all these girls, the only thing they have in common is the way they were killed."

Edwin reaches across his desk. "Here's the file on Janet Cross. She's verified as victim number five."

B.J. sets the paper on the desk. "We just left her funeral. Chris is in a tailspin from the whole thing. It wasn't easy seeing him like that."

Edwin gives the file to Jack. "I'm sorry to hear that about Chris, I didn't realize he was that close to the Cross woman. Next time you see him, give him my condolences."

Jack is opening the file. "We will, Doc, he'll appreciate that."

The doctor is watching Jack with the file. "We got more D.N.A. from saliva on the victim's throat and prints from the front office door, the hallway side of the door. All of it produced a match to what we already had. I think maybe the suspect had to push himself into the office to get to the victim."

Jack is checking out the file. "There was a visible struggle in the office."

Edwin sips his coffee. "The samples match with the Amy Sanders's crime scene, so that indicates the same individual was involved. Not to mention the puncture wounds on the neck and the back of her head was slammed against the file cabinets in the office to render her helpless like three of the victims. But there's one other thing."

B.J. and Jack look at Edwin and speak simultaneously, "What's that?"

"The victim used a lamp as part of her defense."

B.J. confirms the statement, "Yes, it was on the floor in the inner office. We figured she used it like a club or something."

"Correct. We found some blood on that lamp that matched the D.N.A. we have on file. The blood type is AB negative. A rare type; so, now, we have D.N.A. and prints from two different crime scenes and blood type AB negative; tools that can certainly be used in a courtroom for a conviction."

Jack is curious about something. "You've run the results of the blood type through all available records?"

"Of course, but nothing was found, no match. As I've mentioned before, I sent the D.N.A. results to C.O.D.U.S., the F.B.I. records. There were no hits there either. As a matter of fact, none of the samples we have is on file; the blood type or prints and the D.N.A."

B.J. ponders the answer. "So we're still at square one technically."

"Square two. If it's not on file at C.O.D.U.S., and there's nothing on our personal records, we have a local boy more than likely who has no priors and probably won't be going anywhere. The city is his hunting grounds."

* * *

Sam was still at his desk, with his feet on it, the newspaper still in his hands. He had migrated to the sports page by now, enjoying the absence of detectives in the office. His concentration on league standings was interrupted by voices in the hallway. They get louder, telling him the owners of the voices are approaching his sanctuary. He takes his eyes off the paper and puts them on the doorway. Jack and B.J. barrel into the place, with Jack leading the discussion.

"But it doesn't make sense."

"It's the only thing that does make sense in this whole case. How else could he get in the buildings without breaking and entering?"

Jack walks over to a bulletin board that has all five pictures of the victims. Under the pictures are eight-by-tens of the buildings and crime sites. Next to that display is a map of the city, with little red circles bunched close together indicating where the crimes took place in relation to the overall city streets. Jack stands in front of the map and points at the red circles.

"We checked all the key makers and locksmiths in this area and came up with nothing. We checked security and maintenance in all the buildings and found there was no way to enter without violating an access of any kind, and they informed us of no missing keys to those buildings."

Sam drops his feet on the floor and introduces his two cents sarcastically, "Let's not forget, there's no security video at any of the buildings that show anything of use. including the building Janet Cross was found in. Nothing in the lobby cameras to indicate someone was moving around unattended, and the security guard that was there has nothing to report. The image we do have is useless, they identify no one in particular, and we're not even sure of what we do see."

Jack looks at him. "So what's your point?"

"He's a vampire. He moves in the night like the fog, undetected. A vampire doesn't reflect an image in a mirror, maybe the same goes for a camera, except for maybe one camera anyway. And that camera caught an image of a guy with a cape that looked like a vampire. He attacks people and drinks their blood, drinks them dry. Just like a vampire. Even leaves the mark of a vampire on their neck."

Jack turns back to the bulletin board. "Yeah, right, you're not helping any."

B.J. follows that train of thought, "No, he may have something there."

Jack brings his attention on B.J. "What, we start wearing big, iron crosses around our necks and carry wooden stakes for guns?"

B.J. walks to her partner. "Jack, look, you said back at the gift shop in the hotel that maybe he has his own set of keys. Edwin just told us there's a good chance this guy's from here, a local boy. It could be he grew up here, lived here all his life. And he knows where to go and how to go unnoticed because of that. And it could be he has his own source of keys we don't know about."

Jack continues the thought, "He also talked about the vampire murders that have taken place around the country; where the motive was to become a vampire."

"I've said more than once that maybe he thinks he's a vampire and on some kind of mission. Maybe he thinks the blood he takes is something he needs, something for survival, who knows."

Sam jumps in again, "That's what I meant."

B.J. continues, "If he's from around here, he probably knows this city, knows it very well. Knows where to go to live like a vampire and hold up during the day where it's dark and quiet."

Jack scans the city map. "And secluded, like an empty warehouse or vacant building he has keys to."

B.J. goes to the map and refers to the red circles, "All the murders took place in the downtown area, all within blocks of each other."

Sam injects another comment, "He lives right here downtown."

Jack has been listening to all the suggestions, formulating and digesting the innuendo. "And maybe with keys to the city, keys he has possession of somehow. And the only common ground the keys might have would be the buildings the murders took place in—"

B.J. intervenes with a thought, "The buildings may be the connection we've been looking for."

Jack sticks his tongue in his cheek for a moment. "Sam?"

"Yeah, what can I do for you?"

"Check out the internet and see if you can find any connection to the buildings where the murders took place. If there is a connection, and somehow all these buildings are related to each other, it might lead to a suspect with a handful of keys. It could even lead to a key that shows us his location where he might be hiding out when he's not prowling around the city."

The captain breezes into the office, with his hands folded behind him, right at the end of Jack's statement. "Well, now, all my detectives are in one spot, finally. Now that I have all of you together, suppose you bring me up to speed on what's going on. Fill me in, boys and girls."

Sam looks earnestly at the captain. "We're looking for a vampire."

# Chapter 39

Driving in downtown Dallas was always a pain no matter what time of day or night. It was early evening, and Bicks was on his way to pick Missy up for their dinner date. The restaurant they were going to was within a walk to the Crown Fountain where Missy was, and the distance made it almost not worth driving. It was a beautiful day, and it had strayed into the evening with the same value; that special time where a blaring sunlight had dissipated and dulled to a cooler blend of weather. Needless to say, it would be a nice walk to their destination.

Bicks knew Missy would be expecting him to pick her up in his Jaguar and drive to the restaurant in comfort. She was not much on exercise but a real stickler on air conditioning and luxury; a flaw in her character, but a small one. Overall, she was a grand dame, and he was so delighted he had her for his agent. She would be plucking his brain for details on the book. And he was prepared to give them. He had a hunch about the direction he wanted to take in digging for information but had been detained by his visit to his mother. Back in town and back on track, he was looking forward to where it all might guide him to. He was also looking forward to see what Missy would think.

The obliging traffic thinned, and Bicks was able to take his Jag to the front of the hotel. A doorman was standing near the front, and bellboys were dashing about, catering to guests. Bicks did not have to park and look for Missy; she was waiting for him. Before his car came to a full stop, she came out of the glass entrance doors and trotted for his car, unassisted. He applied Chap Stick to his lips while he watched her go to the passenger side, open the door, and slide into the car.

"I'm starved."

"It won't take long before we're ordering."

* * *

Jack and Captain Parks were standing in front of the bulletin board where the map was. Jack has been pointing out particulars in the group of red circles, explaining their purpose and how they related to the case. B.J. was sitting on a desktop feet away from the wall where the bulletin board was, adding to the discussion when needed. Sam sat at his desk, listening to the presentation. Jack is concluding his summary of the investigation to the captain.

"So we thought we'd have fingers over there check the internet. If a connection can be found to the buildings, it might lead to a guy who may have keys to them."

B.J. stands up. "Considering this case, the whole idea might be the piece of the puzzle that fits."

Sam suddenly jumps out of his seat and heads for the office door. He wiggles his fingers in plain sight. "I'm going to put these suckers to work."

The captain watches Sam leave, then turns to B.J. "I've read your profile, more than once. I think it brings some clarity to who we're looking for, at least in theory. Do you stand by it?"

B.J. is confident. "Yes, I do. Keep in mind it's not in stone. No profile is."

Captain Parks reacts to her retort with a smile. "I realize that. For that matter, what is, besides a tombstone?"

He starts for the door, and when he gets to the doorway, he turns to face the two detectives.

"The boys up top are really breathing down my neck on this. They're getting pressured from the media. That article in the paper doesn't help any. Shit rolls downhill, boys and girls; you need to get your teeth into something."

Jack lets him know they get the drift, "We understand, Captain. Consider it done."

"I do my loyal troops, I do, and I'll do whatever I can to ward off the evil spirits. I know you're doing what you can, question is how much time is there do we have to do it in." The captain smiles again, then makes an about face, walks through the doorway, and disappears.

It leaves the office still, bleak, and soundless. Jack and B.J. are standing in the middle of it with no one else around to share the challenge Captain Parks just gave them. Without taking their eyes off the doorway, they speak to each other. Jack enlists the conversation.

"I'm hungry."

"Yes, I'm with you on that."

"I'm thinking of the Blue Note?"

B.J. grabs her purse off a desk. "Let's boogie."

* * *

Bicks and Missy were halfway through their meal. Missy took a big bite of a grilled salmon smothered in cream sauce and checked out the restaurant. The outer walls were red brick. An area tucked away on the backside of the room was sealed off with glass brick. This provided privacy for waiters to pick up orders and busboys to perform their duties, unobserved by the diners.

Original paintings from local artists adorned the brick and interior walls to break the banality of the space and create relevance. Several tables were placed in the open floor where candles flickered on tabletops and where potted palms and peace lilies stood randomly for ambience. This was where the main body of staff could be found circulating around the tables, providing assistance to the guests. Anchored in the center of all this was a big, round, salt-water, fish tank that dominated the scene. It was huge, ten feet in circumference and nearly reaching the ceiling; so big, you could not see any people sitting on the other side of it. Missy chewed on her latest bite and watched the activity in the aquarium.

"I see why you like this place so much. The service and food is great, not to mention the atmosphere. Thanks for bringing me here."

"You're welcome, dear. So what's in store for you tomorrow?"

Missy frowns. "Pitch day."

"Pitch day! What on earth is pitch day?"

Missy takes another bite of salmon. "All the people who have paid to attend the convention get to go and talk to agents of their choice. We're all at tables, and they each sit and pitch their book one after another. If the agent likes what he or she hears, they make arrangements to see the manuscript or at least the first pages of it."

Bicks has been listening with interest. "Sounds like that could be grueling."

"It is. The hard part comes with all the verbal pitches that may not cut the mustard. It makes for a long day, but you never know what might cross the table. What's your day look like?"

"I'll be getting back to my book."

Missy takes a sip of wine. "Speaking of which, tell me about it."

Bicks wipes his mouth with a napkin. “Where can I start? It’s such a fascinating story, I don’t know where to begin.”

“Just give me the details.”

Bicks dwells on a moment to collect his thoughts. “Well, several bodies have been discovered all over downtown. The victims are all women, and all these bodies are bloodless.”

“Stop right there. How do you know this? That sounds like something the police would keep under wraps.”

Bicks shows a knowing smile. “I was an investigative reporter in this city for years. During those years, I developed resources.”

Missy understands what he says. “Okay, I’ll buy that. Go ahead.”

“The women are untouched. What I mean by that is that the bodies are in pristine condition. They haven’t been raped or slashed to death; they haven’t been shot, mutilated, or dismembered. They’re just found without blood. The lack of which is what ends their life.”

Missy pokes at her salmon with a fork. “How’s the blood taken?”

“Sources tell me by two little marks on the neck.”

“Are we talking about a vampire?”

Bicks opens up with a grin instead of a smile. “That’s part of the intrigue of the story. I don’t know if you’ve noticed or not, but a gift shop in the hotel you’re staying at is one of the crime scenes.”

Missy picks up her wine for another drink. “You know; I saw some crime tape roping off an area from the lobby. I was wondering about that. I was going to ask you about it.”

Bicks keeps grinning. “Now you know. There’s also a question about keys.”

“What do you mean, what keys?”

“I overheard detectives talking about keys at that very crime site. Most of all the murders took place in public buildings after hours. Sources tell me these places are not broken into. Somehow, the killer gains access inside without breaking and entering.”

Missy is captivated. “Go on.”

Bicks digs into his pocket for Chap Stick. “There was another set of similar murders that took place in Highland Park years ago that was never solved. I ran across information while I was doing research, that one of those buildings was once called the Crown Plaza. The gift shop is in the—”

Missy interrupts, “Crown Fountain Hotel; you think there’s a connection?”

He takes the top off his Chap Stick. “I don’t know. That’s what I’ll be working on tomorrow. If there is a connection, then I’d say these buildings have one thing in common.”

Missy puts her fork down, folds her hands in a fist, and sets her chin on it. “What’s that?”

Bicks puts Chap Stick to his lips. “Keys; at least that’s the conclusion I’ve come to at the moment. Someone’s got an extra set of keys, and how he has them is part of the mystery. And that mystery, dear heart, is a portion of what I intend to write about in the book.”

# Chapter 40

The secret lair is dark, still, and quiet. It has the feel of a hollow bowel to a gargantuan creature from another time. The reserved and dull placidness has a strange oppressiveness, a pressure that seems to grip the body with invisible hands. Stroking and kneading the conscious to a hypnotizing state of mind. It reaches into the core and chokes it to a submissive consternation. It is a living death.

In the distance, the big, oak table can be seen with the candelabrum lit up with candles. The drippings from them collect on the table surface, creating tiny stalagmites. Beyond that is the big easy chair and lamp. The journal and quill wait patiently to be used on the small table next to it. Across from that are the full-length mirror and the old refrigerator with three, empty canisters sitting on top of it. The glass of the canisters is stained in a deep red, eager to be replenished with life's liquid; that of blood.

The deft silence is suddenly disturbed by a loud *clang*. It penetrates the calm like flying daggers. Moments go by, then, once again, *clang*. The noise invades the mute atmosphere like a charging army of armored knights; *clang*, *clang*, and another *clang*. As if someone were being crucified.

It clangs once more, then the Renaissance man appears from out of the shadows. He is driving a six-inch concrete nail into the brick wall near his curtained sanctuary, *clang*. In his hand is a ten-pound metal hammer, and he is wielding it like a madman. *Clang*, *clang*, *clang*, followed by one more *clang*. Finally, he seems satisfied with the task. He leans into the wall until the side of his face touches it, breathing with difficulty. The hammer he is using rests in his right hand against the wall as well.

He spins in his position and leans to the wall by his back. Staring into the vacant dark, he gasps for breath, fighting for it as if it were his last; the hammer now dangling at his side. Breathing furiously, he abruptly abandons his mark on the wall and trudges heavily to the refrigerator with the hammer in hand.

Once he gets to the refrigerator, he opens the door in a willful motion and grabs a canister of blood inside. The glass containment is close to empty as he brings it to his mouth and gulps down blood like a predator. Careful not to spill the precious red, he drains the canister dry. Finished with the ritual, he slowly closes the refrigerator door, places the extinguished glass on top with the others, then leans into the weight of the cold bulk.

Breathing fiercely, his eyes slide slowly up to glare at the wall and the work left to do. The Renaissance man spends seconds in the torment before he pulls himself from the support of the refrigerator and takes measured steps back to the brick wall between the curtain and old, tarnished sink; the hammer waving gently to his gate.

He grips another nail lying on the old work sink and eyeballs the spot he wants to place it at; deciding on that, he sticks the nail at the designated point and pounds it with the hammer; *clang, clang, clang*. Continuing the violence on the nail, he hammers away while the nail eases into the concrete lining of the brick till it is in a satisfied depth. *Clang, clang, clang*, again and again.

Then, he stops the labor. Done with it, he turns and leans into the wall with his back against it once more. Agonized by his breath, he stands there, looking blankly into the murky chamber. He raises the hammer next to his ear and pitches it disdainfully into the dark. It skitters on the concrete floor, banging and clanking to an eventual stop.

Still leaning on the wall and grappling for breath, a slight curl of a smile traces his lips. It blossoms under the glower of his black, dead eyes. The smile spreads on his colorless face in recognition of the knowledge that the first part of a plan is now finished.

# Chapter 41

Large, neon, electric, blue letters blared into the dark-spelling Blue Note. Located high above the entrance door, it was so bright, it cast a blue tint on the street below. A number of small musical notes in the same blue danced around the lettering to enhance the sign. The small window next to the door still had the blue sign reading Blue Note, but the big sign above gave out a notice to be noticed.

It was slow outside, with hardly a pedestrian on the sidewalk. An occasional car cruised by on the dim boulevard, meandering to some unforeseen destination. From this inactivity, Jack and B.J. pull to a stop in the midnight blue right in front of the place. Jack shuts down the engine, and both detectives climb out of the cab. Jack makes a point while closing his car door.

"Lock it up; this neighborhood isn't the best in town."

B.J. complies by the wish. "Wouldn't you know; a cop hangout in a bad neighborhood. Go figure."

Jack drops the car keys in his pocket. "You never know when you might need one, and you need one around here a lot."

The two of them head for the Blue Note door while B.J. makes a comment, "I like this place. It's cozy, and the food's excellent."

Jack agrees, "I was hoping you would. I knew the food would sell the place."

B.J. employs a satirical note, "You're so intuitive."

Jack overlooks it. "I am to please."

"Think your girlfriend is here tonight?"

His expression changes. "I wouldn't know."

B.J. grins. "Turn on that intuition."

Jack holds the door open for B.J. "She's not my girlfriend."

B.J. strolls in with a snicker.

The bar inside was just as boring as it was outside. One fellow was at the bar, nursing a drink. A young couple was at a table on the far end. Jack and B.J. make a left turn and go to the line of booths they sat at before, next to windows overlooking the street. No one is on this end of the bar, so the detectives have a built-in seam of privacy.

They both slide into a booth in the middle of the row and make themselves comfortable. As soon as they are seated, the waitress, a short brunette, walks to them with menus in hand.

"Would you like something to drink?"

Jack looks at B.J. "Two beers?"

B.J. agrees with a nod to the suggestion, and the waitress sets the menus down, then goes for the beers.

"I guess your girlfriend isn't here tonight."

"She's not my girlfriend."

B.J. grins again. "That's okay; it leaves you all for little, ole me."

Jack picks the menu off the booth table, watching B.J. dubiously. "She's not my girlfriend."

B.J. gets her menu. "Me thinks the lady doth protest too much."

Jack opens his menu and reads. "You have to know me better to call me a lady. I believe I'll have the catfish dinner tonight."

"I'm not tired of the pot roast yet."

The waitress appears at the table with two beers and takes their order, then walks away.

B.J. takes a sip of her beer. "So tell me, Jack, have you ever been married?"

Jack raises his beer. "Once, it didn't last very long though."

"Divorced?"

Jack takes a long slug of his beer. "Years ago; she could never get used to me being a cop; kept after me about quitting it. She wanted to be an artist, so she went to Europe to study. I haven't seen her since. I don't even know if she's still in Europe. What about you, were you married?"

"I've never been married. I got close once, but it went no further than the altar at a church."

Jack looks surprised. "Literally?"

B.J. becomes pensive. "Literally, standing in front of it in my wedding dress; the preacher, my relatives, my mom and dad, and all my friends watching in shock while I watch my fiancé running for the door and out of it, slamming it open. Buddies of his later told me he met a woman a few weeks before that he was crazy about. I guess he decided at the last moment she was the one he wanted."

Jack takes ahold of her hand. "You know what, B.J.? That fellow made the mistake of his life and the biggest favor he could ever make for me."

B.J. smiles. "Sweet of you to say that."

"It's the truth. I hate to say it, but I'm glad the man was so foolish. What did you do when he left like that?"

"I told everyone to go to the reception. We had a big party, and I smiled all night long with a broken heart."

Jack gazes into her eyes. "That must have been tough. I'm sorry you had to go through that."

"It's okay. It's far enough in the past now, it all seems funny. Part of the reason I left the F.B.I. was because of that. The irony of it all, he was the one that talked me into joining the department in the first place."

Jack reaches out to brush her cheek with his free hand. "The jokes on him, and he's never going to know what a joke he made of himself."

Just then, the waitress appears with two, steaming plates of food. Jack and B.J. react to the sudden intrusion.

"Here we are, folks. Can I get you anything else?"

They look at each other and decline her offer. The waitress leaves, and both of them dig in.

B.J. takes a big bite of pot roast. "How long have you been a cop, Jack?"

Jack is grabbing the ketchup bottle. "A long time, years. I started out a patrolman beating the streets. It took about six years before I made detective. I've been a detective for over ten now."

B.J. nods to the answer. "A long time."

Jack pours ketchup on his fries. "A long time."

A lull in the conversation spills between them. They concentrate on their meal for some moments when Jack has a thought and conveys it.

"I have a confession to make."

B.J. looks at him. "Oh yeah, what's that?"

"I took a peek at your personal file the other day."

"You did huh. What did you find?"

"There seems to be a conflict of interest with you."

B.J. pokes a fork at her pot roast. "What do you mean by that? Are you talking about Highland Park?"

Jack realizes he has put himself in a corner. "You don't see many from Highland Park get in the crime business."

"What, you think I'm pretentious and privileged. Hell, my uncle, or at least I consider him my uncle, was the mayor of Highland Park. He's the one that got me on this case. I'm not anything like a typical Highland Parker. Though I have to admit, when I went to high school there, I was. I outgrew that silly shit when I got in the real world."

Jack sips his beer. "That's the conflict of interest I'm talking about. The wife I had, she was from Highland Park. She never could get past it. I still don't know why she was with me."

B.J.'s eyes glitter. "I have an idea why."

"She would never come to a place like this. It would be below her; she would look down her nose at it. She wouldn't even consider it."

"And, yet, here I am."

"Yes, that's part of what I love about you. You come from money, position, education; all the opportunity's anyone could have in life, and, yet, you're just this cool down-to-earth Texas gal. And you're here with plain ole me in this dirty, little bar."

B.J. stops her attention on her meal. "Why do you think that?"

Jack shrugs. "You got me. Why?"

"Because you're a decent man, Jack; you have a sense of integrity and honor, and you abide by it, you live by it. My dad is like that, it's a quality I've always loved in him. And it's just built into you. It's not fabricated or manufactured. And, on top of that, you're so damn good looking."

Jack chuckles. "I don't know about that, but thanks for saying it."

"You want to have a drink on that? Up at the bar after we eat, I'm buying."

Jack smiles. "You can buy the first round."

B.J. grins back. "You know, I can drink all night long, and it never bothers me."

"Bullshit."

"It's true. I never met a man I couldn't drink under the table."

"Are you trying to get me drunk or something?"

B.J.'s grin broadens. "Or something."

* * *

Subdued light was just enough from the outside streetlamps and city signs to give the room and the objects in it outline for recognition. A large source of that light came from the big bay window and the two, narrow, glass, brick windows that bookended the bay. Warm earth tones of the furniture could be defined along with the unpacked boxes sitting against the wall. Some of the paintings with their primary colors seemed to jump out for recognition in the obscure light. A deep red-and-brown carpet in an interesting design covered the wood floor where the furniture was. It was a new addition, and it gave a sense of section to the living space.

Separating the living area and the bright white kitchen at the end of the room was a dark-brown dining table seating six that had also been added. A bouquet of red roses was in the center of the table in a fine, deep, blue vase. Next to the kitchen was the hallway leading to the backrooms. Some of the unpacked boxes had been emptied and left at a corner in a pile, waiting to be disposed of. A few of the paintings that were leaning on the wall by the cardboard boxes were now hanging. It told any visitor the occupant had not fully moved into the place and there was more to come and admire.

The entrance door suddenly opens, with B.J. holding keys and Jack standing behind her. She steps into the room, noticing it is easy to see in the veiled light.

"Come in, Jack."

Jack glances around the room. "You've got a nice place, B.J. I'm impressed, but I should be going."

B.J. turns to him. "Come in for a nightcap. You're not under the table yet."

Jack is still looking around. "I don't know; it's getting late."

B.J. grabs his hand and pulls him through the doorway. "Come on, it's not that late. Besides, I want to show you my little abode. You can see I'm still unpacking, so excuse the unruly mess."

Jack surveys the room. "Don't be silly, you have a beautiful home."

The door closes seemingly on its own effort, and before they get far, they stumble into each other, their bodies touching. In the privacy, neither one of them can help themselves or resist the temptation and neither one wants to. There, in the semi-dark, coupled with the solitude, they are enjoying, the next step produces contact with kissing.

Sweet, slow kisses at first, but they soon move to deep, demanding, yearning kisses. Each of the two explored the other with roving hands, and the embrace quickly migrates to hot quirks. Long moments follow, with both of them tasting each other and, in turn, both start a lazy descent into an abyss that can't be stopped. In the midst of all this, Jack tries to gather himself through a husky voice.

"We shouldn't be doing this. We're partners."

"Temporary partners, and I like it. I never kissed a partner."

Jack responds with fervent words, "I never had a partner I wanted to kiss."

The two of them swim in the currents of the moment. It is unstoppable, and they spill into a tidal wave of overwhelming heat and craving. As if they have never embraced another human being before. Lost in the spinning zeal and moist, urgent kisses, they charge at each other with a hunger neither one has ever felt. It is so good and feels so right, and both of them want to spend eternity in this cove of wrapped arms, groping hands, and warm bodies. B.J.'s mouth abruptly shapes into a naughty smile.

"If you're real nice, I'll show you what my initials mean."

"You mean B.J.? You told me, don't you remember, Billie Jean."

"You don't get it. I said I'll show you."

They are still near the door, kissing wantonly. With deft purpose, B.J. gradually begins to drop to her knees.

Jack wonders. "Oh."

He gazes at the door. A zipper is heard, and Jack smiles. "Oh."

Then, B.J. takes it to the stage far beyond. Jack looks astonished while his eyes fix on the door and a silly grin on his face. "Oh!"

# Chapter 42

It felt good to be home. Bicks was drifting around his residence, enjoying his first morning back from the trip, watering the plants and generally making sure things were in order. He was currently holding onto a big coffee mug and was on his way to feed his betta fish. Dressed in a white, terry-cloth bathrobe, he was relaxing in his sanctuary before his big day in the city. He had a lot to do today and was looking forward to any information he might be able to obtain for the book. While drinking the coffee, he sprinkled Betta mini pellets for the grateful occupants in their respective containers; each bowl different in size and shape. Bicks loved the males with their flamboyant and colorful, flaring fins. These fish came from Cambodian rice patties, and they loved stagnant water. They did not care for the air-induced water aquariums you always see in shops and homes. The males also took care of the young, and they had a most unique way of doing it. Because of the still waters they came from, betta fish had the ability to take in the air, and they would do it by coming to the surface. By their nature, they would blow bubble nests on the water tops. Eggs gotten from the females were fertilized and spit into the bubble nests after the dancing males, with their fins spread out, induced the lady of his attention to join him under the nest. She would shortly swim away, but the male would stay and guard the nest he built. When the babies hatched, they would hang in the nest by locking their heads in individual bubbles and breathing the air in them. If they lost their grip, they would descend to the bottom and drown if the male did not pick them up by his mouth and spit them into another bubble. The romance of these fish was why Bicks had so many of them on his custom-built shelf besides the beauty they possessed. He had a deep love and appreciation for Siamese fighters. And they were called fighters because they did fight. But not to the death, always ending in a defined defeat and nothing more. The vanquished would swim away and the victor would maintain his territory; thus, the reason why they were kept in separate domains. Finished with dropping pellets in each glass container, he stands facing the shelf, watching them feed. They could go weeks without being fed, which made it easy to go for trips his trade sometimes made him do.

"There you go, my little buddies. Did you miss me?"

The phone starts ringing after he is finished with the feeding, and Bicks leaves his concern on the fish and walks to the coffee table where the cellphone is laying around. He answers the call and circles in a 360, surveying his home while he talks.

"Hello… Hi, Missy, having a good morning… I am, it's good to be back home. I guess the convention is rolling along okay… Sure, why not, at the restaurant in the hotel? I'll be there, can't wait to meet your friends… Of course, it's a dinner date."

Bicks hangs the phone up and drops it in the big pocket of the bathrobe. At the same time, bringing out a tube of Chap Stick. With one hand holding his mug and the other applying Chap Stick to his lips, he marvels at his home.

* * *

Jack was walking to the door, noticing B.J.'s apartment was even more inviting in the glorious morning light. He was in a shabby state of affairs, in need of a shower and a fresh change of clothes. B.J. was trailing him in her nightgown, naked underneath and appearing as lovely in the morning as he ever saw her. She too looks a little tossed from the rowdiness they enjoyed but imbued from events the night before. Jack opens the door, then stops abruptly and turns to her.

"I just thought of something; how will you get to the office?"

"I'll take a cab, since my rental is still at the police parking lot."

"I'll go take a shower and a change of clothes and come back and pick you up."

She complies to the suggestion with concern. "Okay, but there's one other thing."

Jack seems perplexed. "What's that?"

B.J. smiles. "No goodbye kiss after last night?"

"What… I'm sorry. This all seems a little weird. I'm not used to waking up in the arms of such a beautiful woman who happens to be my partner."

Jack steps to B.J. and gives her a sweet, lingering kiss. "I don't think I ever had a better time with a woman last night."

B.J. reacts with a grin. "I could say the same thing."

"We've got to be cool at the office."

B.J.'s eyes get big. "Absolutely."

"I'm serious."

"It goes without saying, we're both professionals."

Jack puts a hand gently on her face. "I really liked what happened last night."

B.J. puts her hand on his. "I did too."

They kiss again, and Jack slips out the door. "I'll be back before you know it."

Closing the door, B.J. reports, "I'll be ready."

* * *

Sam was just entering the squad office. There were other detectives dotted around randomly at their respective desks, but no Jack and B.J. He has a cup of coffee in one hand, a folder under his arm, and a newspaper wrapped in a cylinder in his other hand. He looks bushed. As if he had a long night. He sits down heavily at his desk, and, at the same time, the captain appears all in a flurry and impatience. He looks at the office with a miffed expression.

"Where is everyone?"

Sam seems confused. "You mean Jack and B.J.? I don't know. I just got here myself."

The captain sees the folder he has. "Is that your report?"

Sam handles it from his desk. "Yes, sir. You won't believe what I found."

"When everyone's here, I want all of you in my office with that report."

The captain turns on his heels and blusters out.

* * *

George was behind his desk, eating a candy bar. Bicks suddenly pops in, unannounced, and makes a direct line for the hotwire as usual. He acts as if he owns the place.

George responds to his surprising visitor, "You again?"

Bicks views the material on the hotwire. “Me again. How are you, George, anything new?”

“I wouldn’t know, haven’t had the time or the inclination.”

“I thought I’d drop by and take a quick peek at the turn of events before I went to the tombs.”

George is taking a bite of candy. “Tombs! Why are you going down there?”

Finished with his study on the wire, he turns to George. “The internet offers a good overview on most subjects. But if you want to find the obscure stuff, you have to dig. And I usually dig in the tombs.”

George shoves the last bite of candy bar in his pie hole. “Sorry I asked.”

Bicks starts for the door. “That and old habits die hard.”

* * *

The midnight blue was pulling into the police station parking lot. Jack and B.J. sit in it, a little starry eyed. They come to a sudden stop at the mouth of the lot, and Jack articulates a point.

“Why don’t you get out here and go on in the office?”

“All right, why?”

“It’ll look funny if we come in together; don’t you think?”

“We have before, a couple of times.”

Jack thinks about what she said. “Yeah, but, now, it’s different. We have to watch ourselves now.”

“You’re too devious for a cop, but I still love you; yeah, okay.”

They both give each other a kiss, and Jack reaches for more. “I don’t know how I’m going to hide this. I can’t stop kissing you.”

“I know what you mean; I feel the same way.”

They share another kiss or two, and B.J. jumps out of the car and heads for the entrance to the building, all in a flush. Jack drives into the parking lot to find a spot to put the midnight blue away.

* * *

Bicks was scanning a screen to a micro-fish. Going through the machine, shuffling the images of old Dallas Morning News articles, he comes upon something he finds interesting. While he reads, he smears Chap Stick on his lips.

Finished with the Chap Stick, he puts it in his tan suit pocket with a black shirt and black tie. He picks up his recorder sitting next to a matching fedora with a black band. Turning it on, he speaks to what he reads on the screen.

"Three of the buildings the recent murders have taken place in were once old Crown buildings or are still under the Crown estate. I've also got material on the Crown family, the son they kept out of the public eye, and some family tragedy that caused the demise in their global influence on the real-estate empire they had at one time. All this makes for a great story and will be an intricate part of the book. If what I'm discovering is all connected to the murders, and, right now, there's no reason not to think that, I've got a bestseller brewing. From here, I'm going down the street to the state records department to see if I can find out who is in control of what's left of the Crown estate."

* * *

Sam was at his desk, reading the newspaper. The folder he brought sits on his desk in plain sight. B.J. saunters into the office misty eyed, and Sam looks at her from above the paper.

"Where's Jack?"

"I wouldn't know."

"You look like shit."

B.J. is a little taken back. "Well, thanks, Sam, so do you."

"I've got an excuse. I was awake till the wee hours, dragging up information on the case."

B.J. sits down on a nearby desk. "What did you find?"

Sam indicates the folder. "It's all in here, and the captain wants all his Indians in his office to discuss it."

B.J. smirks. "Do tell. I was up late myself."

Sam studies her. "It's funny; I saw your car in the parking lot this morning when I got here. I thought maybe you were with Jack."

"Jack and I went to the Blue Note last night; he took me home from there. I got to work by cab."

Just then, Jack walks through the office door all in a rush. He heads straight for his desk. "Good morning, guys."

Sam checks him out. “Good morning. You look like shit too.”

* * *

The space is full of filing cabinets, rows and rows of them. In the middle of it all is Bicks, moving from one filing cabinet to another; preferring the cabinets over the computer system. He has his tan suit-coat off, hanging on a chair back with his shirt sleeves rolled to his elbows.

He opens a new drawer and thumbs through the contents till he comes to what he is searching for. Five other drawers are opened around the general area like a giant mouth of a hippo. Bicks has his tape recorder in hand. It has been in his grasp since he started the escapade. He pushes a button and the little red light blinks on.

“Note: The city records department has been a wealthy source of information. I’ve found the name of the executor to the Crown estate and where he can be located. Files on the economic and social downfall of the Crown’s and their holdings are available as well.”

# Chapter 43

The black casket in its little enclosure was luminous. As if there was an inner light that supplied a glow from some unforeseen magic lucent. Like a glimmering light from a green or blue swamp gas drifting along in a wet marsh, floating ghostly among the moss-covered trees. Captivating, mystifying, and yet haunting, all in the same mix.

Without warning, a tumultuous breathing erupts from within the confinement, and by creeping increase, the lid of the casket rises. First seen is a white-sleeved arm pushing the lid open. Once the lid is placed out of the way, a stark and ominous figure begins an ascent. Dressed in black except his white silk shirt, the Renaissance man climbs out of his resting place and joins the dim light of his private lair.

Troubled by the disturbance of his breathing, he trudges to the big, full-length mirror for a report of himself. He stands in front of his reflection and laments by the sight of it. The image he sees is still defined by clarity. There seems to be no diminished outline of his appearance whatsoever. Discouraged, he turns to the refrigerator just a step away. Opening the door, he takes out a canister almost full of his red nourishment and gulps a large quantity down.

Recognizing the fact his personal resource needs to be replenished, he glances at the numerous, empty, glass containers sitting atop the refrigerator. Disenchanted and dismayed, he puts his food back in the refrigeration and steps to the mirror once again.

He studies himself for long moments. Staring at the sight before him and becoming more disgruntled as he does. Abruptly, he starts to disrobe. Starting with his cape, he unties it at his neck and lets the thing fall. His silk shirt is next, and as the Renaissance man unbuttons the garment quickly, he also flings it from his shoulders to the air. Then, he begins on his black fatigues, undoing them while kicking his combat boots off at the same time. He drops his clothes on the floor and is now naked in a relative brisk time, then positions himself in front of the mirror for a soulful analysis. His body is emaciated. Pale and slender beyond health and devoid of muscular definition, he looks to be an individual who has been starved by encampment from a ruthless dictator, reminiscent of those poor mortals in World War II.

As he watches himself in the mirror, he turns to the left, then to the right, monitoring his profile. The Renaissance man observes himself over his shoulder, checking the view of his backside; all the while looking for evidence of his impression fading from his watchful eye. Any kind of diminishment from the outline of his body in the mirror would be welcome. He seems totally unalarmed by his frail, depleted frame.

Suddenly, he spins from the mirror, exasperated from the fact he can still see himself. He wants results, confirmation in becoming a complete and natural vampire. The image he sees in the mirror denies him that conclusion.

The Renaissance man marches to the big easy chair, and before he sits, he snaps on the lamp sitting behind it. Falling hard into the cushion, he then gathers up his journal, quill, and inkwell sitting and bunched on the small table next the tattered chair. Lining all of these elements in order so he can proceed with his thoughts for tabulation, he quietly contemplates what he wants to write.

Dipping the quill into the inkwell, he begins. The scratching of the quill on parchment is the only sound emanating in the quiet, dank chamber.

* * *

I need blood. I need blood that is fresh; blood that will come to me directly from the vein. I need it to flow to me like a river. And, tonight, I will find and capture that river. This is the remedy that is needed to cure my malady. Fresh blood is the secret to acquiring and completing my process. This is the realization I have come to, and I will hunt prey with that objective in mind. The quest for my transformation is just a heartbeat away, and I will reach out and take it.

It has come to the point of my recovery to change tactics drastically. It will be a risky and difficult undertaking. But it will be met. I will overcome all obstacles to bring myself to the pinnacle I deserve. A vampire in its truest form; a creature of the night to be feared and respected by all humans, and I will not stop in my endeavor until I fulfill my destiny and attain immortality. It will be done, and it will start tonight.

# Chapter 44

Captain Parks sat calmly at his desk. His hands folded, resting on the desktop, with his posture erect in full attention to the proceedings. Jack and B.J. were seated across the way on the leather couch. They too were attentive to what was about to unfold. They were watching Sam like he was an instructor moving around on the office floor with the folder he had open and undone. He was drawing out copies of the report he had made and passing them around to each of his spectators for their personal use. Sam was enjoying the celebrity of the moment, barking out the knowledge of his research.

"Now get this. Every one of the buildings the crimes have taken place in was once or still is Crown property."

Jack chimes in, "Including the hospital building?"

"Built by Crown Construction and, at one time, owned by the Crown estate."

B.J. jumps in the fray, "And the office building?"

"It was first called the Crown Forum which is now The Deep Elm Business Building. One of the murders that took place years ago in Highland Park, The Becker Building, was once a Crown building."

B.J. makes an observation, "Judging by our map in the squad office, all the murders, including the ones years ago, have occurred in public buildings; except for the housewife in Highland Park and the alley behind the strip joint."

Captain Parks adds to her statement, "And we know about the Crown Fountain Hotel, and, according to this, the apartments the Sanders girl was in was once called the Crown Deluxe."

Sam is savoring his prominent place in the discussion. "That's right, and something else."

The captain looks at him. "What would that be?"

"The building that strip joint is in happens to be Crown real estate too."

Jack eyes B.J. "That connects the alley site."

B.J. agrees to Jack's assumption. "Yeah, it does. Who controls the Crown estate?"

Sam refers to his report, "An attorney here in town, Lawrence B. Fargo."

Jack stands from the couch. "Do the Crown's still own the buildings?"

"Yeah, sort of; a decade ago, the family dropped out of the social scene and merged their property with a corporation. I remember it being a big surprise to the whole city. There was a big buzz about it in the local news at the time."

Captain Parks has his eyes on the report. "I remember that. As I recall, there was some kind of family tragedy around that time as well."

Jack walks over to Sam, fingering his copy. "See what you can find on the Crown family; if they're still in the Dallas area and where that might be."

B.J. now stands up. "They lived in Highland Park. I remember my parents spoke of them as neighbors."

Captain Parks looks up from his copy of the report. "The connections are beginning to be too obvious."

* * *

A nice and spacious office with plush, black, leather furniture and large-potted plants adorned the floor space. In a far corner near the front entrance was a big, rubber, plant draping next to a huge, metal sculpture of the female human body. The other corner contained a big leaf philodendron that seemed to give the effect of a growing jungle. On the walls were depictions of the Dallas downtown buildings and skyline full of color and bright lights. Covering the walls was a thick, wood paneling that gave the place the feel and ambience of a courtroom waiting for a judge. It was a quiet and stately interior that was impressive to walk into.

Sitting behind a front desk was a very pretty redhead in a green dress, with eyes that sparkled blue in contrast to the dress. She was busy with daily activity when Bicks walks in and disturbs her.

"Yes, may I help you?"

Bicks impulsively applies his Chap Stick. "I'd like to see Mr. Fargo."

"I'm sorry. Mr. Fargo is out of town today. He won't be back till the end of the week."

"Will he be in the office when he gets back?"

“We expect him to be.”

Bicks puts his Chap Stick away. “I’d like to set an appointment.”

“That can be arranged.”

“Sometime in the morning he gets back if that’s okay?”

* * *

Jack, B.J., and Sam all file into the squad room after the meeting in the captain’s office. Sam goes immediately to his desk, sits, and lays the folder with his reports down. As he does so, Jack and B.J. watch him. They glance at each other, and Jack decides to throw a bone.

“Damn good job on that report, Sam. You’ve given us a legitimate direction in the investigation.”

Sam folds his arms with a smirk. “Think nothing of it, part of the job.”

B.J. smiles. “Not too good with compliments, are you?”

“Oh no, nothing like that; I’m used to being overlooked around here; it’s nice to be noticed.”

Still smiling, B.J. gives a retort, “Well, noticed you are. I guess our next move is to go see that attorney, Fargo.”

Jack complies to that notion, “Yes, that would be the next move. You wouldn’t have the address to his office, would you, Sam?”

Sam opens the folder and jots down the address. “I would, but he’s not in the office today. I already called.”

“What do you mean?”

Sam hands the scrap of paper to Jack. “He’s out of town on business. Here’s the address and the day he’ll be back.”

B.J. smiles again. “Damn, Sam, you’re just full of surprises today, aren’t you?”

“You mean like the one I had when I saw your car in the lot this morning?”

Jack and B.J. exchange a sheepish glance. They both put their eyes on Sam, and Jack has a reply, “Like she said, full of surprises.”

* * *

The tinkle of silverware filled the room along with the dinner chatter of the crowd. Seated at a table near the center of the affair was Bicks, Missy, and friends of Missy: Gloria Vickers, a pretty blonde, and Pat Rand, a beautiful brunette.

They were in the restaurant of the Crown Fountain Hotel. Featured was a plush, lush, sumptuous atmosphere surrounding the good food and a courteous staff to attend the guests; the place reeked of wealth and prestige. Large palms in hand-painted pots with fine sculpture of well-known sculptors dotted the space everywhere you looked, along with original oil paintings decking the walls and Italian tile covering the floor. All four were enjoying the company, the agreeable décor, and the food.

Missy raises her wine glass and makes a declaration, "To the day, ladies and gents!"

Her companions join her in the toast, "To the day."

Bicks adds to it, "And mine has been especially rewarding."

Missy takes note of the comment, "I've been telling the girls about your book."

Gloria follows that, "Yes, she has. It sounds like a potential blockbuster. Something I wish one of my clients would come up with."

Missy jumps in, "Gloria and Pat are fellow agents invited here to the convention to speak like me. Needless to say, they both have an avid interest in your book. They're like a lioness smelling the blood of money."

Both women chuckle to the statement. Pat continues the train of thought, "I've read a couple of your books, Mr. Bickers. I liked them, liked them a lot. You always have an interesting slant in what you write."

"Please, call me Bicks, everybody does. Thanks for the compliment; it's nice of you to say that. I think maybe this book might be the best one I've found to write. At least, it's shaping up that way."

Gloria wants to know more. "It's about the string of murders in the city, is it not? The recent ones, like the one that took place in this very hotel."

"Yes, that's right, bizarre accounts leaving a trail of unexplainable corpses; a score of bodies that lack blood."

"Sounds like a gruesome story, just the kind that sells books—"

Missy interrupts, "Hands off, girls, this writer's in my stable, and there he will stay."

The two women chuckle again and sip their wine. Missy directs her next remark to Bicks.

"So you've had a productive day huh?"

"Yes, I have. I've come across what looks like a connection to all the murder sites and maybe a possible connection to the very family that built this hotel."

Pat sparks to that. "The Crown's, I know a little about that family. I have an author that did a book on them and their history. It was a fascinating peace."

"What I'm working on will entail some of that, but the line of research I'm following could lead to a whole new revelation of the Crown's. A hidden and dark revelation you might say."

Gloria is curious. "Whatever do you mean?"

"It's something I need to delve into more before I can really talk about it. All I can say is read the book."

# Chapter 45

Jack and B.J. were eating avidly, starved from the day spent tracking more key makers outside the established perimeter they had and following leads that Sam's report had given them. Coming up with very little but verifying the lawyer, Fargo's, office for a future visit; they were seated at the big dining table in B.J.'s apartment. Each of them was halfway through their meal; both had hardly spoken. There was a bevy of what looked like little white castles scattered all over the tabletop containing the Chinese food they stopped and got on the way to her place. The two of them had half full glasses of white wine next to their plates, and B.J. had chopsticks to eat with. Jack used a fork.

He watched her eat with the chopsticks for some time, then finally asked a question.

"How do you eat with those things?"

"I don't know. A little practice; it's not hard."

"I think maybe my fork and your chopstick shows the difference between us. Don't you think?"

"What are you talking about?"

Jack stops eating. "What is a beautiful, cultured, sophisticated woman like you doing with a flatfoot like me; an old detective with no real future."

B.J. takes a moment, watching Jack the whole time. "Don't sell yourself short, Amigo. You know how to use that fork of yours pretty damn well."

She sits, staring at Jack with a glint in her eye, underlying the jest of her meaning in the statement she just made. Jack responds with a slow curving smile crossing his face. During the process, B.J. jumps up from her seat and heads for the kitchen.

"And it's bigger than most too."

She goes to the icebox and pulls out the open wine bottle chilling inside. Jack watches her and thinks about her bawdy compliment. That nature of hers;

the honesty and boldness she possessed is part of the reason he was falling in love with her.

She comes back to the table and pours the remaining contents of the wine bottle into the glasses.

"So, you think Sam is onto us?"

"Oh, yes, yes, I do."

"It didn't take him long to put it together."

Jack smiles. "Yeah I know, a frigging day."

Jack picks up his wine for a sip. "He's had a front row seat on the two of us from the beginning. Probably saw the chemistry between us before we ever realized it."

B.J. sets the empty bottle on the table and drops back in her seat. "You think he'll keep it to himself?"

"Yeah, he will. Don't underestimate Sam. He's a clever, observant cop. He comes off befuddled and incompetent like that detective with a cigar on T.V., but he figures things out."

"Now you tell me. But I already knew he was smart."

The two of them smile at each other over the rims of their wine glasses. Jack makes a sudden announcement, "I'll help you clean this up, then I guess I'll go on home."

B.J. looks surprised. "What on earth are you doing?"

"I should go home, cool things off for a bit. Sam knows about us already, no sense in pushing it."

"We're not pushing anything, but we should be pushing it."

"I guess I'm having a hard time sleeping with my partner."

B.J. puts her glass of wine down and sets her chin on her hands. "Think of me as a woman."

"Thanks for the tip; that never crossed my mind." He takes a moment for a thought. "I'll be right back."

"Now what are you doing?"

"I've got a change of clothes in the trunk of the car."

B.J. looks at him with a knowing grin. "You big faker!"

"Hey, I'm fighting this."

"You don't know it yet, but you've already lost."

* * *

Jack was lying naked under the sheets. His hands folded under his head while he watched the rotating ceiling fan and listened to B.J. fool around in the bathroom. Thoughts were tripping on his mind; thoughts that were entangled with emotions, second guessing, and longings. He was amazed to find himself waiting on this gorgeous, lively, and intelligent woman, waiting for her to join him in her bed of all places. Life had suddenly put him in her arms after years spent in solitude. He was not celibate in those years, but he had been lonely. Almost instantly, that seclusion and loneliness was broken. Dashed away by her presence; by her warmth and humor, the abundant energy she possessed, and the inquisitive frankness she used to express it.

He had doled away years, isolated. It was safe to be alone; simple, uncomplicated, and unchallenged. It was easy to fit his spirit in that desert of emptiness and get lost in the cushion it offered. His wants and needs had lain dormant all this time, but, now, they were awakened. The cherished, uncluttered candor was in jeopardy, by this woman. She was breaking into his private little world with a sledge hammer; shattering the walls that he had constructed for himself. And as they tumbled down, he was getting scared. He was hardly scared of anything or anyone, but this thing she presented called love scared him.

Unannounced, B.J. breezed through the bathroom door, wearing nothing but a bath towel. When she unravels the towel and reveals her nakedness, Jack reacts with a mixture of contentment and concern. It was an odd brew of perturbation.

Observing her, Jack is compelled to comment on what he sees, "You are so beautiful, B.J. You're like something the ancient Greeks molded out of clay; perfect and flawless."

B.J. crawls into bed and whispers softly, "You don't need flattery with me, Lover."

She kisses him with a moist, delicious kiss. It evolves to a moist, alluring, and lingering kiss. They dwell many splendid moments in that zone of attention and touch, response and stirring. They begin to fall into their desires. The want and passion flash-flooding onto them, making them helpless from the volley and rush of their hunger.

Jack suddenly peels himself from the grip of their connection. B.J. counters with an inquiry.

"What is it, Jack? What's wrong?"

Jack rubs his brow. "Nothing's wrong, not with you anyway."

B.J. is confused. "Then what is it?"

Jack replies with a long sigh, "I need to tell you something."

"Don't worry about us being partners; I don't think anyone cares about that."

"It's not that. The only person I care what they may think is you. It's something else."

There is a pause in the moment; B.J. unsure of what was wrong. "What is it then?"

Jack puts his eyes on hers. "I'm falling in love with you. I can't help myself, and it freaks me out. I've been by myself for so long and I'm used to it. There was never any risk. What we're doing together means a lot more than a fling to me. And I can't shake this feeling of being in deep water."

B.J. studies him for long seconds. A trace of a smile begins and crosses her face like a road map. Big eyes look directly into his.

"Jack, don't you know I love you too? I love you, Jack. And it's happened so fast. I'm scared just like you. I'm afraid and question who I am or at least who I was when I first came back to this city. I've met you, and everything, everything has changed for me. It feels wonderful but frightening. So let me tell you, lover man, you're not the only one swimming in deep water."

They both regard each other for what seems like a timeless flash. Grinning, touching, and gazing at one another, dissolving into the quiddity of their being, to the point of almost counting pixels in the colors of their eye.

Jack strokes her face. "I love you, B.J. More than anything, I love you."

They start kissing again. Sweet, slow kisses at first, but they soon migrate to deep, thirsty ones. Their bodies mesh into a divine entwine; hers a soft, fluid flexibility, and him, a strong, hard craving. Swirling in their passion, the only reality they can identify with comes from their desire. They swim in it, and it feels like they could drown. It gets hotter, blazing hot, and the swirling spirals out of control, spinning in circles.

Finally, they fit themselves together and start a rhythm toward each other. Thrashing and hurtling like they were in a fight, they start their climb to a peak. Fast, then still faster, mounting to a crescendo beyond all reason, beyond the intangibles, beyond anything they both knew existed. That fine climb to the peak. Together, they climb while seeing red. Step by step, they climb. They carry each other to that unfailing, unceasing ascension; the eternal nirvana that leads to the foot of the stairway to heaven.

# Chapter 46

A campus library is a location for students to find information on their studies, to ascertain knowledgeable nuggets that will bring clarity to the pursuits in their chosen fields. But it also can be used as a sanctuary for socializing. Not only is it a refuge for students, but the professors too. Both bodies of the campus personnel socialize and have tempered debates on the subjects they teach and study in the library. The resource that it holds offers support for the case of both factions.

Unlike the library, another site for socializing and debate is the campus cafeteria. Rowdy behavior and riotous vocalization can be maintained along with the general chime of the dinnerware at the campus' greasy spoon. Each of these localities is used by the students as a stopover from their habitats besides a neighborhood pizza joint or a sports bar. But the library is a place for quiet reason and earnest thoughts.

The chamber of this particular library was massive. Elongated oak tables with green shades on brass desk lighting occupied a large area in the center of the floor surrounded by bookshelves too numerous to count, spreading out in all directions. A second floor hung over the bottom floor bookshelves, and it too was brimming with bookshelves that was uncountable as well. Black metal railing edged the second floor, allowing safety for anyone who wanted to check the huge first floor and its activity. It provided anyone to lean over and gain the attention of someone sitting at the tables below.

Near the entrance of the building was a big counter where the library staff could be found eager to help anyone who might need it. It was in the shape of a large square, and it was a focal point to the industry of proceedings and goings on in the place. The campus library was full of young people milling about, looking for a book that might enlighten them in their studies or satisfy some curiosity they may have. Like all libraries, it was serene with very little quick or sudden movement.

A young man in his early 20s stood behind the counter, watching a lovely brunette with an armful of books walk up to him. He recognized the girl and, needless to say, was eager to help.

"Hi, Kim, what do you have here?"

"Hi, Colby, I have some pretty dry stuff. Material for a class I'm taking."

Colby flips through the books she has and reacts to them with a sour face.

"Yikes! Is this for American Myths?"

"Yes, how did you know?"

Colby starts taking the library cards out of each book. "I took that class. At times, thought provoking, but it can be boring too."

Kim flashes a smile. "Yeah, I'm finding that out. I thought it would be an easy elective, but it turns out to be something of a time-consuming back breaker."

"These books will help you get through the course. I give you my approval on them. Say, I'll be off in a minute. You want to go for a coffee?"

"I shouldn't. I'll take a rain check though. My roommate, Betty, and I need to study."

Just then, Betty, a nice-looking blonde with a big smile, walks up to the counter and joins them.

"Hello, Colby." She directs her question to Kim, "Did you find what you needed?"

Kim answers her, "Yes, I think I did."

Colby stacks the books. "She did; how are you doing, Betty? Give me a second, I'll have these books ready to take, and you two can be on your way."

* * *

The grounds outside the library are typical for any campus. Lots of streetlamps to light up the night and give anyone an easy pathway through the bushes, trees, and flower gardens that always adjoin a college landscape. Tall buildings full of classrooms randomly dot the view, and sidewalks run in all sorts of directions connecting the buildings and the scenery into a semblance of order.

Something dark and sinister is running gracefully through the vista. It is a black shadow-of-a-figure dashing around bushes and dodging behind trees, undetected. The image jumps a large bench effortlessly. A cape flaps to the motion, giving the look of a stealth bomber while tracking for a destination that will suit motives for one's presence.

It is the Renaissance man, and he stops along the side of a building obscured from sight by a large bush. He stands there, trying to catch a breath. He leans heavily against a brick wall with one hand, desperately breathing deeply. Then, he is off again, slicing through the trees and gardens like an unseen animal.

* * *

Kim and Betty are leaving the library with their stash of books. They both have arms fully loaded with the weight of them as they go down the entrance stairway. A stream of kids is going in and out of the building, passing the girls, locked on their own interests. The two friends take the last step of the stairway and hit the sidewalk. They decide on a direction and leave the clamor and populated activeness of the campus library in their wake while they walk into the veiled, unoccupied grounds.

* * *

The Renaissance man silently moves through the terrain with relative ease. He comes to an enormous clutch of bushes at a cloven where a sidewalk forks. He looks about smartly, then slides into the interior of the bush. It is deftly quiet. Gradually, by degrees, harsh, agitated breathing begins to seep out from within the foliage.

Through a gape in the bushes, eyes are clearly seen revealed by a slash of lamplight. Bloodshot, dead-like eyes. They peer through the obscurity of the leaves with lust gleaming from their orbs. The Renaissance man sniffs the air for inspection while those eyes of his watch for prey.

* * *

The girls are tooling down a sidewalk, lugging their books. They are strolling along in the quiet with no one else around. Both have been chatting about boys and studies when the two come upon a fork in the sidewalk and determine the left fork is their route.

With anticipation, the Renaissance man observes the approach of the girls while he lurks in the junction of the fork. He is still hunkered down in the complex of the bushes, and his eyes flash with the proposition of opportunity. He sniffs the air again and growls with hungry needs.

Kim and Betty move along in the sparse light. Their footsteps clicking loudly on the sidewalk concrete, forecasting their presence. They come near the bushes where the Renaissance man is waiting, veering to the left. Then, they both abruptly stop in midstride. Each of them standing rigid while obscene breathing sifts the area with sound. It seems to come from the bushes to their right. Kim voices their concern.

"What is that?"

Betty counters, "I don't know. What is it?"

"It's some asshole trying to scare us."

It is deathly quiet except for the heavy hammering breath and the taxing retorts of the girls. They both are paralyzed with fright, standing in the dark, wondering what to do next. Kim finally breaks the silence in a loud voice, "Whoever this is, it's not funny. What a jackass you are." She refers to Betty, "Come on, let's go."

They continue their route and dart by the bushes, their footsteps beating the sidewalk. As they clip along, they look over their shoulders several times, the bushes becoming a distant obstacle to their rear. In between their observations, the Renaissance man has dashed from the bushes in the fork to a tree to another bush, tracking them unseen in parallel to their advance and moving silently ahead of them, unnoticed.

Sensing danger, the girls move at a much quicker pace, almost running. They have gotten more scared with each footstep, to the point of being frantic. The two of them still hearing that infernal breathing somewhere in the vicinage. They troop along hurriedly when they come to a part of the sidewalk that has a giant oak tree hanging over it like a canopy. It is darker here because of the huge limbs, and they slow a bit to stop under the shadow the tree presents. Once under the overhang, they stand and gather their wits, feeling they are hidden somewhat. Looking around with care, they scope the surroundings and deduce they are not being followed anymore. For a long moment, it is graveyard quiet, and it settles in with a peace; both of them breathing with effort from the excursion and content that things are back to normal.

Then, out of nowhere, an undiscerning peal of damnable breathing begins to penetrate the calm again. It saws into the repose they were enjoying. Realizing the fact that bedeviled breathing has appeared once more, they look around hastily, the loud breathing disruptive and seemingly close by. Kim suddenly barks out a protest.

"Dammit, who is that?"

Betty answers her, "I'm scared, Kim."

Still standing in the broken quiet next to the big, dark tree, they wonder about where the source of the breathing is coming from. In seconds, they look at each other with recognition. By small measures, they both slowly peer above them, following the sound that seems to be somewhere in the tree. The girls suddenly scream while the Renaissance man, upon discovery, drops on them like a giant, black, baleful bruise. They all hit the ground hard, scattering the books like leaves. The girls kicking and squalling in their defense while tumbling apart.

Kim manages to get back on her feet immediately and starts to run. The Renaissance man clobbers Betty with his fist, and she submits to the knockout blow. Then, he goes after Kim. It takes but a moment to get to the squealing girl; he grabs her by the neck and squeezes firmly. He chokes her scream till it is muffled, and she falls limp and unconscious in his hands.

By now, people have heard the commotion and are shouting alarms for help. The voices get louder as people come to investigate. The Renaissance man quickly gathers both the senseless girls and hikes them over each shoulder with little effort. Then, he scurries off into the dark with unnatural speed. The weight of the women seems nonexistent as a burden. His rasping breath the only evidence he was there as it fades into the ebony night.

# Chapter 47

George was at his desk as usual. He had his feet propped up on the desktop, eating an egg and bacon biscuit. His large belly was causing strain on the buttons of his shirt to the point it seemed to be on the verge of an overburdened dam about to burst. There was a cup of coffee in the other hand, and he takes a big gulp to help swallow some of the sandwich. When the undertaking is done, he is ready for another bite, and he lays into it like a bulldozer.

Bicks glides into the office unannounced, looking chipper and dapper as always; he has a white straw fedora on with a black headband and a little red feather stuck in it. Dressed in a black suit, a white shirt, and a red-and-black stripped tie, there is a matching red carnation in his lapel. He goes directly to the hotwire uninvited, passing George on the way.

"Every time I come in here, you're eating."

George does not seem to mind the intrusion. "A man needs sustenance."

"What you need is exercise. Come with me down to the tombs. I'll put you to work."

George speaks with a mouthful of sandwich, "Yeah, I need to spend time down there with you."

Bicks reads what is on the hotwire. "What's this about abduction?"

"It happened last night at a local college, two girls were taken."

Bicks wheels an about face and heads back for the door, applying Chap Stick while he goes.

"Two girls huh; murders, kidnappings. Are you sure you don't want the tombs? It might be safer."

George takes another hulking bite. "I'm eating, thank you."

* * *

Sam was nice and cozy in the police-squad office. Leaning back in his chair with a cup of coffee on his desk and reading the morning paper, he was once again enjoying the serenity of no one there. He knew that would not last. He had another folder on his desktop from a night's research.

Jack and B.J. sweep into the room as if on cue. Sam looks up from his read and makes a comment.

"Well, well, both detectives come in together all at the same time. Imagine that."

Jack spots the folder on his desk. "You got something for us, good Buddy, besides being a smart ass."

Smiling, Sam reaches for the folder. "Sure do. It's a listing of buildings under the Crown estate."

B.J. walks to his desk and takes the folder. "Are we talking about a long list?"

"It's not a paragraph, and it may not be all of them. I'm going to my playground and see if I can drum up more info on the Crowns in a minute here. Have you seen the paper this morning?"

After looking at it, B.J. hands the folder back to him. "No, not really. Why?"

Sam gives the paper to B.J. "Front page, you might find the article interesting."

B.J. glances at the pages. "Are you talking about the abduction of two girls?"

"That would be it."

Jack walks to B.J. and reads over her shoulder. "How's this got anything to do with the case?"

Sam twinkles. "Witnesses say the guy looked like Zorro."

Jack's head pops up from the paper. "Zorro!"

Sam folds his arms. "Yeah, it says in there he had a cape on and everything."

B.J. responds, "That sounds like our Renaissance man."

Jack is reading. "Could be, by the description, wouldn't hurt to go by there and see what there was to see."

Edwin suddenly strolls into the office, holding a folder of his own. All three detectives notice his entrance. Doc walks to them, holding out his report. Jack reaches to retrieve it.

"What's this, Doc?"

"I was in the neighborhood, thought I'd drop this off. It's the results of the last D.N.A. tests on your case. The second sample matches the first, a perfect match."

B.J. looks at Jack. "Which verifies the same suspect at both murder scenes."

Jack nods. "Yeah, so I guess that bundles up the case a little tighter."

Edwin turns and heads for the door. "No thanks needed; whatever I can do; I will do." He stops at the door and grins back at them. "It's in my D.N.A., later, Detectives."

* * *

Bicks had made himself at home in the tombs. He was working a micro-fish. The screen on the machine tumbles through images of tidbits from past news and articles of interest when he stops handling the roller knob and halts on a subject. He reaches into his breast pocket and pulls out Chap Stick. Reading intensely, he puts the Chap Stick on his lips. After a moment, he sticks the stuff back in his pocket and grabs the recorder sitting next to his straw hat. Turning it on, he reads more of what he found, then relays what he has into the recorder.

"Note: This fits with material I already have, something good for copy; the couple who started and created the Crown estate were Ethel and Sinclair Crown. It seems they gave their last social appearance at a play they financed and sponsored. Their son played the title role. The play was Dracula. Reminder: Bring this info up to the lawyer, Fargo, when I'm able to talk to him. It could be important. At the very least, it will make a few paragraphs in the book. Find out more about it from the lawyer and see what he knows. The Crown's last public appearance for their son's play, Dracula, and now we have bloodless bodies all over town. Coincidence or connection; you couldn't find this in a Hollywood script."

* * *

Sam was sitting in front of a computer. His fingers soar on the keypad and print blinks on the screen. He reads it thoroughly, then pokes the keys some more. Sam sits quietly and cracks his knuckles, patiently waiting for the new print to appear on the monitor. When he reads his findings, he becomes shocked from the score of information.

"Shit, they're dead! What the hell happened?"

He scrolls down on the site and reveals even more material that was not realized. He hits some keys and starts printing what he has.

"I should stop being a cop and write a book."

* * *

The midnight blue pulls to a stop under a tree. Jack and B.J. watch what looks like a crime scene in progress in the distance. Uniformed police are roping off an area with yellow crime tape; a couple of men are taking snapshots of certain points of interest. There were yellow markers with little black numbers sitting around on the ground to highlight those localities of special relevance and possible importance.

Jack makes a comment, "This looks like the place we're looking for."

B.J. agrees, "Yep, let's go check it out."

They both climb out of the car and start for what the two have been watching. After the short walk, the detectives come to the tree where the two girls were attacked the night before. A swarm of customary sightseers are standing around outside the crime tape, gawking at the police and their work. A tall man who seemed in control of the investigation spots Jack and walks toward him and B.J.

"Jack, how are you? What the hell are you doing here?"

"Hey, Carter, how's it going?"

"How's Chris doing?"

"He's good, thanks for asking. This is Detective Dobbs. B.J., this is Detective Carter."

Carter reaches out to shake a hand. "Detective."

B.J. reciprocates the handshake. "Detective Carter, glad to meet you."

Carter puts his attention back on Jack. "What brings homicide here?"

"We were curious about some details on this."

"Not much to tell. We think the initial attack took place here."

B.J. scans the crime site. "What were the eyewitness accounts?"

"People said he was dressed in black and had a cape or something on his back. No one got a clear look at his face. One guy said he saw him jump a hedge with the girls on each shoulder."

Jack is astonished by that statement. "Now how in the hell could someone jump a hedge with the weight of two people on their shoulder? That would be an almost impossible feat."

"I agree. Witnesses say he was average size too, skinny even. They all said he was no weightlifter anyway. We've got dogs searching the grounds for something, anything including bodies. It doesn't look like it will lead too much though. We do have a good footprint right over there. Forensic is cataloguing that. It looks to be a military boot."

B.J. has another question, "So, right now as it stands, we're talking about abduction and nothing more?"

"Yeah, it looks that way. Excuse me a minute. Hey, Gains, take a look at this."

Carter walks off and leaves the two detectives to themselves. Jack watches Carter's backside move away, wondering about the conversation they just had with him.

"You know, I had my doubts on the way over here. Didn't think there was any connection to our boy. The M.O. is totally out of what we're used to. But, now, I'm not so sure. We should let Edwin know about that boot print."

B.J. is looking around. "Yes, we need to red flag that. I think it could be the Renaissance man."

"So do I, but why would he grab the girls and not take their blood; and why two girls?"

"It could be he wants a personal blood bank."

# Chapter 48

It was deathly quiet and motionless. Like a boneyard except for weak moans that filtered the air. The sounds came from the brick wall where the Renaissance man had hammered nails the day before. Kim was tied to them. She was posed in a crucifixion with each arm outstretched and bound by black, silk scarves to the long, concrete nails. Her clothes were torn and tattered, her face smudged and soiled. She seemed to be coming out of unconsciousness, slowly gaining an awareness of her predicament.

When she comes to her full faculty of senses, she looks about frantically, realizing her situation. After moments of deduction, Kim struggles to set herself free. She strains and thrashes with all her might, then decides it is fruitless to try. With that appraisal, she starts to scream bloody murder. The screams bounce and echo off the chamber walls, producing an even more shrill sound.

Out of the gloom, a pair of slender hands with long, black fingernails subdues and muffles the screams with another length of black, silk scarf. The Renaissance man ties the cloth tightly to her mouth while he stares blankly into Kim's eyes. She glares back with confusion, her stricken eyes filled with bewilderment and fright.

When he finishes, he puts his attention on Betty. Already gagged with her hands bound behind her back and her feet tied securely, she lies on the floor just steps away like a pile of rags. The Renaissance man moves over to her, bends down, and picks her up easily. Betty is conscious, and she fights to the manhandling, voicing a stifled protest. She looks at Kim with the same bewildered fright. He slings the girl over his shoulder, then turns and looks dead at Kim for an instant with those cold, black eyes and swings to walk away.

Kim watches them go into the dismal, undefined expanse. She tugs on her bindings without results until she hears a door slam shut in the distance. Still shackled to the wall, her mouth dry from the gag and her eyes full of riddled unpredictability, Kim is unable to move from the restraints. She stands, bound to the iron nails, wondering fearfully for Betty. Her head sways listlessly side to side, dismayed and frightened.

In seconds, the Renaissance man shows back up without Betty. He approaches Kim with heavy steps and comes close, face to face. She is revolted by the stench of his breath. Black eyes bore into hers with a pitiless stare. Out of nowhere, a glass of water appears, and she looks at it as if she wants it. He releases the gag and shoves the glass into her mouth. She drinks it down greedily. Finished, he pulls the glass away, and Kim voices an appeal in mumbled words while he replaces the gag.

"What do you want? Where's Betty?"

The rest of her words are smothered as he fixes the gag, tying it snugly once again; then the Renaissance man walks away, holding the empty glass. She watches the ghostly image trail away and disappear in the nebulous dim.

The area becomes quiet again except for the sobbing moans expelled by Kim. She hangs on the wall, amazed by her and Betty's plight and marvels where it will lead. The Renaissance man emerges back into her view, and she stiffens with fear from the sight of him. He goes to the easy chair and sits. Grasping his journal, he opens it, then dips the quill in the inkwell and begins to write. The only sounds emanating are the scratching of the quill on paper and the feeble sobs of Kim. All through his writing, Kim's pathetic crying floats in the atmosphere. The Renaissance man abruptly stops his verse and sets the quill down. He sits in the easy chair without moving and ponders.

After moments, he gets up from the chair and goes to the full-length mirror. Kim is watching his every move, anxious to what he may do next. The Renaissance man stands in front of the mirror and studies himself. Trying to decipher if his reflection has faded any at all, he comes to the conclusion that if it has, it is undistinguished at this point.

Turning from the mirror, he slowly walks to Kim who squirms to his advance. At first, she was lost in her own misery, but as the Renaissance man gets closer, she is obviously charged by the nearness. He stands in front of her with those dark, lifeless eyes locked on her, and she responds by flailing about wild-eyed with dread. Placing his hands carefully on either side of her head and leaning on the wall, she freezes with shear fright. Her eyes are almost bulging out of their sockets.

He brings his face up to hers, just about touching nose to nose. Again, she repels from the reek of his breath. Then, slyly, almost seductively, he begins sniffing and smelling her. Kim is perfectly still from the odd attention, stricken with panic. Inch by inch, he drifts down the whole of her body, moving in slow motion and taking in the essence of her scent.

* * *

Betty found herself in a dark enclosure that seemed to be something like a closet. It was empty aside from her rolling around on the damp concrete, attempting to free her hands of the cinches the strange man left her in. She twists and turns and pulls at the knots when, suddenly, her hands pop free and allows her to take the gag off. The next thing she does is untie her feet. Shed of the straps, she reaches out at a tiny door, and it surprisingly swings open effortlessly.

When she crawls through the small opening the doorway affords, she looks back at where she was and finds that it was not a closet at all. More like a storage space located under a stairway that led up to some unforeseen dark. She stands there, breathing hard from the toiling task of getting loose, and gets her bearings. There does not seem to be any window, forbidding the notion of what time of day it was or even if it was day at all. She does spot a line of small window high up on a far wall painted black. Betty deduces she must be in some kind of basement and the stairway may be the avenue of escape. While deciding on that course, she hears wailing in the distance. Betty looks over her shoulder, and in the diffused light, she can make out large pieces of old furniture in what seems to be two rows lined in a makeshift order. Around a corner where the furniture disappears, the source of the sound she hears sings out like the calling of a siren nymph from the sea.

Betty realizes it must be Kim. And instead of fleeing the weird place, she decides to go and find out if it is her friend. She cautiously steps to the established corner and nudges down the length of the structure till she gets to the edge. With trepidation, she peaks around it, and, there, tied to a solid brick wall, is Kim. She seems in a miserable state, disoriented and barely conscious, her clothes torn and disheveled, but alive. The rows of furniture are to her left, and she scans the area, searching desperately for the figure that took them to this place in the dead of night.

Scared but sure of what she needs to do, Betty checks the huge inner space carefully and squints at the shadows for the Renaissance man. There is no sight of him, and with opportunity presented, she takes the chance and dashes off for Kim.

When she gets to her, Kim slowly comes to the understanding that her friend is there to help. Her eyes flash with recognition and reacts to the sudden appearance of her roommate. Relieved to see Betty is still with her but concerned for her safety, Kim groans a protest of warnings.

Betty is busy trying to untie one of her hands when she sees Kim is trying to tell her something. She switches her focus on the gag and battles with the knot.

"Let me get this undone. I'll have you out of this in a second. Don't worry, we're getting out of here."

Kim notices something behind Betty and starts voicing her appeal through the gag in her mouth. Betty takes her alarm for relief and continues on the knot that seems so persistent. The Renaissance man has crept silently to Betty's shoulder in full view of Kim. She is totally unaware of the danger she is in while she struggles over the knot.

For the first time, Kim can see the heinous, chrome mouthpiece. Lodged into the Renaissance man's mouth, gaping wide open and poised to strike, the pointed fangs glint in the poor light. He looks like a monster from a bad nightmare or something from the netherworld. The dark creature oozes closer behind Betty. His eyes stark black and death-like, looking into Kim's eyes. Kim begs for attention from Betty while she fusses with the knot, completely oblivious to the menace at her rear, and, good humoredly, she expresses her frustration with the situation to hurry.

"Damn this thing. This knot refuses to—"

The Renaissance man suddenly spins Betty around to face him. In one motion, he snaps out the switchblade in front of her eyes and flicks the blade out. It stands tall, aiming for the ceiling; treacherous and lethal. Then, he quickly slams it into her midsection. She grunts to the assault while Kim becomes berserk over the brutality. He shoves the knife in deeper, and Betty jerks to it. The ominous presence grabs her hair tightly and throws her head back, exposing the neck. Kim is inches away, watching the horror. The Renaissance man places the mouthpiece and fangs in place on Betty's neck, pushes a button on his wrist, and the evil contraption clamps down into her vein. He presses another button, and the pump activates with a pulsating reaction dominating the moment to the sound of it. His dead-like eyes look straight into Kim's eyes. They glisten and tear with the pleasure of the feed. Betty tries to turn in his grip but is helpless in his grasp; she becomes weaker and weaker to the point of collapse.

Kim is demoralized from the ugly sight. Her eyes boiling over with salty tears to what they witness, and her spirit simply melts away. Betty gasps to her death, and her body grows limp in the Renaissance man's arms. The pump keeps chugging away, drawing the life out of her as she falls deeper and deeper into lifelessness.

# Chapter 49

The lab was void of Edwin or anyone else when Jack and B.J. blitz into the room, expecting just the opposite. They each stop short of completely entering the place when they realized no one was there. Both of them drift slowly into the quiet of the space, a little unsure if they should at all, paranoid of being accused of disturbing some project in progress and causing a false result. The two detectives stand next to each other, wondering what to do when Jack breaks the silence.

"I can't remember a time I walked in here and no one was around."

B.J. has second thoughts. "You think we should wait?"

Jack reviews the question. "It won't hurt to wait a minute or two. Maybe Edwin went to the latrine or something."

B.J. has a mischievous glint in her eye. "Aren't we being polite, the latrine huh; why not the shitter?"

Jack replies sarcastically, "I'll quit walking on eggshells on your behalf, since you don't need them."

B.J. grins. "Throw them in the shitter."

All of a sudden, Edwin sails into the lab with an open bag of potato chips in hand. He just put one in his mouth and mumbles through the crunch of it.

"Well, well, someone's in the shop. What are you two here for? What do you want?"

Jack eyes the bag of chips, then glances at B.J. "Hey, Edwin, we thought you were in the shitter. We've got something we'd like you to check out."

"Go on, you have my attention."

B.J. falls into the conversation, "You know about the abduction last night at a campus, right?"

Edwin sits at his desk and sticks another chip in his mouth. "I've got a crew on the crime site as we speak. Why?"

Jack follows the question, "We were there earlier and found out about a shoe imprint they found. We'd like you to compare that imprint with the one we have on file from the murder in the alley."

Edwin throws more chips in his gullet. "That can be arranged, as soon as they get it to the lab. What's all this about?"

B.J. answers him, "We both have a hunch our guy could be connected to that crime. If the imprints match, it will be proof of it."

Edwin sweeps chip crumbs off his desk. "Your wish is my command, Detectives. I'll check it out; you'll have what I find as soon as I'm able to compare them."

* * *

Bicks has entered his place with one arm full of groceries. His briefcase dangles in his fingertips, along with a glass jar with a screwed-on tin top under his other arm. He heads straight for the kitchen, passing the betta fish along the way.

"Good evening, guys, I have a surprise for you."

He rummages around in the kitchen a moment and sticks things in the refrigerator that needs to be put in the cold. When the chore is done, he walks back to his fish, holding the glass jar. As he does so, he twists the top off and sets it on the coffee table. Little dots swim inside the jar. Reaching for a small fish net he has on the shelf, he looks at his friends in their containers. All of them are responding to his presence by dodging around at the front of the glass with anticipation. He dips the fish net into the jar and captures some of the dots.

"I found some mosquito larva in a mud puddle on my wanderings today. I know how much you love them. It's your main food source in the rice paddies, don't you know? That's why the Asians love you so much, you keep the mosquito population down and the virus they carry under some kind of control."

He puts a dab of larva in each fish bowl and watches his pets go after them. "I found some great copy today. Tomorrow, I may fit the last piece of the puzzle together after I see the lawyer and have the whole scoop. If I end up solving this, it'll be news on all the networks; great P.R. for the release of the book."

* * *

It was dusk. That time of day when the streetlights start to blink on one by one to do their job for the night. The midnight blue pulls up in front of a six-story building. A big sign was etched in concrete above the double glass doors, claiming the name of the six-story as the Crown Complex. The building itself is immaculate with several steps leading to the entrance. It is a tall, proud, very well-kept building full of businesses on each floor.

Both Jack and B.J. are looking at the height of the place when Jack offers an observation.

"Obviously this building is occupied. What number is this on the list?"

B.J. refers to the paper Sam gave them, the list of Crown properties he was able to find. "This is the 11th we've checked, and none of them have been boarded up."

"I'd say there are no vacant buildings on that list."

B.J. puts the paper down. "I'm inclined to agree with you. We've spent all afternoon looking for one, and it's been a wash."

Jack drops the gear in first. "We're working the wrong group of buildings. Let's see if we can't get a list from that lawyer or see if Sam can't find more of the properties on the internet that would include empty buildings."

Jack pulls the midnight blue away and joins the traffic. B.J. scopes out the list she has.

"I recognize a lot of these buildings, and they're all in commercial use."

Jack slams the gear into third. "We'll get on this tomorrow, first thing. Let's pick up a pizza on the way to your place. I'll buy."

"Oh, so now you're taking for granted you'll be sleeping with me at my little haunt."

"Well, yeah. It seems to be the natural course of events."

B.J. smiles. "Did you bring a change of clothes?"

"Indeed, I did."

"That's good; my cocky little jackass."

* * *

Sam was at the copy machine in the research department. Once again, he had been busy digging up material he was able to find on the Crowns. He was working in the wee hours of the night to gather the facts and running several copies so everyone would have a set during his lecture on the subject the next morning. He was looking forward to that when he could be in charge of proceedings again and the center of attention. Not that he longed for such a thing, but it still felt good that he was contributing to the investigation in his own specialized way.

Stacking everything in a neat pile, he tucked each version into its particular folder and grabbed them. Ready to leave, he turns the light off and goes through the door and down the hall for the squad office. It was just a short walk down the hall to the destination he headed for, and Sam gets there within steps.

When he enters, he sees a couple of detectives that share the squad office at their desks, doing paperwork. Each of them locked on their task, and neither one look up to greet him. Sam goes to his desk and puts the folders in order on the desktop, then plucks his suit coat hanging on the back of his chair. While he slips on the coat, he glances out the window and notices it has gotten dark outside. Finished with putting on the coat, he straightens it on his shoulders and looks down at the pile of folders all in a nice, tidy group. Satisfied with the work that was found, he grins and a thought crosses his mind.

While he picks the folders up, he expresses the thought, "Stuff of a novel."

* * *

Jack and B.J. were on the couch at B.J.'s loft. She was dressed in a flimsy, white, cotton nightgown, while Jack sat in a navy-blue bathrobe. An open pizza box was on the coffee table along with a couple of beers and a phonebook spread out across the surface. They are both going over the list of property Sam gave them using the phonebook to see if the property is listed in the book, and if so, a functioning building. B.J. starts a conversation.

"So assuming the guy thinks he's a vampire and he wants to stay out of daylight, he'll want to find some kind of refuge in an abandoned building where he won't be disturbed during the day."

Jack responds, "Yeah, but how would he know if it's Crown property? Where would he get the knowledge of that? How does he connect to the Crowns and their buildings?"

B.J. ponders the question. "Maybe he doesn't stay in a Crown building but in any place that's not being used. It could be an empty house or even a space left unattended on that campus."

"I'm banking it's Crown property where it's easy to enter with a key. Like all the murder sites indoors have been."

"We still don't know if he has keys to all those places."

Jack grabs his beer and takes a sip. "It sure points that way."

B.J. sparks to a thought. "I'll bet that lawyer, Fargo, can give us an answer to all this."

Jack picks up the list Sam gave them and shakes it. "This list is useless. All these buildings are in the phonebook. They follow the M.O. of potential crime sites, but we need a list of vacant buildings where he might be."

B.J. handles her beer for a sip. "It makes sense he'd be using an empty building, boarded and forgotten, that wouldn't have a landlord to fuss with; or neighbors to bother him and his activity."

"And to find that building, we have to go to a lawyer. What a pisser."

"I'm not sure I understand what you mean by that."

Jack takes another sip of his beer. "I have an inherent distrust of lawyers, no matter what they practice."

B.J. grins to that remark. "You know I'm a lawyer, or at least I will be."

"That's okay. I won't hold it against you; I'll make an exception. It's getting late."

B.J. puts down her beer. "Yes, it is, and we've got a big day tomorrow."

"What does that mean?"

"It means what it means."

Jack smiles a retort. "You sound like a lawyer."

He sets his beer down and reaches over and gives B.J. a big, wet kiss. This leads to another, then another. Before long, they both know they won't be making it to the bedroom. They ease down on the length of the couch, kissing and caressing, hands on everything and everywhere. Jack is surprised B.J. is naked under the nightgown, but happy she is. B.J. is delighted to find Jack naked under the bathrobe. She pulls the robe off him while his hands travel under the nightgown.

They keep on with each other's pursuits till Jack enters her, and they both gasp to the pleasure and joy of the connection; she with a fluid embrace, and he with a bold intrusion. While Jack strokes her, she throws her legs straight up in the air, and they move at each other with a determined frenzy. Eventually, they come to a wondrous and glorious end, all at the same time, realizing the couch can be as much fun as the bed.

# Chapter 50

The place was so still, it seemed like a desert sunset. So quiet, it was disturbing, like an ambush was about to occur and a predator was waiting to pounce. Kim looked small and helpless, tied up in her restraints. Her head hung loosely, and she was sagging to her binding, unconscious of the surroundings and the activity that had developed during her unwanted stupor. Her clothes draped in rags, and Betty was nowhere to be seen.

Out of the gloom, the Renaissance man appears without his mouthpiece. He is fully dressed as if he were about to join the public in the streets. His hair was smoothly slicked back, the white, silk shirt tucked into his black fatigues, with the black string tie neatly at the collar. The pant leggings to the fatigues were, in turn, tucked into his combat boots. Crowning the whole outfit was his black cape flowing behind him and setting the tone of his attire in the manner he was comfortable and accustomed to. A transition of what he coveted but not quite realized.

He stood in front of Kim while long rows of lit candles tracked the floor, two each on Kim's flank and stopping at her feet, placed there in her ignorance while she was passed out from exhaustion and exposure. On either side of her, just feet away, were two, huge, silver candelabras burning brightly with several more candles mounted on them. They sat framing her like bookends. The two rows consisted of countless candles inches apart, creating a length of at least 15 feet and developing a bright lit lane between the rows of maybe six feet wide. Expanding in a far-reaching berth, covering the floor beyond the two candle rows, were more flickering candles. It represented a sea of them with small flames jumping vividly, all in different containers; bottles, cans, pieces of cardboard, some are simply naked on the concrete. There must be hundreds of them, and all of them light up the area like a monastery.

Coupled with the flashing candles, stuck in melted and cooled wax, are sticks of incense. Their smoke trails up into the rafters, and along with the glowing candles, the spectacle composes a seductive and yet-eerie ambience. Too numerous to count, the incense is collected with the spread of candles all over the floor. The fragrance all these scented candles and incense produce is so heavy, it overpowers any odors in the dank basement space and permeates the air like that of a harem. The sight is striking with a brilliance that seems unearthly and almost holy; the flames dancing in their own light and the smoke of the incense climbing to the ceiling like small, ethereal phantoms.

Slowly, Kim comes to consciousness and is shocked to find such an assemblage of cathedral-like piousness surrounding her rather than dark horror. The picture so quiet, it is captivating. One can almost hear the fluctuating candles and the sticks of incense vaporizing. The Renaissance man stands before Kim in the golden, smoky light. Still gaged, she watches him like he is crazy. Long moments slip by while she stares at the carnival in front of her.

Without evident reason, the Renaissance man reaches down and grabs a corner of his cape. He deliberately raises the cape to cover the lower part of his face. All Kim can see are those black, lifeless eyes glaring at her. Suddenly, the Renaissance man begins to dance. Almost ceremoniously, he starts to move in an extremely bizarre but graceful motion. The animation he expresses seems even more evocative because it is done in complete silence. Contorting into odd bends of his torso and scampering in a catlike jaunt, he leaps and jumps among the candles and incense. The dance is a cross between voodoo and modern, a ballet of sublime formication and bewitched freakish bewilderment. Kim sets her eyes on him in wonderment, tied to the wall, watching a nightmarish fantasy; captured in a hypnotic fright while witnessing the mystic dance.

The only sound discernable is the rustling movement of the Renaissance man in the smoke-filled light. He dances among the candles and incense, the smoke swirling from the flow of his gestures. He hides his face from Kim the whole time with his cape while his black eyes flash with anticipation. She is stretched out against the wall, observing the Renaissance man dance this way and that when, suddenly, he comes up close, eyeball to eyeball. Once again, she is appalled by his breath.

Without warning, he whips out his switchblade. Releasing the edge, it slides out of its housing in an instant and sparkles in the candlelight. The Renaissance man points the blade high in front of her eyes. Kim reacts to the real danger it presents and thrashes about wildly. The Renaissance man dances off among the incense and candles while the smoke twirls around him, enhancing the insane image. He frolics about in a quicker, more-frenetic fashion, as if hearing some ghostly beat of a native drum. He swings around, waving the knife threateningly, and Kim repels to every lunge.

All of a sudden, he jumps at her with daunting speed that surprises Kim. She screams into the gag with bulging eyes while he slices away parts of her clothing with blinding quickness. Dancing off again, the Renaissance man leaves Kim half-clothed and crying from the brazen attack. He whirls around on the radiant floor, wielding the glittering blade, playing his cat-and-mouse game.

In the middle of a grotesque move, he unexpectedly rushes her again, brandishing the knife. Kim stands at his mercy with shut, weeping eyes, too scared to watch. He slashes at her garments once more, leaving Kim naked from the waist up. Then, he spins away while she screams in agony through her gag. The fear she expresses excites the Renaissance man. He can hardly contain himself as he hides his face with the cape, his dark eyes sparking to the moment.

He moves around like a bullfighter now, swinging the knife in a much more menacing way. Kim, bound in her helplessness, can do nothing but wait for the next assault. And the assault comes. With remarkable velocity, he is on her and cuts the girl deep above her right breast. The blood flows, and the Renaissance man jumps at the wound as if it were to avoid death, then grunts as he sucks the blood with gusto. Kim swims in confused hysteria. Having sucked the first wound dry, the fiend cuts her again across the left shoulder. Once more, he vaults to the flowing blood like a frenzied shark. The Renaissance man gleefully drinks down her blood while Kim surrenders to the ordeal in a submissive agony. He repeats the attack over and over again until Kim is quiet and frozen through a transition of a mental shutdown. Her body jerks to the wicked onslaught, enduring the brutality as if in a trance.

# Chapter 51

Bicks comes out of his kitchen, dressed in emerald-green, silk pajamas. He was holding a large mug of coffee in one hand and, in the other, his cellphone. He walks to the custom-made shelf and watches his betta fish become active for the day, expecting to be fed.

"Good morning, guys. I've got a big day today. At least, I anticipate one."

He takes a big sip of coffee, then dials a number on his phone. While waiting for the connection, he puts the mug on the shelf and grabs a vile of food pellets. Cradling the phone in his ear, he untwists the vile and sets the lid back on the shelf next to the mug. He starts dropping pellets in the fish bowls when the connection suddenly comes alive.

"Hello, yes, this is Mr. Bickers. I have an appointment with Mr. Fargo this morning. I understand he's been out of town and... He is... Okay, good. Thank you."

He disconnects, drops the last of the pellets in the remaining fish containers, and replaces the lid. Bicks grips the steaming mug of coffee and takes another big sip. Relishing the stuff, he gulps down another and watches his pride and joys feed.

"I'm looking forward to my little talk with Mr. Fargo, amigos. It should be fruitful."

* * *

B.J. was pulling freshly baked biscuits out of the oven. A pot of coffee was filling the kitchen with sweet aroma, and she set the biscuits on the counter to cool. She got a couple of cups from the sideboard and poured coffee into one of them, then meandered around to the outside edge of the kitchen bar, leaned on it, and sipped coffee.

She pondered over her first morning thoughts and the antics of last night when Jack came in, looking spiffy from a shower. They were both still dressed in bathrobes, and Jack made a dash for the coffee.

"I smell coffee. Man, it smells good."

"I made some biscuits too; they should be just about cool enough to eat now."

Jack pours a cup of coffee, grinning to the hospitality and that wonderful smell. He goes to the opposite side of the kitchen bar, leans on it with his elbows, and looks deep into B.J.

"Is there a time of day you aren't beautiful? Even when you just get up, you're a knockout."

"You're pretty easy on the eyes yourself."

They are both delighted in each other's presence and are quiet for some moments, languishing in the company and solace of the morning. B.J. looks at Jack over the rim of her cup and twinkles with a thought.

"Jack, would you like to meet my parents, have dinner with them?"

Jack is a little taken back by the suggestion. "I don't know; I'd hate to embarrass you with my bull-in-the-china-shop demeanor. I'm sure they'd wonder what the hell you're doing with me."

B.J. sets her coffee down on the counter. "Don't be silly. They're not the starch collars you think they are, and, besides, it's none of their business what I do with you."

Jack watches her. "It's kind of a step, meeting parents. They're going to think that anyway."

"That's the point. I want them to think that. It makes sense, and they'll be happy I found someone I love. I want them to get to know you like I know you."

It gets quiet between the two of them again. B.J. picks up her coffee, and they lock eyes over their cups. Jack reaches over for a biscuit and finally gives an answer to the invitation in his own way.

"You know; we really haven't known each other for very long; a blink of an eye in terms of a lifetime. But one thing I do know. I love you, B.J. I've never loved anyone the way I love you. And I don't want to love anyone else the way I love you. You're the last train stop for me, there's no other place to go to. I'm yours, B.J., if you'll have me. I'd be honored to meet your parents."

B.J. sets her coffee down again, walks around the kitchen bar, and gives Jack a loving kiss. They hold each other, enjoying the warmth they share. Lingering in each other's arms as if the world stood still; Jack then whispers in her ear in a soft tone.

"Come on, we've got biscuits to eat and an office to go to."

* * *

Dressed in his favorite brown suit with a yellow-and-green, hand-painted, silk tie; a matching brown fedora sitting on his head with a little bright yellow feather in the hat band, Bicks breezes into Fargo's office, putting his Chap Stick away. He carries a brown briefcase as he walks to the pretty secretary. He stands in front of her, takes his hat off, and announces his purpose for being there.

"Good morning. My name is Bickers; I have an appointment to see Mr. Fargo this morning."

She refers to her stationary, "Yes, Mr. Bickers. I remember when you set the appointment. I'll let Mr. Fargo know you're here."

The young woman takes the phone on her desk and pushes a button. "Mr. Fargo, your morning appointment, Mr. Bickers, is here… Yes, sir." She puts the phone back in its cradle. "Go right in, Mr. Bickers."

Bicks walks to a door nearby and knocks lightly. He opens the door gingerly and sees Fargo rising from his desk.

"Yes, Mr. Bickers. Come in please, come in."

Bicks goes through the door and closes it behind him.

Fargo gives a gracious gesture. "Have a seat, sir. What can I do for you?"

He walks to the desk and shakes hands with the lawyer. Fargo is a handsome man in his 50s, a little gray at the temples and wears a tailored, dark-blue suit with a red tie.

Bicks sits down at a brown leather chair Fargo indicated in front of his desk. He sets his hat on a small table next to the chair, opens his briefcase, and obtains a notepad and pencil.

"My name is Jerome Bickers. I'm a freelance writer working on a book about the Crown family."

Fargo folds his hands on his desk. "Yes, a sad story. What brings you here?"

Bicks slaps the pencil on his hand. "A sad story but an interesting one; through my research on the subject, I found out you're the legal guardian of the estate."

"Yes, that's right. I have been for quite some time. But I'm not sure how I could help you."

Bicks leans in to the conversation. "Did you know the Crowns before you were appointed the guardian?"

The lawyer leans back in his desk chair. "Yes, I did. I've known the Crowns for many years. I was a legal and financial advisor to them as well as a friend."

"You must have been close to their private lives then. Anything you might recall about them would be a help. The dealings you had with them must have been numerous. I'm not asking you to speak of things you may feel uncomfortable about, things that are of a private nature to you and them. Just a general overview of what you remember fondly. By the way, can you tell me something about their son or where he might be?"

"I'm afraid I can't help you there."

Bicks has been observing Fargo intently for any reactions he may have in the discussion.

"What about the play his parents sponsored for him? Do you remember any of that?"

Fargo leans forward on his desk and places his hands on it. "You mean that fiasco at the old Crown Majestic? I advised them not to get involved. But it didn't do any good. The Crowns would do anything for that boy, no matter what he asked. Anyway, it was a complete disaster. Why would you want to write about any of that? It's just a small occurrence in the vastness of their enterprising story."

"It was one of their last times to be seen in public."

Fargo thinks about that. "Yes, I suppose it was."

Bicks is jotting something down in his notepad. "I didn't realize it opened at the Crown Majestic. That theatre has been torn down since then, hasn't it?"

"No, it hasn't. It's been boarded up for years though. The name was changed after the merger, but it's still Crown property."

Bicks is secretly excited by this piece of news. "I can't remember where that place was at. Where would it be located?"

“You can get an address from my secretary. Why on earth would you want to know the location of the old Crown Majestic?”

Bicks starts to put his notepad and pencil away in his briefcase. “No special reason. You never know what you can use in research of a story. I feel I’ve taken enough of your time this morning, Mr. Fargo. I do thank you for the time though. And I may be back to discuss more about the Crown’s if that’s okay with you.”

Fargo begins to stand. “Yes, of course; whatever I can do to help, Mr. Bickers.”

* * *

The midnight blue is pulling into the police-department parking lot. Not many cars are in the lot for a change. It makes it easy for Jack to find a parking spot near the door entrance. Jack and B.J. are coming to a stop when Jack makes an observation.

“I’ll bet Sam makes a comment we’re showing up together again.”

B.J. looks at the building, “Unless we beat him here.”

Jack shuts the midnight blue down. “That’s a long shot. All these years, I can’t think of a time I might have got here before him; there’s been times, I’ve wondered if he ever goes home.”

“Money says he was here late, tinkering around on the computer last night. I wonder if he found anything that will help the case. And if he did stay late, maybe he’ll get here late to boot.”

Jack starts getting out the car. “Wishful thinking; he’s here, and he’ll make a comment to boot.”

* * *

Bicks is walking to his car at a parking meter on the downtown streets. He gets to it and throws his briefcase on top of the Jaguar, then opens the case. He takes out his recorder and turns it on.

“Note: I had no idea the old Crown Majestic still existed. The ties are there. His infatuation with the theatre, the opportunity it offered, and the play, Dracula, he wanted to do. His failure and subsequent collapse of everything he valued. The obvious embarrassment for the family and the son of closing the first night; it's worth checking out. I'll go back to the tombs and see if I can find some history on the place. But, first, I'll go see the theatre firsthand. Maybe even take some pictures for the book."

# Chapter 52

Sam was sorting out the folders he had collected in neat piles on his desktop. A couple of detectives are leaving the office on the way to start their day; one of them shoots a so long at him.

"We'll see you later, Sam, have a good one."

"You two take care, catch a criminal."

The detectives walk out of the squad office. "Yeah, yeah."

Sam is left to himself in the empty room. He continues with his inventory on the folders when Edwin rolls in with a folder of his own, tucked under his arm. He goes to Sam, eyeballing the stack he was assembling.

"What's all this you have?"

Sam stops his attention on the reports. "Hey, Doc, you're roaming around awful early. What are you doing here?"

Edwin scans the office. "To see Jack and Detective Dobbs; I see they're not around."

"Not yet, but they will be, they usually show at the same time. It's good you're here, you can join in on the fun we're about to have."

Edwin eyeballs the folders again. "What do you mean by that?"

Sam taps the folders with a hand. "These reports have mucho info in them. Stuff I think you'll find very interesting."

Edwin pats the folder he has. "This has got some pertinent info as well. But I don't know how long I can hang around; I've got work to do."

"I sympathize with you, Doc. Right there with you."

Jack and B.J. unexpectedly flow into the office, both grinning like cats with a canary. Sam notices them first.

"What did I say, there they are, together. And they look pretty happy, don't they?"

Jack and B.J. glance at each other and erase their grins. Sam continues his thought.

"You two are just in time; I've got a report you're going to want to read."

Jack walks to Sam's desk. "Yeah, what is it?"

Sam holds the folders up in clear view. "Information on the Crown's; a shitload."

B.J. looks at Edwin. "What's that you have there, Doc?"

"I also have a shitload. And before you get started on what Sam has for you, I've got something you two should see."

B.J. and Jack glance at each other once again and amble over to a desk that Edwin is using for his presentation.

"When you asked me to compare the shoe imprint from the campus abduction with what we had from the alley murder, I couldn't figure out why. I was skeptical because of the difference in M.O. But now I know."

Edwin lays two photographs out on the desk and shows them to the detectives. Sam, being curious, gets out of his chair, joins them, and peers over shoulders.

Jack is checking the photographs out. "They look like the same by my eyes."

Edwin handles the pictures. "Not only do they look the same, but they're a match. More than that, they're an exact match."

B.J. examines the prints. "What do you mean by that?"

"Both imprints come from a military boot. They are both from the left boot, the same size. The patterns of these boots are the same, but you see this mark on the heel here on this one?"

Sam answers, "I see it."

Edwin points at the other photograph. "This imprint has the same mark. It's like a fingerprint, probably caused by stepping on a nail or something. These two imprints were made by the same boot. They are an exact match, and you two were right in your hunch. The same guy made these imprints and was at the same crime sites. This is proof of it."

Sam toots his horn. "My hunch was in on that. I had a feeling about that abduction and put these guys on it."

Jack responds to Sam, "And I take my hat off to you. That goes for you too, Doc, good work; both of you."

Edwin gathers the photographs. "Thanks, it's a good piece of evidence."

B.J. takes notice of the folders on Sam's desk. "What is that you've got on your desk, Sam?"

He heads for his desk. "You're not going to believe what I found."

Sam gets to the desk and hands out folders to everyone. "At one time, Ethel and Sinclair Crown were the pinnacle of the social scene in the metropolis, in the world for that matter. They were considered the Fitzgerald's of their generation."

B.J. thumbs through her folder. "Where can they be located?"

"They can't."

B.J. looks at Sam. "What's that supposed to mean?"

Sam gives his answer. "They're not with us anymore. But we're getting ahead of ourselves."

Edwin shuffles through his folder. "I have an uncle that knew the Crowns well. They travelled all over the world."

Sam continues his little lecture, "They built an empire in real estate. You could find a Crown Fountain Hotel in several of the largest cities around the globe. And they started it all right here in this city."

B.J. has been listening to the conversation but is not satisfied with the answer to her question moments ago. "You two speak of them in the past tense. What happened to the Crowns?"

Sam, again, answers B.J.'s question, "Some years ago, they were killed in a house fire."

Jack follows the trail Sam is leading. "No survivors?"

"They had an adopted son."

Edwin sparks to that revelation. "That's right. I remember my uncle said they always wanted a child but could never have one."

Jack continues the line of thought, "Where was the son at the time of the fire?"

Sam grins. "In a mental ward, the boy was adopted at the age of six. By the time he was a teenager, he started showing signs of psychotic behavior."

B.J. thumbs through her folder. "Was that about the time they merged their business?"

Still grinning, Sam replies, "Yeah, they dropped into seclusion and liquidated a lot of their property as well."

Edwin adds to the answer, "My uncle used to say that boy sucked the life out of them."

Jack intervenes, "What's the son's name, and have you a snapshot of the guy?"

Sam refers to his notes, "Carlton Sinclair Crown. I do have a picture; it's in the folder you're looking at."

Jack finds the headshot and studies it. "Was he institutionalized after those murders years ago in Highland Park or before?"

Sam looks up from his notes. "After. You already know the Crown's lived in Highland Park."

B.J. is checking the picture she has of Sinclair in her folder. "You have any idea where he might be?"

"I did till six months ago."

B.J. follows her inquiry, "Six months ago; what do you mean by that?"

"That's when he escaped from the institution. Apparently, he just walked off the grounds."

Jack puts his folder under his arm. "What's the name of that place, and is there an address?"

Sam hands a paper to Jack. "It's called The Green Oak Hospital. A privately owned place located out at Lake Dallas. A little over an hour drive from here. This is the address and how to get to it."

Edwin has a comment, "Just in time for the murders."

Jack turns to him. "What's that, Doc?"

"He's locked up after the Highland Park murders and escapes right before our set of murders."

"Yeah, it kind of points a finger at this fellow as our primary suspect, doesn't it? Not to mention he may have access to keys. Have you given a copy of this to the captain?"

Sam grabs one last folder off his desk. "Not yet. But I'm going to his office from here. He'll get a personal tour on the subject."

Jack backs up the suggestion, "The captain will want that tour."

Edwin heads for the door. "I'm getting back to the lab, got work to do."

"Thanks for the info, Doc, again good job."

Sam starts for the door. "Hey, wait a minute, Doc, I'll walk with you. What are you two going to do?"

Jack goes to his desk and sets his copy on it. "First, we're going to that lawyer, Fargo's, office. He should be back in town today. We'll find out if he knows anything. Then, I think we'll take a drive out to Green Oak and talk to Carlton Sinclair Crown's doctor. See if he has any idea of his whereabouts and get a professional view on how that brain of his ticks."

B.J. has been standing quietly, detached from the office bustle. She has been reading her folder, avidly going through the contents. She suddenly looks up from it and barks out a revelation.

"You know what? It says here the son of the Crown's was home, visiting from Green Oak the night of the house fire."

# Chapter 53

That faucet was dripping again. Each drop produced would descend to the work sink and send out a noise that seemed to explode like an artillery round in the deep quiet. Mixed with the sound of the water drops were haunting moans randomly surfacing into that same calm quiet. Kim was the source of the moans still strung up to the wall, hanging to the binding limp and barely coherent. To her right, the coffin can be seen through the open curtain, with the lid open. The black enamel-and-silver trim glances the obscure light like a firelight was dancing on it.

What was left on Kim's upper clothing is gone, except for torn rags in pieces dangling from her waist. Her torso, shoulders, and arms are covered with nicks and cuts. Raw, red slashes are everywhere on her body, making Kim look like an incomplete Salvador Dali painting. She moans pitifully out of the tortured state.

The Renaissance man is at the big, oak table, writing. Bent over and concentrating on the task at hand. A lit candle and a glass of water is on the table along with the inkwell and journal. He scribbles his words on the parchment with his quill for some moments, recording thoughts and events. Finished with his tabulation, he puts the quill down and closes the journal.

Standing from his crouched position, the Renaissance man goes to a bookshelf and places the journal carefully away. Next to that shelf is the full-length mirror. He puts himself in front of the mirror and checks his image out. There seems to be no discernable difference from when he last observed himself. All through the activity, Kim's distant moans echo off the walls. They bounce and reverberate in the atmosphere, causing a lonely and wailing cavity of horrors. The Renaissance man slowly shuffles back to the table and caps off the inkwell; then walks toward a new object in the chamber. It sits among several other bookshelves on a simple, small, wooden table. An old record player made of birch with a record already in place on the wheel. He switches the player on and sets the arm to the spinning record.

A startling piece by Beethoven bellows out. It is his *Symphony No. 5 in C Minor, Op. 67 the 1st Movement.* It rings in the space, drowning out the dripping faucet and searing moans from Kim. She, in turn, becomes alive to the sound the record makes and starts to watch the Renaissance man move about. While the music stabs the air, the Renaissance man, in measured steps, crosses to the dismantled Kim with the glass of water. He carries it out in front of him as if it were a sacrificial token in a religious moment.

He comes close to Kim, approaching her face until they are eye to eye, staring at each other; he with passive satisfaction and she with consuming terror. They stay frozen in this macabre statue for a long minute till the concerto stops and the record player shuts off. Once again, it becomes quiet. Heavy, settling in like the aftermath of a loud thump from a judge's gavel. All that can be heard is the distressful breathing from the Renaissance man.

He looks intensely into her eyes while she repels from the contact. His left hand holds the glass of water. With his right hand, he reaches to her gag and pulls it down with a finger. Then, he offers her the water. She drinks it down gratefully, and before she can mumble anything, the gag is replaced, leaving her mute once again.

Still close, his breath an unnerving foul to Kim, he gazes longingly into her eyes. Without warning, he suddenly kisses her hard, full on the gag against her will. She squirms and squeaks her protest of it. Backing away after the deed, he turns and trudges away, leaving Kim in a confused misery.

He throws the empty glass on the concrete floor, and it shatters in splinters. With a deliberate and solemn gate, he heads for the coffin. When he gets to it, he fondles it like a lover, climbs up, and sidles into it. The lid slowly closes while Kim watches. The only thing left are her anguished moans cascading off the walls in despair and obscene breathing from within the coffin.

* * *

Jack and B.J. are walking to the door that opens to Fargo's office. As they get closer, Jack extends a thought.

"Hey, I'm curious. The Crown's lived in Highland Park, I'm wondering if you knew them?"

"Afraid not; I never knew the parents or their son. I was probably out of high school before he started it, if he did at all. I have no idea if he went to Highland Park High School."

"What about your parents. You think they knew the Crowns?"

"I don't think so. I never heard them speak of them anyway. They might have met at a function or something, but they weren't a part of their lives. A lot of people live in Highland Park, and you can be there for many years and not know a portion of the folks. My uncle might have known them though, since he was a mayor there, but I'm not sure about that."

The two of them get to the door they were heading for, and Jack opens it. B.J. steps into the office, followed by her fellow.

* * *

Captain Parks is behind his desk, reading the report Sam has gathered. Sam is by the orchids, admiring their beauty. The captain looks up from his reading.

"Is this your full report?"

Sam turns from the orchids. "Yes, sir, it is. All I could find anyway."

"Has Degree and Dobbs seen it?"

"Yes, sir, they have."

"I want this lead followed out, the whole nine yards."

"We are, Captain. Jack and B.J. are on the streets as we speak. I think they're on their way to the lawyer's office right now; the one that controls the Crown estate."

Captain Parks puts his eyes back on the report. "I've finally got something the brass can put their teeth into. Good job, Sam. You've made my morning."

* * *

Jack and B.J. are sitting on a brown, leather couch along a wall. Plaques, certificates, and pictures of Fargo shaking hands with people at events are above them. Fargo is in a big easy chair facing the pair. His secretary has just given him a paper and leaves the office, closing the door. He, in turn, hands the paper to the detectives after looking at it.

"This is a list of all the Crown properties in the city. Highlighted are the buildings boarded up and not in use."

Jack takes the sheet and studies it. "Can you tell us where Carlton Crown might be?"

"No, I can't. Not at this time. But, then again, there's no reason for me to know."

B.J. peers at the sheet Jack has. "Would he have a way of getting keys to any of the properties?"

"Not to my knowledge. That's not to say he couldn't. We're not talking about rocket science here."

B.J. is curious. "Doesn't he make money from all this real estate?"

Fargo folds his hands. "His finances are managed by a trust fund. He hasn't been in contact with it. As far as I know, he hasn't anyway. They would inform me if he had. You know, it's funny."

Jack looks up from the sheet. "What do you mean; how's that?"

Fargo adjusts in his easy chair. "A man named Bickers was in my office earlier this morning, asking about Carlton. He wanted to know about his theatre interest."

B.J. flashes to that comment. "Theatre interest; was he an actor or something?"

"He wanted to be. He was a dismal failure at it. I really don't know him very well, never have. He was always so strange. Every time I was around him, he made me feel uncomfortable."

Jack passes the sheet to B.J. "What do you mean by that; why did he make you so uncomfortable?"

Fargo ponders on the question. "I don't know; he just put out this aura of darkness, like he could become something extraordinary right before your eyes. Something you wouldn't like."

Jack is watching Fargo. "You don't remember anything about him besides being odd, do you?"

Fargo visits his memory of the man. "I do remember one thing."

"What would that be?"

"Asthma; he had the worst case of asthma I've ever seen. It was difficult for him to breathe, let alone being able to speak on a stage."

Jack and B.J. lock eyes from the statement Fargo just made. It rings a bell for them.

* * *

The midnight blue was waiting in a parking lot outside Fargo's office building. Jack and B.J. are walking to it at a good clip. B.J. gets to the vehicle while Jack unlocks her door.

She's curious about their next move. "Where to now?"

Jack starts for the other side of the car. "Let's take a quick drive out to Green Oak. See if those doctors out there can tell us a little more about Carlton Crown. Maybe they can clear the fog on details for us. At the very least, they'll be able to give us a mental history on the man."

"What about Bicks?"

"Our man Bicks; he's good, too good."

B.J. starts getting in the car. "We need to talk to that guy."

Jack has unlocked his door and is getting in the car too. "We will. I'll give him a call when we get back from Green Oak."

B.J. slams her car door shut. "What do you think about what Fargo said, about Crown having a case of asthma?"

Jack shuts his door. "I'd say that's a big nail in the coffin."

# Chapter 54

The soft crunch of gravel is heard as Bicks pulls up in his Jaguar outside an old, abandoned building. Gargoyles peer down from pedestals, and crumbling concrete erodes what was once a beautiful construction in the heart of the city. Above him is a marquee with missing letters spelling incomplete words. The windows are boarded shut, and graffiti marks the elaborate brick walls. Bicks reaches into his glove compartment and retrieves a flashlight, blinking it on and off to make sure it is operable, anticipating a use for it. Opening his briefcase on the passenger seat, he grabs his recorder, then closes the case and leaves his hat sitting on it.

Getting out the Jaguar, he slips the recorder in his shirt pocket and takes his suit coat off while looking the place over. Placing the coat in the driver seat, he closes the car door and locks it. Checking out the front, he sees weeds, bramble bush, and trash is everywhere as he finds a way to an overhang of the building. Feeling around, looking for an entry into the interior of the place, he loosens his tie and rolls the shirt sleeves up. No admissible access is shown, so he decides to round a corner on the side of the structure. Before he goes around the corner, he takes out his cellphone and shoots some pictures of the front, then slips the gadget back into his pant leg pocket to keep it handy for want of more pictures.

Bicks goes down the side of a tall wall several feet high, obstructed by all kinds of overgrown shrub and debris, causing a hardship to travel through. There are old cardboard boxes used as housing for homeless vagabonds along with dirty blankets and empty wine bottles strewn everywhere. About halfway, he spots an old, rusty door. He assumes it was used as an exit door. When he gets to it, he looks around cautiously, making sure of the desertion the place seems to hold. Satisfied with the seclusion, he reaches for his hip pocket and exposes a small leather lock-pick kit. He liked to think of it as a tool of his trade. Unzipping the pouch, he chooses the lock picks he wants and starts to work on the door.

Finally, the lock unlatches with a snap. The door is still tight from years of settling, so Bicks puts his tools away and jams a shoulder into it. The door shudders from the blow and shows a gap. Bicks shoves a little harder and widens it. He sticks his head in and peeks into the unused theatre. The inside is dim with a musky, damp odor permeating the air. There is row after row of cobwebbed, red, theatre seats, junk tossed about in the aisles and corners, and torn-down curtains faded from neglect. It has the stamp of dusty disregard everywhere you look.

Bicks forces the door all the way open, and it protests with a loud screech. Fresh air and sunshine rushes into the stale, old building in relief. He turns the flashlight on and steps into the dank atmosphere. He flashes the light around, and it exaggerates just how alone he is.

"Hello, is anyone here?"

Complete silence answers him. He moves deeper into the place and speaks to himself, "Nothing here but the rats."

Bicks vigilantly makes his way through the house of the theatre and begins to climb the side stairs leading to the stage. He picks his way across the stage carefully. It is full of props from long-forgotten plays. There is an old wooden mantel for a fake fireplace; racks of grimy wardrobe clothing and floor vases of assorted sizes, colors, and shapes. Chairs of all kinds are set about, some tilted off their legs and lying on their sides. Among the cobwebs are hat trees, lamps, small tables, and boxes full to the brim, with objects to put on those tables. Upstage, there are a sundry of wooden crates large and small, stacked on top of each other. Lodged against them is an old trunk sitting on its end, with numerous, long spears wedged between it and the crates. They are pointing to the rafters just above the crates and the trunk, one of them is prominently sticking viciously at the catwalks high up at the ceiling. These are period props placed and lost with all the other clutter found everywhere on the stage. Bicks turns and finds his way downstage above the orchestra pit. He stands there quietly and takes in the view of the house. After a long look at the whole area and dumbfounded from the scope of the place, he utters some words.

"This was a grand theatre at one time."

Bicks decides on pictures and fumbles for his cellphone. The vastness of the red, theatre seating stretching to the back surrounded by the multi-tiered balconies was well worth capturing. He snaps off many shots, then replaces the cellphone once again in his pant pocket.

Satisfied with the pictures taken, he turns from his position and looks at the backstage. The backdrop curtains barely hang, torn and rotted. It has the appearance of an old horror movie set that was, at one time, a beautiful piece of scenery and now left dismantled and buried from memory.

"I wonder what's back there."

As he proceeds to the back of the stage, he gets to the center and stumbles over something. Bicks looks down at what it was he tripped on.

"What the hell is this?"

He kicks at a big metal ring protruding from the boards of the stage. Its home is a deep indention carved into it, but the ring is sticking up like it has recently been used. Bicks bends down and grabs it, then pulls with some effort. A huge trapdoor eases up from the floor. He gets it all the way open and leans it on a large box. Bicks shines his flashlight down in the dark.

"What have we here?"

There is nothing but silence as he stands, regarding the unexpected find. Perplexed by it, he starts to climb down through the trapdoor way. His light beam bounces off the walls as he clambers along the steep staircase. He gets to the floor and acclimates. Waving the light around, he sees the place is very dim and seems unattended. The first thing he notices is an open, tiny door under the stairs. He shines his flashlight into the interior of the little room and ascertains it is empty. He does observe scuffmarks on the concrete but nothing more.

After a moment, Bicks begins to move for the rest of the immense chamber. There is a glow from some unforeseen source around a corner, and he decides he does not really need the flashlight. The quarters have lit candles decked randomly around, giving an ambience of an unpredictable and spooky region. Seeing the rows of bookshelves and odd, knot furniture defined within the candlelight, he is amazed at his discovery.

"Somebody lives down here?"

He walks closer to the furnished section and comes to a brighter glow. Bicks can see around the corner now, but the murky light makes it as if he is looking into binoculars out of focus.

A distant moan ripples through the expanse, and Bicks becomes very conscious of what he is doing. He is now sure he is not alone. Another moan penetrates the stillness. He immediately moves toward the sound, apprehensive but determined.

By small measures, the clarity of the place is enhanced, and with a sudden start, he sees Kim hanging limply on a brick wall. Bound and obviously in distress. The red, bleeding slashes jumping out against her clear, snow-white skin. She moans listlessly through her gag, unaware that Bicks has ventured into, what appears to be, a living nightmare.

"What the hell."

Without fear, Bicks dashes to her and begins to untie one of her hands.

"Are you okay? You must be one of those kidnapped girls."

Kim tries to speak but cannot formulate words from the gag. Bicks recognizes the effort and switches his attention to the secured tangle on the gag.

"Here, let me get this. Don't worry; you're going to be all right."

In response, Kim expresses muted screams. Terrified by what her eyes tell her. Over his shoulder, in the little cubbyhole where the coffin is, she can see the lid of the black box slowly rising. Her eyes bulge with terror and warning. Bicks misreads the attempted alert.

"I almost have it. It'll be okay."

Bicks is oblivious to the danger from behind. It has not even occurred to him there might be another presence in the dark. Kim watches the sinister figure creep toward the unsuspecting man. Each mounting moment, she sounds off the alarm in futile screams; the black form inching closer with the knife out.

The point of the switchblade is easily seen gleaming next to the ghoulish face of the Renaissance man. Suddenly, the black image zips across and hits Bicks hard with a loud thud, followed by an even louder roar. It knocks Bicks away from her instantly. The Renaissance man stands by Kim, outraged by the intrusion.

Bicks staggers back, stiffly stepping on his heels, knocking over shelving with flailing arms and bewildered eyes. The switchblade stuck deep in his neck. He clutches his throat and gasps for breath. The Renaissance man walks quickly toward Bicks while Kim goes crazy from the insanity. He gets to him, reaches out, and rips the knife free. It tears a gaping, bleeding wound that Bicks cannot contain, spewing blood like a broken waterline.

This is the fatal blow, and Bicks collapses to the concrete. The Renaissance man stands still, quietly watching, fascinated by the sight of him squirming on the floor, his legs kicking about in vain for life while Kim screams into her gag with muffled terror. In a flash, the Renaissance man pounces on Bicks with that alarming speed. He gets to his throat and begins to feed as Bicks tries helplessly to push him away. Kim, witnessing the ghastly crime, swoons in disgust and wretchedness.

# Chapter 55

B.J. was drifting around a large office, observing the contents of a long wall. Covering the wall were plaques and certificates expressing the credentials of a doctor the office belonged to. They were a collection of imposing achievements the doctor had attained during his career. There was no mistaken the prestige and position he had acquired over the years and why he was now in charge of such a place as Green Oak. Needless to say, B.J. was impressed by the display as she surveyed the doctor's accomplishments.

To her left rear were bookshelves behind a huge mahogany desk. An extensive library burdened the shelves with books containing subjects on psychology, neuroscience, and the study of the human brain. To the right of the shelving and desk, situated in the corner joining the wall she was checking out, a door could be found. To the right of B.J., down the wall of awards and documents, was another door that she and Jack had entered from. The first thing they noticed when they were shown into the office was a nameplate at the front of the desk declaring the occupant's name, Dr. Brian Kane.

Across the room, opposite the wall B.J. was standing at stood Jack, with his back to her. The wall he was at was nothing but a long window. An enormous one, overlooking the grounds of the building the office was in. Immaculate, lush, green lawns sloped down to where the midnight blue could be seen. Dotted on the lawn were massive oak trees with limbs so gigantic and heavy, the branches bowed and touched the ground. One could actually walk up to these limbs and reach the midsection of the colossal oaks. The view offered a deduction of why this institution might be called Green Oak.

Groundskeepers with hoes and spades were scattered about, attending the colorful gardens and emerald-green lawn. Patients dressed in white could be seen everywhere, roaming walkways like dinner napkins caught in a breeze, spending idle time enjoying the serenity. Surrounding the whole affair were clean, white, stucco buildings two and three stories high. Beyond the parking lot where the midnight blue was, Lake Dallas could be seen glittering in the sunlight. Sailboats were zipping along on the water, appearing to be American Indian teepees on the move. The entire area held a sublime charm and reeked of wealth and distinction.

Jack throws out an observation while looking out the window. “It’s beautiful here, a good place to be if you’ve got problems with your brain.”

B.J. turns to face Jack and takes in the view he had been watching. “Yeah, I could live here.”

“With that brain of yours, you could end up here.”

B.J. goes to the window, next to Jack. “I’d say you’re a better candidate than I am.”

Jack smiles and pokes a finger on the tip of her nose. “You might be right about that.”

Just then, the door by the bookshelves sweeps open, and a gray-haired, middle-aged man with a matching, manicured beard, wearing a white smock walks in; a tall, handsome gent with obvious breeding. He joins B.J. and Jack at the window, with his hand out to shake.

“Hello, I’m Doctor Kane. I understand you wish to speak with me.”

Both detectives shake hands and bring out their badge. Jack makes the introductions.

“Glad to meet you, Doctor. We’re detectives Dobbs and Degree. We’d like to take a few moments of your time if that’s all right.”

“Of course, please, have a seat, and make yourselves comfortable. Can I get you something, coffee or tea perhaps?”

B.J. answers him, “No, thank you, Doctor. We don’t intend to take that much of your time.”

Doctor Kane takes a seat behind his desk while Jack and B.J. settle into chairs at the foot of the desk. The doctor touches the fingertips of his hands, holds them in front of him, and smiles.

“What’s this about? What can I do for you?”

Jack starts the interview, “We’re here to discuss a patient you had, Carlton Sinclair Crown.”

The doctor’s eyes light up. “You found him?”

“No, but we’re looking for him. We think he may be a primary suspect in a string of murders we’ve been investigating in the Dallas city metropolis.”

B.J. follows that statement, “You wouldn’t happen to know his whereabouts, would you?”

Doctor Kane reacts stiffly. “No, I’m afraid not, no. I’m sorry to hear he may be connected to murder. They wouldn’t be the murders I’ve been reading about in the papers, would they?”

Jack answers, “They would.”

Doctor Kane expels a long sigh. “I’ve been wondering about that.”

B.J. chimes in, “What can you tell us about Mr. Crown, Doctor?”

The doctor contemplates his answer. “I can sum Mr. Crown’s disorder in one word, psychopath.”

B.J. leans forward. “Does this assumption come from your study of him? I mean, do you have something substantial that could be used in a courtroom?”

Doctor Kane takes a moment to gather his thoughts. “Decades ago, the diagnosis of psychopathy came from simple observation, but, today, we can actually take a look at a psychopath’s brain with an M.R.I. We found that Mr. Crown’s scanning revealed his brain data fit within the percentile on gray-matter density. That his density measures had a strikingly similar Para limbic system with other psychopaths studied. His Para limbic gray-matter values were even more detrimental than most psychopaths.”

Jack looks at B.J., then back at the doctor. “Meaning what?”

“He’s a classic mold of a psychopath. There’s also a checklist that’s been developed through observation over the years, a very reliable checklist. There are 20 items on this checklist that make up psychopathic behavior. Mr. Crown has most all of them. Psychopaths can be pathological liars; they lack empathy, guilt, remorse; they have a grandiose sense of self-worth; they’re manipulators with a complete failure to accept their actions. Psychopaths are a specific breed of cunning, bloodthirsty predators that readily violate social rules and exploit others for their own gain. And they have no fear in results to the crimes they may commit.”

Jack points out what the doctor just said. “You mean the law doesn’t scare them.”

The doctor almost chuckles to himself. “No, they will break certain laws over and over without fear of repercussions.”

Jack looks at B.J. “That’s quite a testimony, Doctor.”

Doctor Kane leans back in his chair. “There’s a lot to be said about a psychopath. Research suggests one in 100 people are psychopathic.”

Jack is astonished. "One in every hundred?"

"Yes. They're like cold-blooded chameleons. Fortunately, the distribution of psychopathic traits is diverse in the population. Most people have some of the traits. A few have a bit more, but those that have high grades are usually diagnosed as psychopaths."

B.J. has been watching the doctor with a pensive expression. "What else can you tell us about Carlton Crown that is not in his diagnosis?"

"To start with his I.Q., most psychopaths are very smart. Carlton's I.Q. is in the high 140 levels."

Jack follows the train of thought. "That makes him a pretty smart cookie."

The doctor smiles. "Smarter than most in the cookie jar."

B.J. gets everybody back on track, "Can you tell us when he might have started his bloodlust?"

Doctor Kane thinks about the question. "I would say it surfaced from the play he got his parents involved in."

Jack and B.J. look at each other with recognition. Jack continues the pursuit, "What does that mean, Doctor? How could something simple as a play set him off that way?"

"He talked his parents into financing a play."

"Yes, we're aware of that."

"Were you aware the play was Dracula, and that's the role he cast himself in; he transformed into Dracula by the wardrobe he wore and the words he spoke in the play, not to mention the motives of the character he pretended to be."

B.J. jumps in from that comment. "No, we weren't. You think that had something to do with triggering his bloodlust?"

"Yes, I do. He got so carried away with playing Dracula, he fell so far into the role, he emerged thinking he was Dracula or a least a vampire. It wasn't long after the play closed that his parents admitted him for help."

B.J. continues, "So you're saying his quest for blood started with his acting as Dracula in the play."

Jack follows her, "The M.O. we've been following certainly points at the logic in that."

"I can't answer that for sure. I only know the problems seem to stem from that. But the grandiose image he has of himself began there. He believed he was more than human, a special entity that demanded special treatment. He was under the delusion the hospital here was trying to make him human again with prescribed drugs, and staff doctors were all a party of that delusion. He was convinced he was a vampire, and we were trying to deny him of his rightful inheritance. And this whole concept of his surfaced while he was performing as a vampire in the play, Dracula. He believed his place was at the top of the food chain so to speak."

The conversation folds to a stall in the flow of words for a moment. Each of the participants locked in their own thoughts on the subject they were discussing. A long ten seconds drops in arcane quiet while each of them soul-search when Jack glances out the window and sparks a thought.

"I've noticed, Doctor, that the patients here have a lot of freedom. They pretty much go where they like on the grounds. From what I've seen, it seems that way. Is that true?"

"Yes, it is. We try to keep an atmosphere that is of a free will. We don't want our patients to feel like they're incarcerated. It's part of the therapy we practice here."

B.J. ponders that practice. "Do you have many patients leave, escape if you will, from the practice of free reign?"

The doctor puts his elbows back on the desk. "If you're asking how Mr. Crown was able to get away, we don't know. We haven't been able to figure out how and what he did to get away from here. Despite the appearance of casualness on the grounds, we have a very tight guarded and carefully watched perimeter at this institution. Keep in mind Mr. Crown's I.Q. and that helps explain his disappearance to some degree."

Jack is curious. "Did he ever show any special interests on anything around here?"

The doctor ponders the question a moment. "He spent a lot of time in the machine shop."

"Machine shop; what would be the purpose of a machine shop for the patients, Doctor?"

"We have several facilities that we supply our patients with. It's another part of the therapy here. We encourage them to find an interest, a hobby, maybe even create a potential way to a job for their future."

B.J. has one more question, "Can you tell us what Mr. Crown did in the machine shop?"

Doctor Kane picks up a phone. “No, but I can call Mr. Gambles. He runs the machine shop, and I’m sure he can answer that for you. I’ll see if he’s busy, and, if not, I’ll have my assistant show you where the shop is.”

# Chapter 56

Bill Gambles was a happy man. He was a man in his 30s, relatively good-looking, and single with a job that paid well. And the job he had was a perfect gig. It was something he loved. All this made a happy man of Mr. Bill Gambles. He smiled all the time and laughed at a drop of a hat, and when he laughed, it was a hearty belly laugh that was infectious to anyone who heard it. This very contagious and pleasant demeanor was equated to one very important fact. The love of his job and the freedom he enjoyed in it.

He was the boss of the machine shop. The beauty of that was he did not share that responsibility with anyone else. He was in charge and that meant no one ever looked over his shoulder. Unlike many of the jobs he had in the past, he had the run of the place. He fell into the position almost three years ago right after a layoff occurred operating a table drill in a metal shop. He saw an ad in the paper, applied, and low and behold, a week later, he was hired to take care of this machine shop. Which lead to be the captain of his domain; something good had finally happened for him, and he never looked back. Heck, it never crossed his mind to look back. Not even once.

At the moment, he was busy sweeping the floor. It was part of his duties to keep the shop in order, and since the place was empty at this point in time, it was an opportunity to do just that. And the shop could always use a good sweep. Nothing was too good for his domain.

While he worked the broom, the door flies open unexpectedly, and Doctor Kane's pretty assistant walks in, escorted by two visitors he was sweeping the floor for in the first place. He was expecting the drop in from the doctor's phone call just minutes ago. The nurse introduces the visitors as Detective Dobbs and Detective Degree, then leaves them in his care. He puts the broom away, wipes his hands clean with a shop rag, and asks about their visit.

"I understand you two are interested in what goes on in here. Is there anything in particular you had in mind to know?"

Jack scans the shop and acclimates. “As a matter of fact, there is. Can you tell us anything about Carlton Crown and why he hung out around here?”

Gambles recalls the memory of him. “Carlton Crown, yeah, I remember him; one strange fellow.”

B.J. follows the thought in the conversation, “We’d like to know why he spent so much time here. What was he interested in?”

Gambles mulls over the question. “Carlton Crown, well, he was in here for any spare time he had. He learned how to operate all the machinery we have, and he picked it up really fast.”

Gambles heads for a huge, metal, mega box. It has the length of four yards or so and a width of about eight feet. The height of the thing was at the chest level of a man six feet tall. As he moves to the instrument, Gambles voices his lecture on Crown and the purpose he seemed to have in the shop.

“The machinery in here is state-of-the-art, totally advanced stuff. This Japanese-made baby is called the Horizontal Machine Center. Crown spent a lot time on this thing. He learned to operate it with as much efficiency as I do.”

Jack asks, “What was he doing on it?”

“I don’t know. He kept it a secret whatever it was.”

Jack has another question, “Is that allowed? To let patients do whatever they want around here without any surveillance of any sort? I mean, this looks like an expensive piece of equipment.”

Gambles had his back to them in the process of fiddling with the machine, throwing switches and turning it on. “They make a big deal around here not to run the place like a prison yard. Besides, what would someone make, a gun? If so, where would they get the bullets for it? I usually know what’s going on with the patients, but Crown took special effort to keep his work to himself. As long as he didn’t mistreat the machinery, and he took great care in that, I saw no harm in his business. Everything he did seemed in line with the rules.”

B.J. pops a question while watching Gambles, “What does this machine do?”

“I’m fixing to show you. This thing is a work of wonders, there’s nothing you can’t do if you have the right program for it.”

B.J. pursues the curiousness Gambles has created. “What do you mean by program?”

“First off, you develop the program on that computer system over there. It’s called the Master Cam program, and when you have what you want, you transfer the program to the center. Sometimes, there's more headache in trying to get the program right than operating this thing." Gambles tapped the big metal box affectionately.

Jack puts in a comment, "It's complicated then, the programming."

"It can be, but Crown never seemed to have much trouble. Part of the reason he kept things to himself."

"What do you mean by that?"

Gambles scratched his head. "I don't know; he just knew what he was doing. He never seemed to need any help on anything, much less the programing."

Jack wants to know what he is being shown. "What's the purpose of the program?"

"It gives the machine directions. I already have a simple program in place for a demonstration."

Gambles smiles and picks up a small hunk of metal off a nearby table. He shows the piece of metal to the detectives, clearly letting them know what it is.

"Here, we have a chunk of grade 416 Stainless Steel. Now I'm going to take this and fit it on this thing here, called a tombstone. When I get it connected, you'll see what this thing can do."

He attaches the stainless steel to a giant, rectangular, solid-metal pedestal that must weigh a couple of hundred pounds. It sits on a large metal spike inside the machine. Gambles pushes some buttons on the control panel, and the tombstone starts making 360 degree turns. Carbide bits begin to work, contouring the stainless steel to the will of the program. The action of the machine can be viewed behind a Plexiglas shield using water streams as a coolant system. The machine drills, pounds, grinds, and cuts the steel into the shape it was assigned to do. Assorted bits are used for each individual task from what looks like an enormous bicycle chain. It appears to be heavy and strong. The bits are transferred to a holding clip apparatus and replaced by other bits of a particular use plucked from this chain. The mechanism whirls franticly to accommodate what the program tells it. At the same time, the tombstone spins in circles and angles to match the projected commands and comply to the bits while they eat at the hunk of stainless steel until it begins to take shape according to the program.

By increments, the lump of stainless steel begins to take a form, a miniature replica of a Mustang sports car.

Gambles, watching the procedure with fascination like he always does, adds the final stage that takes place. He points to an elongated room with a glass wall.

"When the piece is done, you take it over there and give it an electro polish for a finished look."

Jack and B.J. look at each other and hold it for a moment. It is a glance with a knowing only they share, understanding the significance of the illustration.

# Chapter 57

The midnight blue was sitting complacently in the parking lot under one of those giant oak trees. All about the landscape were staff members from the hospital along with the patients dressed in white, milling around on sidewalks and sitting on benches seemingly with nothing much to do but mill around. Jack and B.J. were walking briskly to their car. While Jack unlocks the passenger door, B.J. makes an observation.

"I guess we know where he got his custom-made tool to extract blood. I'm sure he must have used that machine to build the thing he uses."

Jack unlocks the door and starts for his. "Curious to see what it looks like."

"We will. I'm positive we're on the right track for our guy. He fits a lot of my profile."

"Yeah, I noticed that when Dr. Kane was talking about psychopaths."

Jack goes around the midnight blue and unlocks his door. "Now all we have to do is find him."

They both get in their respective seats for the ride back to Dallas. Jack fires the car up, and it roars without complaint. He puts it in gear, and the two of them start their trek off the grounds of Green Oak.

As Jack takes the roads that will lead back to I35 and Dallas, B.J. is pulling out the list of buildings Fargo gave them earlier. Jack notices her checking the list and mulling over it.

"What are you doing?"

"Like you said, all we have to do is find him."

"Let that wait. By the time we get back to Dallas and find our first location, it'll be getting dark. And by the looks of it, we've got some ground to cover. We'll go after it in the morning when there's plenty of daylight to work under. I don't relish the idea of stumbling around in the dark in buildings I'm not familiar with and where a killer might be lurking."

B.J. puts the paper away. "I agree. We'll get back to my place and take a good survey of what we need to do. We can decide on which buildings to check out first. Did you bring an extra set of clothes?"

"It's in the trunk. I know a great burger joint we can stop at and get fries, cheeseburgers, and shakes to take back home to eat."

B.J. grins. "Calling my place home huh."

Jack looks surprised at himself. "Yeah, I guess I am."

B.J. turns her eyes on Jack. "That's okay, I won't ask for a share in the rent." A long pause slides by as the scenery outside the car windows slip along in sequence; she turns her head to watch it. Then, she smiles to herself. "Not yet anyway."

* * *

The loft was sedate, diffused in light and waiting for occupants to bring life within the walls. Outline of the furniture was discernable only because of the windows glowing from an outside source. It was dead still as if it were a breezeless forest.

The entrance door opens with a flurry, and B.J. and Jack tramp into the place with armfuls. B.J. is holding onto the folders from the day's business along with Jack's carry case of clothes, and Jack with bags of burgers and shakes. They make their way for the kitchen counter while B.J. barks out an intention.

"I'm getting comfortable before I eat."

Jack returns the intent. "I'm doing the same. I'd like to take the day off me."

They both set their bundles on the kitchen counter when B.J. makes a sound suggestion.

"Could you put the milkshakes in the refrigerator, they'll keep better till we're ready for them."

"Good idea. Your wish is my command, dear heart."

Jack follows the request and puts the shakes in the icebox. Then, they start for the back bedroom.

The moment they get to the bedroom, they start to disrobe. Jack notes the soft beauty of his companion while she undresses and puts on her flimsy nightgown. It is all he can do while she gets naked and not grab her for a tumble. He has never known a woman that stirs him to such heights in just a simple thing as she was doing. And he knew the novelty of it would never wear away.

She too secretly watched her guy undress with fascination. She loved looking at him with his bulging muscles and the smoothness in which he moved that strong body of his while throwing on his robe. His skin was a dark tone without the use of sunlight to tan it, and she realized she could never tire of such a masculine presence that he presented. Not in a million years.

They both finished with the task of getting comfortable about the same time and started for the front room with jubilant fantasies tripping on their minds.

* * *

Finished with their meal of burgers, fries, and milkshakes; the remnants of it sprayed all over the kitchen counter, they both stand at the counter, contented and well-fed. She was in her white, cotton nightgown, and he in his blue bathrobe. The folders and papers acquired during the day were nearby on the counter, and B.J. reaches for them to work. She digs into the list of buildings they got from Fargo and also pulls the head shot they have of Carlton from the folder. Without reservations, she declares what needs be done for the following day.

"Going by what we found out today, I think we have a real line on the suspect we've been looking for." She views the head shot. "He really doesn't look that dangerous, does he?"

Jack glances at the picture. "I think Fargo was talking about what he felt when he was around that dude instead of what he saw."

He gets his cellphone and begins to dial. "We have a name, a history, and a motive. It shouldn't be too hard to decide where the guy could be; aside from the fact it's a needle in a haystack. I'm going to give Bicks a call right now and ask him how and why he was in Fargo's office today. He might even have a suggestion where to look."

Jack finishes the dial and waits for Bicks to connect. "He's not answering."

It rings several times before an answering device receives the call. "Bicks! This is Jack Degree. I need to talk to you, Amigo. I spoke to that lawyer, Fargo, today, and he brought up the fact you were in his office earlier. I'd like to speak with you about that, so when you get this message, give me a call. You know the number. Call me back."

He kills the phone call. "Shouldn't be long before we hear from him."

B.J. has been running a finger on the list of property Fargo gave them. Paying attention to the ones highlighted as abandoned. It is a sizeable list, but she falls upon a very promising prospect.

"Jack!"

He is startled. "Yes, what?"

She is reading the list on the sheet. "Remember how Dr. Kane spoke of Crown acting in the play, Dracula. How it seemed to be the start of his bloodlust."

Jack is listening. "Yeah, another nail in the coffin."

"There's a theatre on this list." B.J. hands the sheet to Jack. He takes it and reads the contents.

"It was once called the Crown Majestic. It's there in the middle of the list we have."

Jack finds the reference. "Are we talking about another nail?"

B.J. is watching Jack. "It's just a couple of blocks from the campus where those girls were abducted. See the address?"

Jack looks at B.J. "Yeah, too many connections to ignore; we'll go by there first thing in the morning before we ever get to the office."

B.J. is excited. "It fits like a glove, doesn't it?"

"It does, you're right, it does; the Dracula thing, the abduction near this address. It would be the one logical place to check on out of all these locations on this list. We'll do it first thing in the morning."

B.J. takes in the mess on the counter. "I guess I'll clean this up and get ready for bed. We've got a heavy day tomorrow."

She grabs some discarded wrappings and her empty milkshake container. Jack follows suit, puts the sheet on the counter and gathers his stuff.

"Here, let me help you."

They both go around the counter and into the kitchen to get rid of their trash. As they move about in the small space, they crisscross each other, going through their domestic chores.

Eventually, they bump and touch. And when they do, it is like two atoms colliding. A nuclear explosion erupts full of passion, heat, need, and want. They reach out to each other, fumbling for an infusion they cannot resist. An infusion of confusion, neither one of them understanding the attraction, but it is transferring into something beyond their control and coming from their blood; like it was in their D.N.A. A bystander would think they were in a fight.

They swirl in the moment. As if the kitchen were spinning with them to a climbing frenzy. Caught in the nucleus of the infusion, it leaves them dangling on the end of their lifeline. And they surrender to it.

In a stormy breath, B.J. cries out, "Fuck me, Jack, right here, right now."

Picking her up like she was weightless, Jack puts her on the cabinet counter next the microwave. He pulls her nightgown up over her shoulders and arms and whispers, "I love you, B.J."

He drops his bathrobe, then drives himself head on inside her, and they both gasp to the sudden pleasure of the union. As they pound their bodies at one another, each of them realized they have never had someone like this. They have never loved someone through the sex they share. A whole new horizon in the expression of loving evolves, and it soars with wonder and delight. As if they have never made love with anyone before while they join like two, wild, sentient beings. It is a limitless pursuit of gratification; a supposedly unreachable plateau of splendid perfection; a once-in-a-lifetime coupling of souls; that beautiful infusion of love and the gambol it brings.

# Chapter 58

The old theatre was like a time capsule. It sat among all the towering glass structures that were the landmarks of downtown Dallas. Modern architecture as opposed to the forgotten theatre, with its gargoyles and masonry work whose detail had been lost through time. It was like an obsolete monument stuck in the middle of the metro activity that thrived today. It seemed like a sad bygone yet still carried the disregarded name, The Crown Majestic, with a dignity it always had. It stood proud in its own decay.

A soft crunch of gravel can once again be heard while the midnight blue pulls to a stop beside a white Jaguar. The weed-infested parking lot glittered with dewdrops from the new sun striking it as Jack makes an observation.

"If I didn't know better, I'd say that Jag belonged to Bicks."

B.J. eyes the car. "I wouldn't be surprised; he never called you back last night."

Both of them get out of the car, and Jack makes a comment, "I'll check the car; see if you can spot Bicks."

Jack goes to the Jaguar and discovers the doors locked. He looks through the glass window with his hands like visors to protect the vision from glare.

"It's Bicks all right. I see his fedora in the passenger seat."

He puts a hand on the hood of the automobile. "This car has been sitting here for a while. The engine is ice cold."

In the meantime, B.J. has gotten to the front and tries to peer into the building through small openings of the boarded windows and doors. Seeing nothing, she drops the purpose and steps toward the corner of the place.

Jack is going where B.J. is. "You see him around anywhere?"

By now, B.J. has gotten to the corner and inspects the far side of the wall as it extends to the backside of the building.

"Can't see anything in those windows; it's too dark. But I think I see a door down here that might be open."

Jack makes it to B.J.'s side at the corner. He too scrutinizes the long wall and sums up the door could be open, "Yeah, I think it is open."

The both of them high step down the length of it, bypassing all the rubble, thorny bushes, and debris that causes obstacles on the trek. They notice the unoccupied cardboard boxes, the dirty blankets, and empty wine bottles as they near the gap in the wall.

When they get close to the old rusty door, they find it is ajar wide enough to allow someone to enter the building. The two detectives take turns squeezing through the opening to get inside.

Once they gain entrance, the detectives stand still a moment and give their eyes a chance to get used to the puzzling obscurity. In short time, they determine the same sea of neglected red chairs and disposed junk Bicks did. Adjusting to the shadows, they pick their way toward the stage through all the litter.

The two of them get to the stage and climb the side stairs. As B.J. walks along the rim of the orchestra pit, she remarks on the house.

"It doesn't look like anyone's been here for a while."

"No sign of Bicks either. Let's check back there."

They head for the backstage section. Feeling their path between all the props Bicks did. B.J. is choosing her own way through all the curiosities when she stumbles and almost falls. She breaks her topple by grabbing a rope tied off to the leg of a table with boxes stacked on it. When she clutches the rope and leans her weight on it, the grip releases a tension to the rope.

Suddenly, Bicks comes swinging out from the wings of the stage a few feet above all the props. The rope that is tied to his feet disappears into the darkened rafters. His loose arms sway to the motion of the swing like a dead man urging to join him. He flies across the length of the stage like a giant ghastly pendulum. The two detectives are frozen with the grotesque sight, watching spellbound. All is quiet except for the grind of the rope.

Jack's head is turning side to side, following the movement. "It's Bicks!"

They both track him another moment. "His throat has been cut."

B.J. follows the statement, "And not much blood."

They draw their guns and move to the backstage, taking care to avoid the oscillating Bicks. Jack scans the location, then comes to a decision.

"Take a closer look. I'm going to the lobby at the front and check that out."

"We should call for backup."

“I will. I’ll use my cell, but, first, let’s secure the area. Watch your ass, B.J.”

“You watch yours.”

Jack takes off for the front of the theatre, leaving B.J. to finish securing the stage. She takes a few steps when she notices something center stage throwing light. She goes to it, bends down, and picks it from the floor. It is Bicks’s recorder. She is careful to handle it while she turns it on. His voice blurts out, disturbing the quiet. “Failure there and subsequent breakdown, worth checking out.”

B.J. turns the recorder off, recognizing his voice. “He must have been around here.”

She drops the recorder in her pocket and starts inspecting the floor. In seconds, she spots the handle to the trapdoor at her feet. B.J. reaches down to tug on it. With a little strain, the door creaks open. She opens the door all the way and leans it on a small table she gathers and scoots in place, then peers down into the dark apprehensively.

B.J. decides not to wait for Jack and descends the stairs, confident he will find the open trapdoor and follow the trail. Moving slow and deliberate, she reaches the lower level, steps off the last stair, and waves her weapon in directions covering her presence. B.J. sees nothing important and takes it upon herself to go deeper into the dim chamber, her gun pointing the way.

In short order, she comes to the furniture and candle-lit space. It still has that unholy golden glow. Dead quiet lures her on while she strides along, making sure no one is there. A moan floats to her ear somewhere in the murk, and B.J. heads toward the sound quickly.

In ticking moments, she finds Kim tied to the wall. B.J. looks about smartly, making sure it is clear to go to her. Deciding it is, she dashes to the bound girl and begins to untie her gag. Kim’s eyes bulge with recognized help from B.J., grateful for her appearance, then enlarges to an unnoticed warning from what she sees in the short distance.

B.J. gives her encouragement, “I’m the police. I’ll get you out of this; you’re going to be all right.”

The Renaissance man silently drops out of the gloom of the ceiling during those words like a black spider would on a strand of silk. He lands softly like a cat right behind B.J. He stands still, with his chrome mouthpiece glinting in the pale light; the fangs of the mouthpiece shines silver in the candlelight as the ebony figure comes closer, right off the shoulder of B.J. Kim is squirming wildly, full of fear for her and her safety. B.J. is unaware he is there, consumed by Kim's berserk behavior. The Renaissance man then delivers a big, windmill blow, smashing an unforeseen arm into B.J., knocking her several feet away. She goes sprawling for the floor, landing hard. The sudden attack sends her gun skidding across the concrete and coming to a stop several feet away.

The angry Renaissance man stands next to Kim, glaring at B.J., breathing heavily through his mouthpiece. The fangs exposed as a detrimental hazard and hungry for the taste of blood. B.J. jumps to her feet, a bit dazed from the shock of the assault. Defenseless without her weapon, she searches for it while the Renaissance man vaults for her, the fangs snapping at the air.

He gets to B.J. and lays his hands on her. She counters with a swipe and arm pivot. The Renaissance man then lunges at her, and she slips his grasp, sending him reeling away. He growls a response and comes at her again with infuriated force. She slides to his left and delivers a sharp chop between the shoulder blades while he flusters by.

He smacks into the wall. Turning, he thunders toward her with the violence of a ravenousness beast. His cape flying, his arms outstretched, fangs snapping viciously, and screaming his rage, the rush is too much for B.J. She backs into the bookshelves Bicks knocked down before and trips, falling to the floor among the contents they held. The Renaissance man is on her instantly. He gets on top of her, pinning her down with his weight. The fangs are wide open, inches from her throat. B.J. struggles to keep him away with all her might while Kim screams into her gag in the background. Out of nowhere, Jack's voice rings out.

"Hold it right there!"

The Renaissance man freezes and looks in the direction the voice came from. Jack is pointing his weapon dead center on the man. An instant goes by. No one moves.

All of a sudden, the Renaissance man bolts for the stairs with that unnatural speed. Jack tracks him with his gun. He looks like a big, black asterisk while rushing away.

"Stop or I'll shoot!"

The Renaissance man keeps running.

Jack yells out, "Final warning!"

He does not hesitate for the stairs. Jack fires. The black form gets to the stairs, and he fires again. Flying up the staircase like a vampire bat in an old black-and-white horror movie, the dark frame is gone.

Jack keeps his eyes on the exit. “You okay?”

B.J. gets up on an elbow. “Yes, I’m okay.”

Jack keeps pointing his gun at the stairs. “I know I hit him. See if the girl’s all right; I’m going after him.”

B.J. is getting to her feet. “He knows this place. Be careful.”

Jack looks at her. “I will.” He takes off for the stairs.

* * *

The detective climbs up the staircase and out the open trapdoor, uneasy to the exposure. It is quiet as a cemetery when he gets his feet on the stage. Bicks still hangs like a light bulb in the middle of it. Jack looks around, pointing his gun everywhere he goes. He starts weaving through all the props and old stage scenery, alert for any sound or unusual occurrence. Jack comes to the spears lodged tightly to the stack of crates from the old trunk wedged into them. He puts his free hand on a crate and stands motionless; silently leaning on the crate, waiting for a clue to appear.

Contemplating on where his quarry might be and wondering what to do next, a surprise clue comes his way. A drop of blood smacks on the hand he leans on, prompting Jack to look at it. He sees a spot of crimson and then looks up. Just as he does, a 50-pound sandbag is falling down feet above him, and he jumps aside with athletic prowess in time to avoid the lethal attack. The bag lands harmlessly on the stage floor, bursting apart and spilling its contents.

He can hear a terrible sound of vexing breath above him as he keeps his eyes to the sky. Standing high up in the fly area, on the catwalks the old theatre has, is the Renaissance man. He grips the railing with both hands, bleeding from a gunshot wound; his orbs glowing with hatred. The cape flows in the inner space breezes while he looks down with that grotesque mouthpiece. It gives the impression of a master villain from a comic book. He grabs a tied rope, releases it, and lets it go, watching another sandbag fall. The bag descends and barely misses Jack again.

Jack checks the extent of the stage and tries to determine a way to the catwalk. His eyes come upon a metal ladder bolted into a brick wall. It is located in the wings stage left, and it leads to where he wants to go. The Renaissance man registers his every thought and watches his every move.

Jack runs to the ladder and starts to climb. The Renaissance man realizes he has to stop him. Various ropes are tied off next to his shoulder, and he knows which one to use. He feverishly unties one of them.

The detective is well up the ladder when a sandbag sails out of the shadows. He regards it from the swishing sound the rope makes and slips off the ladder on one leg, holding on with one hand, dangling on the side of the ladder. The bag hits its mark, but Jack is not there. The ladder shudders from the blow, and the bag bursts into loose sand. The weightlessness of the thing floats away, and Jack continues his climb.

A moment later, and the Renaissance man lets go another rope. This time, it is the body of Kim's friend, Betty, that flies out of the rafters tied by her feet. She barrels into Jack like a side of beef. He hugs the ladder while she stiffly strikes him with a heavy thud. The bash causes Jack to lose his grip on the gun. He watches it tumble to the floor and smash. After the collision, Betty sweeps to Bicks's side, leaving them both to hang above the stage together, bumping into each other and causing them to toss around in awkward, macabre, brittle movements.

Jack casts his eyes on the Renaissance man who's been viewing the events. The mouthpiece is still in his mouth and still giving that grotesque effect. His breath is loud and in deep heaves. Their eyes lock on each other in a frozen moment. Jack can see a bright, blood-soaked, red stain on the right side of the Renaissance man's white, silk shirt. He seems not to be phased by it. After the moment passes, Jack scampers up the ladder.

He clambers onto the catwalk. The Renaissance man is not far away, ready for their duel. His mouthpiece chomps at the bit. He still breathes with tortious effort. Reaching inside his flowing cape, he brings out the switchblade. The blade slices into view. It glints with the danger it presents. He comes at Jack, slashing the blade furiously and the fangs snapping for blood. Jack ducks the blade, avoids the fangs, and manages to land a couple of jabs; the Renaissance man backs away to regroup. He detects a nearby rope and cuts it with the knife. One more sandbag falls at Jack on the catwalk. The unexpected sandbag is a near miss, causing Jack to lose his balance and titter perilously on the railing. The Renaissance man is on him instantly. He comes at Jack in a blur and, using the switchblade, stabs him deep in the left thigh. Jack yells from the sharp pain, and the Renaissance man counters with another thrust to his right shoulder. Again, Jack hollers from the pain, and the second wound leaves him seriously disabled. Jack suddenly brings his right knee up to the Renaissance man's crouch, followed by an elbow to the face. He sends a left hook into the gunshot wound, and the caped fiend comes at him with a roar and more fury. He grapples the weakened detective against the railing and bends him over it. Jack holds the knife hand at bay with his left hand and grabs the Renaissance man by the throat with his right. The fangs bite at Jack, inching closer to his face while Jack's position worsens from the overpowering maniac.

Down below, B.J. is helping Kim get through the trapdoor opening. The girl has an old blanket wrapped around her as she gets clear from the passage. B.J. hears a rumpus in the rafters and looks to see the disturbance. She observes Jack in a dangerous predicament and immediately concludes he needs help. Realizing the two men are too close together and too far away to use her pistol, she looks about for another solution. Spotting the ladder Jack used, she recognizes it would take too long to help if she took that choice. She resolves to use her gun in desperation and fires a calculated wild shot near the men.

The round hits the railing a few feet from the fight and causes sparks off the metal. It makes the Renaissance man transfer his attention to B.J. on the floor. He views Kim standing next to her, and with that hesitation, Jack levels on the man. He throws another elbow from the grip he had on the throat to the side of his head. Then, he spins and ends up on top of the Renaissance man who, now, finds he is now leaning on the railing. Jack slams his knife hand on the metal railing several times till the knife dislodges from its grasp and hurtles to the stage floor.

The Renaissance man lunges free of the weakened Jack's clasp and stands face to face with him. A frozen portion of time passes once again, his black eyes flashing above the abominable mouthpiece at Jack. His breath tormented from the effort of the fight. In an instant, he leaps off the catwalk for a hanging rope. He takes hold and climbs even higher toward the ceiling where another trapdoor lies. It leads to the roof of the theatre and a way out of his folly. It has been open and exposed to the elements for a long time.

As he scurries up the rope with that speed of his, he transfers from one rope to another like a spider in a web. Jack, too hurt to follow, can only watch helplessly, looking for a better way to get there. B.J. is tracking the nefarious creature, but she cannot muster a clear shot.

The Renaissance man gets ever closer to the unlatched hole in the roof. Bright blue skies glitter through the accessible square. He grabs one more rope to finish the climb. All these years, it has been exposed to the unpredictable weather and has become an insecure link. Old and rotten from age, the rains, and the beating sun, the rope tears apart by his weight. The Renaissance man falls like a screeching black raven. The blood-curdling scream follows his furious descent, the cape flapping like a broken wing, till he lands badly, slamming hard on the crates where the spears are pointing.

Jack looks down from the catwalk. There is a sudden quiet that leaves everything with an unsettled feel. B.J. and Kim are next to each other and speechless at what they have in their sight. Across the way, Bicks and Betty dangle by their feet like sleeping vampires. In front of them, the Renaissance man lies on his back, all sprawled half on and half off the crates; the spears sprayed everywhere on the floor. His arms reaching out aimlessly and flailed in directions. His head drawn back with the fangs like two, small, crafted killers glistering in the limited light. His mouth wide open and poised in a silent howl. The part of the torso that is supported sways half off the crate and is braced by one of the spears thrust neatly through the Renaissance man's heart. The witnesses are stunned. Frozen with awe at what their eyes are telling them. A cold stillness in the old stage drops down like a leaden snowfall bloodstained by the glum and burdened by the sudden silence. The abrupt wicked display of the Renaissance man's demise is left to an enigmatical conclusion.

# Chapter 59

It was rowdy in the squad office. A handful of detectives were in the back, working their cases with files and speaking loudly on phones. Sam was at his desk, reading the journal that belonged to the Renaissance man. Jack ambles in using a cane to support the leg that got stabbed and a small sling on his bad arm. Sam takes his eyes off the journal and spies Jack slowly getting around.

"Hey, Jack. How's the leg?"

"It's getting there."

Sam indicates the journal. "Have you read this?"

Jack hobbles for Sam's desk. "I looked at it."

B.J. shows at the office door, lugging a cardboard box. She heads for the guys discussing the journal.

Sam continues his point, "The poor bastard thought drinking blood would make him a vampire and cure his ills."

B.J. sees Sam with the journal. "A repeat of a phenomenon with people's infatuation on vampires; he thought drinking blood would complete a transformation into one. It's not such an uncommon pursuit."

Sam closes the book. "A psychopath that thinks he's a vampire, a psychopire. But there is one thing."

Jack chimes in, "What's that?"

"Where's the body? When your backup got there, they couldn't find the body. At least, it wasn't where you guys said you left it."

Jack frowns. "It's there. He crawled off somewhere and died. There's no way he would have gotten up off the damage he had from that fall and spear."

Sam smirks. "Well, they're still looking for it. Maybe he really was a vampire and couldn't be killed. You know; the walking dead."

B.J. adds to the discussion, "Like Jack said, he's there. There's no telling where he might be in that old stage. There must be a hundred little nooks he could have gone to in that old theatre, and they'll find him in one of those. He knew that building with all its secret hiding places. Better than anyone he knew it."

Sam shrugs. "Well, like I said, where's the body? From the description you guys gave, how could anyone get up from that fall, not to mention the spear in the heart?"

Jack counters the comment, disgruntled, "They'll find him. The fact he was able to rise from that fall really makes him a walking dead. But he is dead, I guarantee that."

Captain Parks walks in with a wingman in the form of Edwin. "Good morning, Detectives. Look who I have with me."

Edwin is holding a file. They both join the huddle of detectives, and Edwin lays the file on Sam's desk. "I wanted to come by and drop this off. It's the file on the case, all neatly wrapped up. This is your copy for the department."

Captain Parks has more to say, "And, also, I have a little surprise for all of you."

Chris appears in the doorway all mended and ready for duty. "I'm back!"

He walks to the group while everyone slaps him on the back with greetings. "Chris, you're here! Chris, how are you!? Glad to see you! You look great!"

B.J. drifts over to a desk while the gleeful salutations continue with her cardboard box and sets it down. Jack leaves the activity with the guys and limps over to her.

"What's with the box?"

"You got your partner back, so I'm leaving."

Missy surprisingly fills the office doorway and looks around the room tentatively. She observes the boisterous activity and decides on intuition that the two detectives off by themselves are who she is looking for. She goes to them, unsure of her deduction.

"Are you Dobbs and Degree?"

Jack responds, "Yes, what can I do for you?"

"I'm Missy Hampton. I spoke to you over the phone about Jerome Bickers's recorder."

B.J. reaches into the cardboard box. "Yes, we've got it right here. It should be okay to let you have it."

Jack backs her up, "It is. The case is closed, we don't need it for evidence, and I'll sign the release papers on it."

Missy takes the recorder. "As I mentioned on the phone, I'm in town for the funeral. I was Jerome's literary agent. I've gotten permission from his family to collect all his research on the book, and this makes the last piece to the puzzle. I'm going to finish it for Bicks and dedicate the book to him."

B.J. smiles. "A noble gesture. I'm sure he would like that."

Jack reinforces the gesture. "Bicks was one of a kind; they broke the mold after him. He was an excellent news investigator and a great writer. B.J. and I are responsible for catching the guy, but it was Bicks who got there first. I only wish we were able to help him."

"Thanks for saying that. He was more than a client to me; he was a good friend."

They all shake hands, and Jack adds to the farewell, "If you need more information for the book, you know how to get in touch with us."

Missy smiles. "Yes, I do. Thanks again."

B.J. speaks warmly, "Good luck on the book, Ms. Hampton."

"Thank you; thanks to both of you." Missy turns and walks for the door. She goes through it and disappears.

From out of nowhere, Chris walks up to the detectives with his hand out. "Hey, I believe you've got something that belongs to me."

Jack digs in his pocket. "Your car keys; I've been looking forward to giving this back to you."

Chris looks concerned. "What do you mean?"

"You asking for the keys says you're all right in body and soul."

Chris shifts on his feet. "I'm much better than I was, about everything."

"I see that, good Buddy."

Chris taps Jack's cane. "How's that leg of yours?"

"Better every day."

Chris winks at B.J. "Watch out for this guy; he'll hurt the other one just for sympathy."

B.J. answers, "I'm beginning to catch on to his prankster ways."

Chris throws a smile to both of them. "It really feels good to be back."

Jack pats him on the shoulder. "It's good to see you back. And don't worry about the car. It'll be okay."

"What! What do you mean by that?"

"It tends to bog down when you accelerate. Probably needs a tune up."

Chris is alarmed. "What kind of gas were you using?"

Jack breaks out a big grin and waits for Chris to catch on.

"Oh, I see; another prank from the prankster. Funny, very funny; payback can be bloody, my friend."

Chris chuckles amicably and salutes his comrades; he spins and meanders to the rest of the gang at Sam's desk. Leaving the two of them alone; Jack nudges the cardboard box with a finger.

"What's with the box?"

"Its things I'm going to need."

"You can tell me about it on a ride home."

"You got your partner, have him do it."

"He's mad at me. I was hoping you'd be my ticket."

"I'm not your partner anymore. I've been reassigned to City Hall. I'm going to work for the D.A.'s office. So I guess our partnership is over."

Jack puts his weight on his cane. "That doesn't mean we can't be partners."

B.J. has an impish look in her eye. "We're cops, remember? As I recall, you have a problem being close to female cops, especially those who are partners."

Jack is catching on. "We're in different departments now."

B.J. looks deep in his eyes. "Is that going to matter?"

"It really doesn't. Not anymore. You're the only thing that matters, B.J. And I still need a ride home."

She picks up her box. "I'm willing to work on it if you have no qualms about sleeping with a cop."

Jack looks deep into her eyes. "Who said anything about sleeping?"

They each stare at each other a long moment, their eyes sparking from the jostle of words. Then, slowly, by small increments, their lips curl into Mona Lisa smiles.

**THE END**

CPSIA information can be obtained
at www.ICGtesting.com
Printed in the USA
LVHW081613240223
740350LV00025B/246

9 781645 758624